Conglommora

Conglommora

Andy Hunt

Photo credits: NASA: Large liquid hydrogen tank for NASA's Space Launch System, Orbital ATK; Soyuz TMA-08M spacecraft; Shuttle super light weight (SLWT) external tank; NASA/Hubble: Hubble Deep Field starfield. ESA/Hubble, NASA: IRAS 05437+2502, a small, faint nebula near the constellation Taurus. NASA: Chandra X-Ray Observatory.

978-0-9992560-0-8 Softcover

978-0-9992560-1-5 Hardcover

Published by Cyclotron Press, www.CyclotronPress.com
Second Printing, June 2018.

Explore the mysteries online at

http://www.Conglommora.com

Acknowledgments

Thanks to my reviewers for taking the time and energy to slog through my early attempts:

Greg Turnquist, Ron Jeffries, Peter Sommerlad, Jared Richardson, Todd Palmer, Ken Weinert, Gregory Brown, Bill Turner, Bob Martin, Cheryl Citron, Kathleen Howard, Phillip Wills and Charlie Payne.

Thanks to my copyeditor, Tracy Seybold, for correcting my occasionally errant linguistic and orthographic confusions. Any remaining errors are sadly and exclusively my own.

And special thanks to my wife, who was busy getting her doctorate while I frittered away the evenings writing.

Dedication

To the late Jared Richardson, whose enthusiasm for the project made it actually see the light of day—long before that meteor comes back.

One

SUCH EXCITEMENT. You'd think this was a once-in-a-lifetime event.

I guess for the kids it genuinely was. Most of the ships had made it here at least a generation ago, a couple of hundred years after leaving Dead Earth. When I was young, one or two straggler ships still showed up each year to connect with the other ships in our Conglommora. But then that became every couple of years. It'd been a long while since anything new at all showed up on our doorstop out here, all alone, in deep space. No planets, no systems nearby. Just us. Only now, something was coming.

The streams indicated it was literally headed straight for us. Well, at least about a dozen houses from here. That family, the Rheads, had an exposed docking tube. They kept watch and waited—for decades—for a relative who never made it. Hope is a hard thing to let go of. Looked like they were getting company now, at long last. Whatever it was, it was on a direct course for their docking tube.

I had met the Rheads more than a few times over the years, and we sort of knew each other, but I didn't know them very well. My wife and I used to hang out with other couples and families more when she was alive, but I fell out of the habit without her encouragement. But now, a ship was headed for us. That would be something to see first-hand.

What if it wasn't even a ship? Could be anything, really, from a dull piece of space junk to a derelict ghost ship. That had happened a few times—everyone on board died at some point and their ship just kept going, hurtling through the void. I shuddered a little at the thought of a desiccated skeleton at the bridge of a dusty hulk.

The Rheads' house was on the large side, as I recalled. I think their family had combined resources with several other families when they first got here. There would be room enough for a bunch of us locals to go visit and greet the newcomer—and everyone else in the world would probably be watching on a stream.

Okay, it really *was* exciting. I didn't exactly want to go, but how could I not?

Alain was already en route to his friend's house. I debated telling him to stay put. How many times had I warned him not to wander too far off? Maybe he wouldn't see the news. Yeah, right. He was probably over at the Rheads' already. So much for sticking close to home. Sigh. Kids.

Fear of missing out was only slightly stronger than my personal discomfort of leaving the house. But it was enough. I put on a clean coverall and headed out of the house through the convoluted set of tubes and corridors that would eventually get me over to the Rheads' house.

Well, me and virtually everyone else in the world.

I walked, climbed and made my way through the immediate neighborhood of connected ships over to the Rheads'. I pinged the hatch and it opened nearly immediately, sliding up quickly and silently.

"Charlie Neylan! Wow, been a long time, how've you been?" Bil Rhead warmly greeted me.

I stammered some sort of polite but perfunctory reply.

Bil was ushering everyone into his main living area, where he had his largest screen installed. The room was pretty packed. Most of the local kids were here already—including Alain—playing on the kids' screen while waiting for something to happen. I knew many of the folks here, but not all. But it wasn't like anyone was looking at each other; the nearly black starfield on the main screen was the center of attention.

Against that endless black, there was a single, tiny, glowing dot. Slowly, inexorably, it was getting bigger.

"Has anyone called them?" someone asked.

Bil answered, "I've tried raising them on the qradio a few times, but nothing yet." The quantum radio was great for very long-distance comms. In fact, you could send a message all the way back to Dead Earth if you wanted. People used to do that, to keep in communication with the handful of family members who stayed behind, who were too elderly or too sick or too stubborn to make the journey. But before long, there wasn't anyone left to respond.

Back in the day, when ships came to join the Conglommora more regularly, they'd qradio ahead with a stream that they were coming, make arrangements with friends, or like-minded folks, and dock alongside them. But this ship hadn't sent anything at all.

"Maybe their qradio is down," my next-door-neighbor Jef offered. "If that's the case, they'll be coming into range for standard pretty soon." He nodded toward the screen showing the approach.

It was a good point, and while you could fix almost anything yourself with a functioning reclaimer and printer, there were times when you needed someone else's to help fix your own—and a lone ship out in the void wouldn't have had that luxury. Maybe that wasn't the only thing that was broken. Watching the dot get bigger, heading straight for us, I really hoped that they at least had brakes.

Now, if this were a script I were writing for the gamers, I'd get all dramatic and have the lead character ask the computers if there was any imminent danger, like, "Arty! Does the approaching ship pose any danger to us?" and the soothing synthetic, computer voice would reply, "There is no evidence or forecast of imminent danger at this time."

But that's not how things work in the real world, of course. Arty would tell us if there were a problem. No need to ask, but it does make a nice dramatic device. I've used that in the scripts I write, sometimes. And it's not like you just chat with Arty. You could, of course, but people would think you were a little crazy. Conversing with the computer itself just wasn't something people did.

"Okay," said Bil. "According to my screen," he looked at the small black shiny in his hand, "they'll be in standard radio range in about eighteen minutes."

We'd have to wait until then. I supposed even if standard radio was out, we could probably still make contact once they'd docked and were in range of the mesh. That's what our pocket screens and everything used for comms. Unless the ship was completely dead, surely that would still work.

Unaccustomed to hosting this many people in his house—no one would have been, really—Bil Rhead started visibly, as if he had a sudden thought. He looked around at the crowd and asked, "Can I get anyone anything to drink? I've got some great brew from a trade with the barley farmers a couple of sections past the Marlins' place."

Well, that got everyone's attention. A good quality brew wasn't the easiest thing in the world to manage. And Bil was offering it to us freely. Well, not really free. The implication was that we'd stay and protect him and his family—if needed—from this curious interloper. It was a pretty smart investment on Bil's part, if you asked me.

Of course, everyone would have pitched in and helped Bil out if there was a problem, refreshments notwithstanding. Apparently, folks back on Dead Earth weren't real good about that. They would have just as soon have killed you and stolen all your goods. But we take care of each other out here. We take care of each other even if we don't always like each other. Forgive, assist, and move on. That's the Conglommoran way. Bil knew that of course, but still better to have a good crowd close at hand already.

His wife, Li, had the printer spit out a few dozen cups quick-and-dirty, and started pouring for us. It was nice, a little more faux-citrus flavor than I would have cared for, but hey, it didn't taste like algae *at all*, and that was a definite plus.

The few remaining minutes passed quickly, and quietly. No one really wanted to speculate on our impending visitor. They could be publicly wrong with some outlandish, fearsome theory, or far worse.

They could be right.

———————

We paced, we drank, we nibbled on some wafers that Bil had graciously offered. Finally the ship was in range.

"Unidentified ship, this is the House Rhead. You are approaching our docking tube. You are welcome to dock, but please identify yourself and your house," Bil transmitted over standard.

The screen was silent.

A faint crackle dripped out of the speakers, like it was trying really hard and just couldn't make it. A sudden, sharp burst of static made us all jump, including me.

Then a youthful voice, maybe not even thirty Earth years old or so, stammered across the void to us,

"Hello, oh, hello, House Rhead. This is the ship *Uten*, and if that is your docking tube we're headed for, thank you, thank you, a million thank yous."

Bil looked back at the room full of people, then to the screen. "My name is Bil. Bil Rhead. What's yours?"

The voice coughed, not out of evasion, but perhaps more out of a lack of talking out loud recently. Hey, it happens. If it weren't for Alain, I could probably go a month or more without speaking to anyone, really.

"Robert. My name is Robert," said the voice. "Robert Brandeis. Our ship is the *Uten*," he repeated.

"Hi Robert," replied Bil. "As I said, you are welcome to dock here. How many on your ship? What cargo or supplies do you have with you?"

"Thanks again, Mr. Bil," came the unsteady voice. Not exactly trembling, or shaking, but just… unsteady. Small pauses, odd dips in pronunciation. "Uh, it's just me now. My sister died last year. Maybe it was the year before. Our chronometers haven't been very reliable. Never did figure out why she died. One day she just didn't wake up. My screen couldn't tell me what to do."

He paused, a little extra gravel in his throat.

"But we were all that was left. Now it's just me. Oh, and cargo—I've got a hold full of Raw that I can trade.

Good stuff, too. Most of it is pure metal base, ceramic base, organic base, that sort of thing."

The crowd perked up. Pure Raw? That was a little rare in these parts. Not unheard of, but not very common. The reclaimers could only do so much; most of the Raw bricks were a mixture of different kinds of base matrix material. You could still do a lot with it, but not exactly everything. You could make Pure Raw, of course, but it took specialized equipment, skill, and time, so most folks didn't bother.

Pure Raw Organic Base seemed especially difficult to come by. Visitor Robert would be able to trade that for almost anything.

Bil didn't miss a beat. "That's great to hear, Robert," he said with genuine enthusiasm and relief. "I'd be happy to let you dock for, oh, three bricks of Pure Organic."

Bil's wife, Li, punched him in the arm, hard.

Bil shot her a glance and rubbed his arm. "Oh and not just dock," he quickly added. "You can stay hooked up as long as you like."

"Sure," said Robert's voice. "Actually, what I need to do is hook into your power grid for a few days while I take my engines offline. I ran into some trouble just after my sister died, and I need to make repairs."

"No problem at all," Bil assured him. "Your approach looks good. Stay on track to the docking tube, and we'll see you in a couple of hours. Rhead out."

There was a kind of sigh of relief in the room. Only *kind of*. It wasn't some raiding party from a crazed former Dead Earth death cult, it wasn't bug-eyed aliens, though. As far as we knew, there weren't any of those in real life, anyway. Just some weirdo in an old ship that took a lot longer to make his way out here to the edge of nothingness.

But hey, that's where the party was.

———————————

The *Uten* continued to decelerate and re-oriented itself to present its docking tube to match with the *Rhead's*.

The docking procedure itself was automatic and uneventful. It's easy to take tech for granted, I suppose. But it's a good thing that the circuits, computers, AI and such just take care of things when they need to. If I had to dock a ship, for instance, I'd probably crash it right through Bil's bedroom. People forget things and end up doing them wrong when they're out of practice. Not a problem for automatic systems. Perfect every time. Decades, even centuries later. The *Uten* made its approach and gently slid into the docking tube attached to House Rhead easily and seamlessly.

The inner hatch—on Robert's side of the airlock—opened, and he entered into the airlock proper. Arty would be scanning him now, checking for any known infectious diseases, viruses, and so on. For the most part, that sort of problem had been solved long ago, but there were stories from some of the ships of new super-viruses that had evolved on the way here. No sense in taking chances. After a few minutes, it was apparently okay, and there was a faint hiss as the seal opened for the first time in who knows how long.

All eyes were on the hatch as it slowly cranked open, revealing a youngish man with brown hair and a very pale complexion. Robert.

He seemed a little overdressed for space travel. Instead of just a simple coverall and grip shoes, he was wearing a strange outfit of heavy boots, a cargo vest with quite a few supply pockets, and a protective top coat/jacket thing. Over that, he had a belted strap with some sort of small bag. Pays to be prepared for anything, I guess. I wondered what he was expecting?

Robert ambled cautiously through the hatchway to meet and greet the dozen or so folks in the tube area, Bil and Li first among them. I was about three rows back, but I could see pretty well. Certainly no need to get closer.

"Hi, uh, I'm Robert," said the young man, more than a little awkwardly. I didn't think he'd had a whole lot of experience at talking to other people. Or even talking out loud, for that matter.

"Welcome to the world." Bil extended his hand, and Robert shook it with a light, token grasp.

"The world?" Robert asked, "Where are we? And how many people is that? What happened to everyone else who left Dead Earth?" He looked around at the dozen or people and the kids.

Bil waved his hand to encompass the crowd. "Well this isn't everyone right here, of course. There are some many millions spread over all of Conglommora. I don't really know exactly. Maybe Arty does. I don't. And yeah, we're it, as far as we know. Maybe a handful of stragglers such as yourself, but no other colonies or any-thing. Nothing planet-based. The People stick together, hanging here in deep space itself."

"Con-glow what?" Robert was trying to piece this all together.

"Conglommora," Bil explained quickly. "As most of the near-Earth systems were explored and abandoned, the remaining masses of ships headed out more-or-less this way. Right about here was as far as anyone could get without engine failure. The maps—folks had mapped out the destructive regions, and if you avoid all that, the longest viable path leads you here. There was an original mass of ships, and then the rest joined up. So, yeah, this is it."

"Oh," said Robert. "I just was expecting a bigger crowd here, I guess."

Bil pointed at the big screen on the wall. "I set our stream on public, so anyone who's curious is watching us live now. That might actually include everyone." He smiled, a warm and inviting grin, hoping to keep things friendly and civil.

Not that that seemed to be a problem, Robert min-gled with the guests in Bil's living room, quiet and re-served. Shell-shocked even. Still, Bil stayed close at hand, feeling some responsibility for him—at least while in his house.

"I didn't know about the maps... our ship was locked in on the signals from here. That's how I found you," Robert said quietly, almost to himself. But then he seemed to gather his wits a bit, and addressed most of his remaining questions directly at Bil. "Do I need to sign in, or register, or get some sort of IdentChip or anything?"

Bil shook his head. "In a close-quartered society like this, you'd expect rigid rules of decorum and protocol," he said with mock formality. "Nah, not here." He laughed at the thought of it.

"Everyone behaves themselves, or else their neighbors get together and throw them into a reclaimer. That's pretty much the sum total of the law. There's no central government or authority, police force, nothing like that. We take care of our own, and we stick to our own."

I snorted to myself. That was a bit of a fairy-tale told to kids. I don't think anyone had *actually* ever been thrown into a reclaimer as punishment. Maybe once or twice back in the old days. But the rest, about sticking to ourselves and taking care of each other, that part was true. And Robert noticed. A strange look passed over Robert's face, like he either didn't believe or our life here was such a foreign concept that it just didn't even register with him.

I suppose that's reasonable; ship life was probably a little different than life here on Conglommora, which probably was *very* different from our grandparents' life back on Earth. He'd have some adjusting to do.

And speaking of adjusting, now he was fiddling with the strap to the bag, and the large metal buckle snapped off and fell to the deck with a solid, convincing thud. The chatter of the crowd dimmed just a bit.

Justin, one of my immediate neighbors, was the first to ask, "I'll trade you fresh eggs for the metal." Justin had a chicken pod, and while we were really lucky to have him close by, it occurred to me that I didn't trade with him much anymore. Eggs were an even better trade than Raw.

Not that any trading was strictly necessary, of course. It had become more of a *sport* than a survival need. Sport, variety, novelty, tuning one's tastes; those were the ideas that drove trade. We are all self-sufficient, but maybe life requires more than mere sufficiency.

"Umm, sure, I guess," Robert sort of mumbled. "Eggs. Wow. Starting to feel like home on Earth already." He gave a wan smile. Not that he'd know anything first-hand about Green Earth, of course. Must have been an expression his grandparents used or something.

After a fair bit of small talk, and a couple of trades— the eggs set off a chain-reaction of friendly trading as usual—Robert started getting a little antsy.

"I'd like to get repairs started as quickly as possible, but I'll need some help. I don't really know much about engine tech." Robert gestured in the general direction of his ship. Bil nodded and steered them through the crowd my way. Straight toward me, in fact.

Turn. Turn around. Walk briskly and businesslike to the hatch and out into the corridor. It wouldn't be running away, exactly. Just… I'd rather not engage this stranger right now. I'd just rather not. But I wasn't fast enough.

"Hey Charlie." Bil came up to me, ignoring my sudden pale expression and the slight sweat on my forehead, despite the perfectly regulated temperature. "You're good friends with Ronny Sullivan, aren't you?"

"Sure," I admitted dully. Ronny and I had been friends for a long time, and I used to trek over a few tubes to visit him all the time and vice-versa. Not as much these days, but...

"Ronny" Bil turned to Robert, interrupting my internal excuse-dialog, "is a real first-class mech head. If he can't help you fix your issues, he'll know who can. He's into that whole crowd."

"Hi Robert." I offered my hand. "I'm Charlie. I'll take you over to Ronny's place when you're ready to go. It's not far."

I regretted the words nearly as soon as they left my mouth, but it was too late of course. Like a rock thrown into the void itself, once you let loose with a word, it will just keep going.

"Now's good," Robert said unceremoniously.

I called over to my son Alain and said I'd be back shortly. He spared a quick glance away from the kid's game and flicked his head in a slight approximation of a nod.

Robert and I headed out of the *Rhead* and into the corridor tube together.

———————

The corridors don't see a tremendous amount of traffic, in general. Just a few neighbors headed here and there to make a trade, see a friend, that sort of thing.

No mass migrations, transit, or cargo shipping. So, you might run into a few folks as you pass through. Nothing like the vids of the massive cities of Green Earth, where the streets were packed with people like bolts in a box.

People being people, of course, means that they're all crazy. And every now and then, you get a guy who's crazier—or maybe just more vocal—than most.

Our local somewhat-crazed orator went by the name of Edward. He particularly didn't like it when you called him by the nickname "Eddie," so I sort of made a habit of that. What can I say? I think I used to be a nicer guy when I was married. But left to my own devices, well, add it to the list…

"Hey, Eddie," I called over as we approached. "What's new in the cosmos?"

Edward stopped in mid-mumble and pinched his lips with disdain. Or maybe just displeasure. Or maybe he was trying to think of something to say.

"The cosmos?" he whispered. He always whispered, and barely that. Not like the old-time vids I've seen of Dead Earth figures delivering shouting, thundering speeches with dramatic hands pushing the very air aside to make a point.

"The cosmos," he repeated, a shade louder, "are sick of us. God is tired of us. He cast us out once, but we got too full of ourselves. Then we cast ourselves out. All the way out. Out here to the void, to the nothingness that mirrors your empty soul."

Well, that was a little pointed. Shouldn't that have been "our" empty souls, if he was indeed out to condemn all of humanity? Hmm, no, it seemed a bit more directed. At me, in particular.

"Oh, Eddie," I sighed as we passed, "you're such an uplifting sort."

"But I can fix it!" he insisted. "If you'll just let me. I can fix it all, for all time, for… for eternity itself! Charlie, listen to me!"

We passed him and continued up the corridor.

"Follow me!" he coughed in a hoarse stage-whisper. "Both of you! I am Edward. I can fix it! Just *let me fix it!* Follow your Edward. Right now! Drop what you're doing, drop your very selves, and join me—join all the awakened—to bring Conglommora back from the void, back to Earth itself! God didn't cast us out. I need you. Need all of you. I will find what you seek!" he croaked. "I can lead you!"

We kept walking.

In a whisper so quiet that it didn't register with me until much later, he hissed after us, "The Earth isn't dead, you know."

"Uh, what exactly was *that* all about?" Robert asked, looking back over his shoulder at Eddie. "What did he want from us, and where are these followers he was on about?"

I glanced back at Edward, who now seemed to be counting the lines in his palm. And talking to them. Or something. We turned into a side corridor.

"No idea. And it's never quite the same each time, either. Once he wanted us all to go outside and get some fresh air. Another time he heard the voice of God telling him to do something or other. Lately he's been on about getting followers to do something, or go somewhere." I waved my hands in a woo-woo gesture, indicating *my* disdain at his foolery.

"He says if we follow his plans we will return to our home and find God at last in the cosmos, but he needs a lot of followers first to do that. If you ask me, I think mostly he just wants to be in charge, to have power like in one of the ancient governments."

"How many followers has he attracted so far?" Robert asked with unusual interest, perhaps even a tinge of alarm.

"None. Zero. Not a single person," I explained. "I think it's pretty self-explanatory, really. We all know the truth of the matter.

"Don't seek God from someone seeking Power."

Robert's face was unreadable.

Two

THERE WAS DEFINITELY SOMETHING a little off about this Robert fellow. But I couldn't really put my finger on it.

Much as I hated it—or at least, wasn't used to it—I thought I'd try making conversation on our way over to Ronny's and see what else I could find out about him. Curiosity, I suppose, is a stronger emotion than I imagined.

Some of the corridors were very narrow; we had to walk single-file. That wasn't a problem, Robert tended to hang back a pace and walk behind me anyway, even if there was room.

This next corridor was broader, a circular tube with a flat walkway, lit in muted colors of amber and blue from various bits of equipment and safety lighting. I slowed so he had to come up alongside me.

"So, tell me about your family, your ship. You say you're the only survivor?"

"Yeah," Robert replied quickly. "My parents died when my sister and I were pretty young. Eight or nine maybe? I'm not really sure. Our chronometers weren't very accurate. In fact, I'm not even that sure what year it is now," he admitted with what seemed to me to be a tinge of guilt.

I nodded. "Happened to all of us, to one degree or another. When we finally got out here, none of the chronometers agreed with each other. Some were close, but others were wildly off. I guess folks realized that it didn't really make any difference anyway. So no, I don't know what Dead Earth year it would be now, either."

"Huh," Robert sort of grunted in acknowledgment. "That's… I mean, I was hoping all ya'll knew what year it was."

"Why?" I asked.

Robert didn't have an answer and just gave a slight shrug. We walked to the end of the tube in silence.

One more corridor tube—a narrow one this time— and we'd be at Ronny's. So much for conversation. Robert slipped behind me again, a strange, silent shadow.

Even though I had pinged Ronny, and he knew we were coming, I rang at the hatch. It was only polite.

The hatch hissed open, revealing a balding man with alabaster skin who would have passed for his late fifties on Green Earth. Here, that wasn't a very reliable guide. Apparently, we live longer out here than our ancestors did back on Earth, and have much better medical technology. A lot of that was developed on the generation ships on the way out here. So Ronny could have been anywhere from thirty to seventy, really. Just approaching middle age.

"Hey, Charlie, been a while! Good to see you as always, come on in." He grinned. "So this is Robert?" he said, peering around me to our visitor after pumping my hand.

"Hi." Robert gave a small and unceremonious wave of his hand.

Ronny got right to it. "I hear you need some advice on your engines?"

"Seems it," Robert replied. "We started having trouble maybe a couple of years ago, but my sister managed to keep ahead of it, and keep it going. After she…" He swallowed, blinking hard a few times. "I um, I didn't really know what I was doing with all that newfangled tech. Not as well as she did."

Newfangled? What did he mean by that exactly?

"I'm not sure I follow," I said carefully. "What was 'new' about it? Wasn't it the same stuff you'd grown up with on the ship ever since you'd been born? Even with your qradio down, and none of our latest streams, didn't your parents leave you streams and vids on how to work the basics even if they weren't around?"

That was common practice, especially on smaller family ships, which this seemed to be.

"No." Robert shrugged. "My sister and I didn't have much in the way of onboard streams, and the qradio had been out for almost as long as I can remember. And my parents died sort of… suddenly. I don't think they were expecting it."

"Ha!" Ronny barked a humorless laugh. "Like anyone does."

Ronny was great with machines, chips and tech, but not exactly the most tactful person you'd meet. I remember a couple of years back when the Johns boy burned to death after playing with a loosened power conduit. The circuits and systems noticed; Arty tried to warn the kid and cut power to that section, but it was too late. Ronny wasn't sympathetic in the least, blaming the boy and his parents for an obviously avoidable accident. He was right, but that didn't make it right.

Ronny's partner, Janel, came in, bearing a few tumblers. Where Ronny tended to the short, stout, and pearly luminescent white skin, Janel was the opposite in nearly every respect. She was tall and lanky, her skin and hair jet black like the void. They were fun together, Ronny the gas giant planet orbiting her inky blackness. Or something.

"Welcome to Conglommora, Earth man!" she enthused grandly and with theatrical energy. "Heya, Charlie. Care to join us for some of the finest sweetbrewed algae in all the world?" Ronny gave her a hug, and they lit up the room with their contrast.

Robert startled at Janel's presence. Like he'd seen a ghost? No, not a look of familiarity. Not that at all. Instead a look of shock at the *unfamiliar*. Like something totally unexpected—and unwelcome. He seemed to stiffen, and stood back a half a pace. Had he given them both a dirty look? A fleeting scowl of, I don't know, disapproval? Maybe I imagined it.

Ronny, meanwhile, rolled his eyes, but grinned at Janel's hospitality. He took a tumbler from her and passed it to Robert.

"Bottoms up, Bob!" He grinned as if having discovered a new nickname for our guest. Ha, that might just stick.

"Ah, thanks. Sure." Robert took the drink with a little apprehension at first, but then downed the rest in one gulp. Okay, not much in the social graces department there. Not that that's anyone's strong point these days, but man, this guy has clearly not been around people much... maybe it was more than that, though.

Janel jumped back in, nodding to the hatch she had come through. "I overheard that your parents didn't leave you much in the way of onboard streams. Anything about your background and history?"

Janel was a major history buff. The comings and goings of Green Earth were a central fascination with her, and she'd done a lot of research on the old governments of Earth and all the myriad causes of the Critical Point that eventually destroyed the ecosystem and forced us out here to the void.

There were many folks who liked that sort of stuff and whole banks of streams devoted to historical info and records, speculation and hindsight. But there were many more of us who just didn't care. What did it really matter which faction or which government was responsible for what? None of that mattered now. There was no one left to punish, there was nothing we could do now to change the outcome. Whatever happened, and whoever did it, this was our life now; our fate. Our species will be out here for as long as it is, and then it won't be. Just like every other species on Dead Earth. We'd bought some time, for sure, but nothing lasts forever.

Robert spoke up, interrupting my reverie, "Our parents didn't share much personal history, and there wasn't much recent general history in the onboard streams. Mostly older stuff." He licked his lips, fidgeted a bit. He seemed a little guarded, or uncomfortable. Apparently, he wasn't the only one.

"Janel," Ronny looked downright annoyed, "we can talk about his family history later." Ronny didn't care much for Janel's hobby. It's not that he didn't value it, he just simply wasn't interested in hearing about it. Janel shot *him* a dirty look.

"Mostly I've just been working the plants," Robert continued, ignoring the side interruption, hands outstretched and palms up in the air. "And as I said, I don't know much about engines. That was my sister's department, and why I need your help."

Ronny, master of tact that he is, stepped right in it and asked, "So why isn't she working on your engine problem? Save us all a lot of bother."

Now it was my turn to give someone a dirty look. That, and Robert's downcast eyes and muttered, "She died last year," really stopped the already sluggish and awkward conversation.

Silence draped the room like a foil bed blanket. Stifling, inescapable. A heartbeat passed, then several more.

Ronny cleared his throat. It wasn't a pleasant sound. More like a stuck hatchway; the grating of metallic and ceramic composites. But it was an honest start.

"I'm sorry," Ronny grated.

A moment passed. Robert looked up. "I really depended on her a lot. She was my older sister and took care of me once our parents died. Without a qradio we were kind of flying blind, keeping to a route our parents had plotted. Didn't really know where we were headed."

Janel couldn't resist. "That's basically how we all ended up here," she said and wound up for a rant. "No one planned to park all of humanity on the edge of nothingness and stay here until the heat death of the universe. No, that was never the plan. At first, the big Earth governments, back when they still had such things, built a couple of immense generation ships to find and colonize other planets. But that didn't work out so well.

"Turns out there aren't any other truly habitable planets in this region of the galaxy, at least as far as we could get with the electromag drives. Once we invent faster-than-light drives, then, maybe. Oh sure, we thought that there were a good dozen candidate planets within reach—they looked real good on paper. Or through a telescope. Even probes seemed favorable. But that's not the same as being there. And it's *really* not the same as living there.

"Plus the big ships had a lot of problems; most of them didn't make it for one reason or another. Our smaller ships were a lot luckier."

"I guess luck doesn't scale well," Ronny chimed in darkly.

Robert cocked his head. "What happened to the big ships? I do remember my parents saying that large ships were bad, and that's why ours was so small."

I tried to explain, "Comments on the streams thought that the big ships got snagged by some kind of exotic matter that reacted with our electromag drives, and blew up if your mass was great enough. Bigger the ship, the bigger the boom."

Janel looked exasperated. "Charlie, that's just a myth. Exotic matter doesn't interact with ordinary matter, so it couldn't have been that."

I was never good with details. "Maybe it was exotic energy, then, or some other unknown form of matter out in the vastness. Maybe it was space ghosts, or demons." I smiled and threw up my hands. "What do I know?"

Janel rolled her eyes and picked up where she'd left off, "Big ships had big problems. So the big ships didn't work, and time was running out on Dead Earth. The great Kain Mimulus broadcast the plans for everything out to everyone in the world: the printers, the reclaimers, the ships. So everyone scavenged, salvaged, and mined to toss into the reclaimers, making bricks of Raw. We probably didn't leave much behind on Dead Earth besides roads and larger buildings. We used the Raw, printed our ships, and off we went, abandoning Dead Earth for a new happy planet we could settle on."

"Right," Robert added, "I thought that's where we were headed."

Janel smiled. "Just as with settlements on ancient Earth, the People stopped and built a city where the horse died. In this case, here at the edge of space. We converted our ships to houses, stuck them all together. We're not in orbit, there's no planet, no systems—there's nothing here. Just us.

"We tried going further, sent probes and ships and stuff, but they didn't make it. More aggressive weird space matter maybe? Perhaps the universe was just sick of our shit and penned us in here?"

"Okay, enough of this," Ronny was bottled up and out of patience at the same-old. He'd heard this all before, more than a few times. "Come on over to my workbench, and let's talk about drive engines." He motioned to a semi-circular hatchway leading into another area of his home.

Robert followed silently.

I leaned against the wall and slid down; a chairform popped out to greet me. It was more fun than waving at the palm screen in the wall.

Janel plopped down next to me and motioned for a small table to pop up from the deck. It did, and she rested both elbows on it with a heavy sigh.

Janel and I waited, idly discussing a little history of Green Earth, her favorite topic.

Three

IT WASN'T TOO LONG before Ronny and Bob came back out from Ronny's workshop to join us.

"Well, Robert is screwed but good," Ronny said diplomatically.

I blinked, "What do you mean?"

"I can't fix it, not with my printer and the equipment I have here." Ronny shook his head. "His ship's gear is pretty old, even for ships of that time. And it wasn't very well built. Kind of a miracle he made it out here alive. But it is repairable without having to replace the whole thing. I know a couple of guys who can do it."

Of course he did.

"Avi and Why, they are some of the brightest mechs I know," Ronny said matter-of-factly. "I'm sure they can get you fixed up, good as new. Better even."

"Why?" I asked innocently.

"Why what?" Ronny asked with a mischievous grin. He knew the conversation was going to go this way.

"Why is Why's name Why?" I asked with as much of a straight face as I could muster, trying to avoid the lengthy word play.

Ronny chuckled, his eyes lighting up. "He's a bit of an... instigator, I guess. I think he just likes the reaction, and the ensuing comic conversations. But he and Avi are top-notch. The best. They can fix or build anything. The downside is that they are a fair long bit away. A long walk, a ride on the hyperloop, and another few long walks. It's going to take you two a while," he cautioned.

Wait, what?

"You two? You're not coming?" I asked with just the slightest hint of panic. Well, hopefully only a slight bit leaked out. On my insides, however, there was a lot more than slight panic. He wasn't coming with us?

Ronny shook his head, "I know Avi and Why. I've visited them a few times already. Plus you'll make better time and have an easier time with lodging with just the two of you," he waved at us.

Ronny took out his screen and tapped and drew for a while, then looked up. "Here's your path."

I got the route on my screen. It wasn't arduous, especially, but it was long. It would not be a quick trip.

Didn't seem like there was enough air in the room all of a sudden. And it got cold. In the pit of my stomach, anyway. In hindsight, I'm not sure how I got snookered into this adventure, but I was. So I took a deep breath and owned up to it.

"Okay, I'll take him," I offered, with a manufactured assurance. "I'll walk Robert up to the mech section. We'll need to stock up on Raw for trade, for nightly lodging, and a few other things we'll need."

The words that tumbled out of my mouth were calm and assured. I have no idea where they came from. Not me. I couldn't believe I was saying this. What was I thinking?

"Bob, you head back to the *Uten* and I'll get ready on my end, and we'll head out in the morning." Ronny's choice of nickname had stuck. Robert looked like a Bob to me.

Robert took his abbreviated moniker in stride and nodded, "Okay, will do. Thanks guys. I really appreciate this. My sister Ann," again the catch in the throat, "took care of all this kind of stuff. I never paid much attention to the engineering parts of the ship. I really miss her."

He looked off in the distance, which was a neat trick in Ronny's small living area.

"I'm sorry," Robert continued, "for so long, it was just Ann and me. When she died, I really didn't know if I could go on. Alone on the ship, no idea where we were going… just the course left by our parents. It felt like we were just… wandering. Didn't see any other ships, no habitable planets, no colonies, nothing. I had no idea you guys were out here. No idea where we would end up."

Ronny helpfully offered, "Well you found us, didn't you?"

"Yeah," Robert nodded, and said dully, "My lucky day."

———————————

We walked back over to Bil's, to the docking tube where the *Uten* was docked.

Most of the crowd had gone back to whatever they were doing, the mystery of the day solved. Just another straggler from Dead Earth. Nothing much to see here. I filled Bil in on our plan.

Robert had an idea. "Charlie, can I give you a couple of the bricks of Raw to carry? We can take more if we split up the load."

Sounded reasonable. "Sure." I nodded, but without much enthusiasm. Just another complication.

He motioned for me to follow him, and he opened up the hatch to the *Uten*. I followed him in. No need for scans anymore; the inner airlock door was left open for convenience.

It sure was a smaller ship. Pretty claustrophobic design, if you ask me. There were no large living areas, just a small central corridor leading to the control center, or hub, with smaller bedrooms/living quarters leading off on the sides. The doors were all open and the rooms almost all completely empty.

Claustrophobic and hollow.

To the rear of the control center was a hatch leading into the storerooms. The first was a much larger area, and Robert went over to an impressive stockpile of Raw and started counting out a few. I looked around while he did. Couple of dedicated storerooms, a large biodome filled with plants, algae tanks and some aquaculture. There wasn't much else to see.

Robert handed me the bricks and a carrying sack.

"Charlie," he said haltingly, kind of avoiding my eyes, "I really want... I just..." He couldn't quite seem to come up with the words.

"Thank you," he said at last, "for offering to take me up to the mech section. I really do appreciate it."

I took the bricks. "Oh, not a problem," I said, as much to convince myself as anything else.

"I've been meaning to go out on a walk myself anyway. This gives me a great excuse," I lied.

"See you first thing tomorrow," I said, and I walked out of the *Uten*, back out through Bil's and home to the *Neylan*.

Words. Such simple words, like "sure" and "okay." But they aren't simple at all, are they? Just a few of these words, and it becomes a promise, a commitment. Just a few words, and then there is no going back.

Four

DOUBT IS A PACK ANIMAL. Like the feral rats of Dead Earth, taking over the rubble that was left of the former cities. Gnawing, ceaseless, coming at you from all angles. Overwhelming. A dark sea of individual doubts, crashing in wave after wave, tearing me up.

What was I doing, taking a stranger to some remote spot in Conglommora, leaving my boy alone, exposing myself to… who knows what? And not just for a day or two, but maybe many days. I hadn't left the house for that long since my wife died. And I hadn't left Alain alone in the house either.

But… maybe I should. Maybe it was time, time to get out a bit, stretch myself. There's a reason folks don't leave their comfort zones. Comfort.

I slept only a little. Couldn't get my breathing to slow down, and there was this knot in my stomach. I think I twitched and rolled over more than I actually slept.

It wasn't quite time to get up yet; not quite a full sleep cycle. But I slid out of the bedform in the darkness.

"Good morning, Charlie," Haily said, seated at the table.

"Hey," I replied. "How's my favorite wife this morning?" I asked, somewhat rhetorically.

Her easy laugh and gentle smile still melted my heart, even after all these years. "I'm your only wife, silly," she admonished.

"I have to do this thing, ..." I started and halted. "Well, I don't *have* to, I suppose, but I said I would. Not sure I can." Suddenly it was hard to meet her eyes.

"I know," she replied. "Don't worry, you'll be fine. Whatever it is, you'll work it out just like you always do. Remember when you didn't think you'd make a good father? Wasn't even sure you wanted kids? And look how that turned out. Alain adores you, looks up to you. You've been great for him."

A smile snuck out onto my face despite my angst. Alain was a bright spot in my personal galaxy; that was for sure.

"And all those writing projects you were sure you couldn't finish, all those times you were convinced you'd run out of ideas? But you always made it work. For me. For your son. You can make this work." She stood, hands outstretched.

"Sure." I tried to agree with a confidence I absolutely did not feel. But for Haily, I always made the effort. Maybe that was the difference now; I no longer made the effort.

"But,…" It was hard to keep this up. I wanted to talk, to argue, to be convinced. But that would take energy I just wasn't feeling.

Haily said nothing, just looked at me expectantly, waiting for me to finish.

"It's not the same now. Not the same at all."

I shut off the vr, and Haily disappeared. The darkness alone embraced me now. But that's how it really was, wasn't it?

———————————

Had breakfast with Alain, laid out the plan for the next ten days or so and double-checked that he was okay with being alone. He was technically old enough, I supposed, but parental worry never ends. Especially as a single parent. One has to worry enough for two.

"Dad, I'll be fine," he assured me. "Go. Have fun. See the sights. Are you walking the whole way, or riding a grav sled, or…"

"Walking. There are a lot of neighborhoods between here and there. It's not all straight-up corridors. I think having to wrangle and re-align two sleds with us through those would be more trouble than it's worth. It's not *that* far, and I'd rather travel light."

He nodded, and I hugged him goodbye. Maybe for a little longer than I should have.

"Dad, really. Nothing to worry about. Go already."

One last squeeze and I was out the hatch, closing it behind me.

Stopped just outside the hatch. Took a deep breath. I'd rather not do this at all. It would be so much easier not to. But these were areas of Conglommora I'd never been to, never seen. And it wasn't that far. I tried to convince myself it wasn't that big of a deal, which was enough to get my legs moving again.

I walked back over to Bil's, met Bob as promised, and we set off. Just like that. I didn't bring a whole lot with me, just a small screen, a few compressed algae wafers, some compressed water, and the bricks of Raw to trade.

Robert had more; he had his backpack filled with the Pure Raw bricks from the *Uten*. That should be enough to trade for food and sleeping quarters for our whole trip, the specialized parts he needed, and then some. Ronny had explained that the parts were small, intricate. Big stuff—girders, beams, hull plates—were actually easier to fab. But the smaller the piece, the trickier.

I carried the Raw he had given me, plus some Raw as a bit of a hedge in case something happened to Robert. Nothing should, of course. But traveling in person was not an everyday thing, and who knows what might happen out there in the world? Arty would protect against any overt danger, if it could, but even all that nanophotonic artificial intelligence wasn't magic. And Arty certainly wasn't as proactive at fighting inconvenience.

We started walking, and it didn't take long before we were out in the corridors.

Well, I call it walking, but only some of the travel was actually in a straight line, with one continuous floor underneath. Within the neighborhoods, the way was often convoluted—a zig zag up and around one house, down the other side, around an edge, through numerous ports and hatches.

So it was more like an obstacle course, or glorified wiggling than walking. A grav sled would be great on the straightaways, but just a burden the rest of the time. Adjacent ships didn't always agree on which direction gravity went, and you'd have to recalibrate the sled when the field changed. Not hard, but sleds were kind of a pain. Couldn't remember the last time I used one.

I hadn't actually gone out of our immediate neighborhoods at all in the years since Haily died. It felt a little odd leaving the house and not having a partner to kiss goodbye. A pang of sadness. Yes, that's what it was.

Which reminded me; as Bob and I were leaving Ronny's house, Ronny gave Janel a kiss wrapped in a passionate embrace before they headed back into their house. And I swear out of the corner of my eye, it looked like Robert *recoiled* a bit. What the hell? Hadn't he ever seen people kiss before?

Well, to be fair, perhaps he hadn't. Last survivor on what was a small ship to begin with, no qradio streams from Conglommora or anywhere else, few onboard streams. What strange circumstances.

Strange on many levels. First, family ships that small weren't unheard of, but they were rare. It was risky. You needed at least enough room for several generations of families. It's not like you could get away with a small ship and stick everyone in suspended animation.

Oh yeah we tried that. Never could get it right. Janel said there had been some pretty good attempts just before the Critical Point. Freezing people always worked great. It was the waking-up part that no one could quite get to work reliably. Mostly, you froze; you died. If they did get your heart beating and lungs pumping again, you were just a thawed-out vegetable.

And what good is a defrosted vegetable, really?

I hadn't seen anything on Robert's ship that looked anything remotely like cryo gear, at least not like the stuff that folks used for food preservation. It would have to be human-sized at least, there'd have to be a few of them, plus large cryo tanks and whatever other extra outboard gear they needed. His ship just wasn't that big.

Their qradio broke. Okay, stuff like that happens. Not often, but it's still plausible. But why would you build an under-sized ship, and not fill the onboard screens with a full set of archived streams? I'd heard there used to be people who didn't trust nanophotonic computers or the AIs, who were afraid of them. But those weren't the sort of people who flung themselves out into the void in a ship, either, so it probably wasn't that. I don't think any of those sorts of folks made it out here at all.

What if his family had left Green Earth before the Critical Point? Before the exodus? What if they weren't even planning on coming this far? That almost made some sense. Except that he had plenty of Raw, and that wasn't invented until after the Critical Point. Ship designs existed, I suppose, but weren't popular until the big broadcast.

It just didn't add up.

Robert and I made our way from Bil's docking tube, past the entrances to his neighbors, in a gentle zig zag. As we came toward the end of his neighborhood, the smaller, round corridor joined with a large square hatch. We cranked it open to the sound of a slight hiss as the air pressure equalized. Closing it behind us, we walked up a wide, square corridor with blank gray walls, a bare metal floor and minimal lights every twenty meters or so.

This was more of a connector-style corridor where we could really walk in a straight line; there weren't any docking tubes in the walls, and no other corridors joined in yet. So we walked straight on, Robert shadowing just behind me and to the side, for as long as the artificial gravity spill from the houses lasted. As soon as that ran out, we'd propel ourselves along using the hand-holds on the wall in zero gee.

At least that was my plan, and what one normally did.

I had fond memories of playing in zero gee as a kid, bouncing around with my parents and the neighbor kids. But I hadn't been in zero gee in ages. Probably not since Alain was small. This might actually be fun. Ah, there's nothing like the anticipation of a guilty pleasure.

But as we turned a curve, the gravity field fell off sharply, and Bob's feet left the floor all of a sudden.

He panicked. White-knuckled, white-faced, a silent scream inside desperate to find a way out, but he was clenched too tight even for that.

I doubled back a pace. "Robert, are you okay? What's wrong?" I took one flailing hand; the other had the hand-hold on the wall in a death grip.

He didn't answer, not right away. Too busy panting for breath. I pried him loose and towed him back around the corner, down the corridor just enough to float lightly back to the floor. After a few minutes, the panting eased, some color came back to his face, and he was able to speak.

"S-s-sorry," he stammered, "I just… the last time… I… I remember the gravity being off."

He sat on the floor. Slumped, really.

"That's when my parents died," he said quietly, to the floor. "The gravity… something had happened to the ship. The gravity was down. We were floating around. Helpless."

Well, this was ironic. Here I was afraid *I* was the one who would have some sort of breakdown along the way. But Robert beat me to it. He seemed to be pulling himself together now, though.

"There had been an accident, something about the engine," he said. "We lost a couple of systems all at once, I think. They fixed it, somehow, for me and my sister, but…" He trailed off.

"It killed them. They died right after that."

Bob shook his head, "I hadn't thought about that in years. Hadn't really remembered it at all, I suppose, until now. Until feeling that weightless, helpless, out-of-control feeling again. Can't have that," he said with new determination, looking up at me.

"Oh, remembering, even the painful stuff, is a good thing," I said thoughtfully, "Really, when it comes down to it, our memories are all we have."

"That's one memory I can do without," he said firmly, standing up. "Okay, Charlie, show me how you do this."

We went back around the corner, and I demonstrated "proper" zero gee technique, at least as well as I could remember myself. He caught on quick—it's not really that hard, just don't worry so much about "up" and "down" anymore.

And along the corridor we went.

———————

Lights turned on as we approached and off behind us a pace. There really wasn't a specific need to be so conservative with energy demand, but when these corridors were first built, maybe there was. I didn't know. At any rate, lights of pale blue, and sometimes amber, lit up before us and gave at least some color to the otherwise drab walls.

It had been an hour or more, I think, since Bob's meltdown, and we hadn't said a word to each other since then. We did pass a handful of other travelers; streamlined nods and greetings were exchanged and we each kept going.

Other than that, the utter silence started to wear thin, so I thought maybe I could pry a few more details from our recalcitrant guest.

"So Robert, tell me," I said over my shoulder, "what do you think of Conglommora so far?"

There was a pause. "It's so quiet in the corridors," he observed. "On the ship, there was always the background hum of the drive engines. But there's no drive here. Just... quiet."

Huh, hadn't thought about that. But it made sense. Ship life would certainly entail running drive engines at fairly close quarters, not something we need to do here. And with his smaller ship...

"Your ship seemed a little on the small side. Do you know how many families you started off with?" I asked Robert.

"Six families in all, most had three or four kids each," he offered.

Three or four kids each?? Well, Robert was just full of surprises. Chalk up another strange point. Most regions of the Earth had limited children to no more than two per household by the end. Three was unusual and four was unheard of.

Out here, you're lucky to get one good child, and maybe a do-over or two. Was that not the same on Robert's ship?

"Wow, you guys were lucky. Janel told us that in most areas, you couldn't have more than two kids. Four was unheard of," I said out loud, echoing the mini-conversation I'd just had with myself.

"Seemed normal to us at the time, I guess." Robert shrugged a little.

The corridor made a sharp bend to the left. The thrill of even a little change against the mind-numbing boredom of the straight, featureless corridor was more than I expected. The next section offered yet another unrelieved straight tube of gray to the horizon.

I exaggerate; actually it wasn't that bad. And we were about done for the day. About halfway up from that point there was a tangle of tubes and hatches. I checked on my small screen, and indeed this was where I had arranged for us to spend the night. I rang at the third hatch.

A young woman, with black and violet hair, fine cheekbones, penetrating, round blue eyes and light, pale blue skin answered the door. "Oh hey." She casually scoped us out. "I'm Hua. You're Charlie? This is the guy from the ship?" she asked, looking straight at Robert.

"Yes ma'am, that's me," admitted Robert. He was staring at our host a little weirdly. Okay, honestly, I was beginning to think everything this guy did was a little weird.

Hua was scanning Robert up one side and down the other. "I've never met anyone who wasn't born on Conglommora," she opined with a curious but still diffident air.

"Well I've never met anyone with blue... ah... anyone like you either!" Robert blurted out.

I quickly interjected, "Robert's been alone on his ship for quite some time. He doesn't seem real comfortable around folks yet."

She looked him over again and asked, "Okay, but you got the Raw, right?"

Robert pulled out a brick of Pure Metal Raw. Hua ran her screen over it, confirming its purity.

"Fair enough I guess." She opened the hatch the rest of the way, and two more figures approached.

"These are my husbands, Ezra and Jalal." The two gentlemen nodded, but didn't say anything and kept a respectful distance behind Hua. One was a sort of light pink shade, the other a brilliant, shimmering purple-black. Couldn't really make out any other features.

"We've been trying to have kids for a while now, but haven't had any luck. So we've got some extra rooms. These two rooms here on the left are empty and all yours. We'll share dinner with you in about two or three hours from now. Is that okay?"

"Certainly," I agreed.

Robert chimed in, "Yes, ma'am." So polite. Except for, you know, staring at the husbands, Ezra and Jalal. I guess his people weren't into custom colors.

We filed in and made ourselves comfortable. It had been a long day of walking, twisting, and turning, which I surely wasn't used to, and of course the zero gee flitting about. That stuff strains your core muscles if you're not accustomed to it.

A nap before dinner sounded like a great idea.

Dinner was quite lovely. They had access to a large chicken pod nearby, and the fresh meat was a wonderful treat. Large, flavorful mushrooms, some root vegetables I didn't quite recognize… they trade well. Perhaps that's something I'd been missing lately. Really no reason I couldn't do the same—Justin still has a chicken pod, and we used to trade a lot. I guess I'd gotten out of that habit after Haily died.

But more importantly, I hadn't realized that was even a problem until now.

"So what do you do for fun, Charlie?" Hua asked me, interrupting my inner monologue. I doubt if any of them really cared, but it was probably a nice gesture before setting on Robert and grilling him just like tonight's chicken.

"I like to write," I said after swallowing a sporkload. "I write stories and plot lines for the vr gamers, and sometimes short stories for the readers."

One of the guys—Ezra maybe?—perked up at this. "Do you play vr a lot?" he asked.

"Not really," I confessed with a shrug. Hmm, maybe that's where my boy gets it from. "I mean, I check out works in progress, and work with folks on them, but I don't really play. I'm more of a sunset and waterfall kind of guy. More relaxing and meditative, less quest and struggle." I smiled. I didn't mention that I regularly "talked" with the AI-enhanced vr simulation of my dead wife. I felt my face darken at the thought and quickly moved on to disclose my more productive habits.

"But I come up with all manner of tangled plots, puzzles, and sticky situations for characters to figure out."

There was the briefest of polite pauses, and Hua turned her sharp eyes to Robert and began peppering him with a fine spray of pent-up questions. He answered slowly and thoughtfully, but even though his lips were moving and perfectly fine words came sliding out, he didn't actually *say* anything. Didn't really answer the questions well. He wasn't evasive, particularly. Maybe he just wasn't that interesting.

Or maybe he was hiding some vast, dark secret plot. Hey, that's what a writer's imagination is for, right? To see the hidden, conspiratorial patterns in normal, boring old daily life.

Even when they're just not there.

Dinner over, finally, we retreated to our respective quarters. It was comfortable enough, but of course nothing is the same as one's own bedform.

Sleep fled before me, as it often does. The unfamiliar surroundings didn't help, and the nap before dinner probably was a poor idea.

I don't think I even had time to dream before it was time to go.

———————————————

Our next stop was closer than ideal, but you can't always space these things perfectly.

Jocelyn and Emmea greeted us at the hatch. They were clearly old, not quite elderly yet but definitely getting there. They had both let their hair go to a natural gray, and the lines on their faces suggested there had been plenty of tales to tell. Some of them may even have been true.

"Come on in, don't just stand around!" Jocelyn effused and waved us into their house with great fanfare. We stood in a large, partial sphere with hallways leading off. At least, I think it was a sphere, once. There was so much decorative hangings it was hard to tell—fabrics, paintings, what I guess were sculptures. Every bit of every surface was covered with something.

"Let me show you around," offered Emmea. "It won't take long!" She laughed at her own comment.

"Charlie—which one is Charlie?" she asked. I held my hand halfway up as identification. She could have looked more closely at the note I sent.

"Charlie this is your room." She waved with a large motion to the first quarters off the main room. "And Robert you can take this room. Jocelyn and my bedroom is here," she waved to the last doorway in the set, "and the galley is right through there." She pointed to an open archway.

"And that's pretty much all there is to it!" She beamed.

Jocelyn chimed in, "Well there's the workshop, on the other side of the galley."

"Well, sure, but they won't be making any quilts or tapestries tonight now will they?" Emmea shot back.

And so it went.

These two were hilarious. All through dinner they entertained us with their... I'm not sure what you'd call it. Personality is too generic; effervescence sounds like a drink recipe.

I don't think Robert got a word in edgewise until after dinner. Spun protein was unusual, but tasty. Long, browned, crispy filaments, endlessly flowing and hopelessly entwined, towering over a bed of greens. It's not that hard to make, but it does take several extra steps, and most people don't bother. Well, I don't bother. Maybe I'm not most people.

Emmea was showing us their other handiwork, hung throughout the galley and entry hallways. Jocelyn joined us after tidying up and finally asked Robert a question.

"So, Robert. Welcome to Conglommora, of course."

"Oh Jocelyn I'm sure he's heard *that* a hundred times by now!" chided Emmea.

Jocelyn kept right on going as if she hadn't heard. She probably hadn't. "What do you do, Robert?"

Poor Robert looked like he'd been thrown in a vat of cold water. He clearly didn't know what to make of any of this. I don't think they had spent much effort on any artistic endeavors on his ship.

He stammered a bit, trying to think of a response and finally muttered something about tending to the plants, working with aeroponics, soil-based formulas, fertilizers, that sort of thing.

Emmea didn't seem to understand.

"But that's just a chore," she said with puzzlement. "Like cooking meals or repairing power conduits. What do you *do*," she asked again. "You know, to be human?"

Now it was Robert's turn to show open puzzlement. "You mean, to write like Charlie does, or make things out of fabrics like you... two?" he said haltingly.

"Sure," Jocelyn chimed in. "Or sculpt, or play music, or dance, or paint, or build things, or..."

Robert's sad nod of his head cut her off. "We don't... we didn't... we never really had time for that." he said.

"Well then we really did rescue you, didn't we?" Emmea said jubilantly. "You got here just in time!"

I don't think Robert agreed.

Five

ANOTHER DAY, ANOTHER BATCH of twisted, randomly connected tubes going every which way. You'd think these folks would at least vaguely agree on which way gravity should go, but no. Through a hatch and the floor was now above us. We tumbled gently into the new gravity. Sometimes the transitions weren't so gentle; it just depended.

More gyrations through some neighborhoods followed by another really long corridor, gray and featureless.

I shouldn't complain about the long corridor this time; we were skirting a large section of houses that thankfully *had* a long corridor to bypass yet another warren of tubes and hatches.

But neither Bob nor I were used to this level of exercise. Sure, I used the equipment at home to maintain baseline health and keep my muscles from atrophying completely. Everyone did that, ever since the ship days. But I wasn't one for much more than that.

So, this was getting tiresome. Fortunately we didn't have that much farther to go, just a few more typical neighborhoods, the hyperloop, and then we'd be there. But as we drew closer to the end of this segment, I saw a problem. A huge problem. An insurmountable problem. I stopped short, and Bob nearly ran into me. I really wish he'd walk next to me more, instead of behind. It was kind of creepy.

The way ahead was blocked; a giant ball of some recently hardened, gray and smooth gelatinous mass filled the end of the corridor.

"Charlie, what's that?" he asked. It was a fair question.

I pulled out my shiny flexi-screen from my pocket, which stiffened as I gestured. Scanning the area in front of us, and any recent news streams for this community, I quickly saw what had happened.

"Looks like there was an explosion," I conveyed, as I read. "Sometime early yesterday. Explosive decompression took out a few houses behind this corridor. Right where we were headed."

"Explosion? Why? What happened? Was it chemical?" Bob insisted, with a sudden and unusual interest. "Was it a bomb? An attack?"

"From who?" I made a face. "No, not that, but I'm not sure what it was," I replied as I scrolled, flicked, and gestured my way through a bunch of different eyewitness reports, sensor logs, and such. "These things just happen sometimes." I put the screen away and turned to face him. "Poor maintenance procedures, bad shielding and a small meteor, a drive failure, whatever. Space is harsh, you know. But the auto seals kicked in and Arty sealed off the adjoining corridors to prevent any further decompression." I pointed at the big ball of sealant. "Which is great for safety, but inconveniences us a bit."

We'd have to take a detour. There was an adjoining corridor about an hour behind us; we'd have to backtrack to that and work our way around.

The route was pretty clear according to my screen, but I wasn't familiar at all with these neighborhoods. There was no telling what we might find.

I pinged Alain, letting him know about the delay.

"Wow, giant sealant balls," he said as I showed him the pics. Was that sarcasm? Where do kids get these things from?

"Still fine here," Alain was wrapping up quickly. "See ya." He didn't seem overly worried about us.

Robert was a little glum at the detour, but still oddly interested in the explosion itself.

"I don't know anything about chemistry or bombs," I admitted, "but tell me, what did you mean by asking if that had been an attack?" I asked.

"Don't you have some sort of political or social violence here?" Robert asked back. "There's always someone who isn't happy with the government, with their social class, their living conditions, that sort of thing."

I laughed. Well, not really, it was more of a snort; a sudden short exhale of derision, mixed with a bit of dismissiveness.

"No," I said, and was going to leave it at that. Would have been easier. But really any conversation was welcome at this point, so I stuck my neck out, and offered my thoughts. "Life here is much more like on the ships than it was for our grandparents, great-grandparents back on Earth. There is no government, not any notion of classes, really. People do what they want, and sometimes move to hang out with people who share interests—like in the mech section. But ultimately, everyone is self-sufficient. So, no. No violence. No riots. No... bombs or anything." I was a little uncomfortable at his interest. But he dropped the topic and didn't pose any other questions.

We continued heading back the way we came, back along the gray corridors lit with the just-in-time amber and blue lights. There was the side junction just as my screen had suggested. We angled over in near-zero gee and started around that way. One major drawback: this was a *really* long, uninterrupted corridor. Two days walk at least without interruption, friendly face, or stopover.

But it couldn't be helped; that was how we had to go. So we went.

———————

If this journey had been boring before, now it was straight-up torture. Hours of just walking up the corridor slid slowly by us, and hours more lay ahead. Now I wished I *had* brought a grav sled. Even a tangle of houses would be a welcome diversion at this point.

And it wasn't like the conversation was particularly scintillating. Trying to get more than a few sentences at a time from Conglommora's newest resident was nothing less than wishful thinking. Still, I quite literally had nothing else to do, so I tried digging in again.

"Not to pry," I obviously lied, "but you seemed a little uncomfortable at our hosts on the stopover. What..." I really wasn't even sure how to phrase it. 'What is your problem' seemed a little hostile. 'What did you see here that you had never seen on your ship and wigged you out' was too wordy, and not even useful either. I decided to go generic.

"What were you expecting?" I asked, simply.

There was a pause. As usual. Robert was not particularly quick on his feet in the thinking department, as near as I could tell.

"Well," he began, "I... I don't know that it's fair to say what we expected. We didn't even know about Conglommora until I saw you come up on the sensors. I mean, we knew there were people out here somewhere, but I figured everyone had found a planet, or system, and had settled it all nice by now.

"I was sort of brought up to believe that, I guess," he confided, in what seemed like a real genuine moment of honesty. "That we were settling on a new Earth, starting a branch office of humanity or something." He smiled a bit.

"But just a branch office," he continued the metaphor. "I always thought that after a sufficient amount of time, the Earth would have healed, and we'd all head back there."

He looked uncomfortable for a moment, like that was something he wasn't supposed to have said. Dark shadows washed over his face.

"So no, this is not what I expected at all. Humanity stuck out here, at the edge of nothing, in the middle of empty," he gestured at the walls, "and not living as people... as I would have thought."

I was puzzled, "How do you mean?" I took a bottle of compressed water from my hip, expanded a swallow and downed a slug, awaiting his reply. We kept walking.

It took a minute. Maybe several. Time played tricks on you in these endless, sensory-deprivation tubes. I remember reading a stream about explorers on Green Earth, who ventured out in the frozen, near-uninhabitable regions of the frozen arctic wilderness, before they melted into the sea.

Back then, you could walk for tens of days or more in the endless, white-on-white world of cloud on snow on ice. Researchers reported hallucinations, both audio and visual, as a result of the unrelieved, featureless panorama of bleached reality. With nothing for the eyes to see or the ears to hear, the mind would just start to make up things. All sorts of things. Voices of friends; loved ones. Dragons. Impossibly vivid colors and yawning, aching empty blackness to contrast the eternal white. All in the space of a few minutes. Or maybe it was hours. Or days. Tough to tell after a while.

We hadn't started hallucinating just yet, not at least as far as I could tell. Maybe he only paused a moment before replying. Maybe it was some tens of days.

"It's just…" he started in finally, "it's just that there is a *right* way for people to live, to love, to act, to behave," he mused, "the natural way, as intended. And what little I've seen of Conglommora," he rolled his eyes a bit, "that just doesn't seem to be the case anymore. You tell me that no one really knows what Earth year it is… how is that possible?" he demanded, suddenly adamant.

Why the Earth year made any difference, I don't know.

But that was only the beginning. He was revving up. "You've got man and wife… and another man! and different races, different colored people all living together, and even different colors altogether!" he exclaimed, his own unique birth color flushing into his face.

"It's wrong! It's just plain wrong!" he flustered.

I wasn't sure I understood.

"What does skin color have to do with it? Color comes from an epigenetic pill. You can pick any color you want, and folks do. Sure, it's not the color you were born with, but people have been coloring their hair and painting their faces for thousands—tens of thousands of years, at least!"

Exasperation took hold and snapped through my normally mild demeanor. "I don't understand how you can judge people by what colors they choose, or how many spouses they have. How does that matter at all?"

"It's not natural!" Robert spat.

"Oh hell, living in a tin can in the literal middle of nowhere ain't exactly natural either, Robert," I sighed and stopped to face him. Almost confrontationally. Almost.

"Lots of women have many husbands out here, because having children isn't as easy as on Earth. You get a lot of failed pregnancies and do-overs."

"Do-overs?" Robert halted, with a tinge of concern.

"You know, when the baby is born well enough, but it's damaged. Damaged enough that no pills will fix it, no replacement parts will make it whole. So it's a do-over. Back in to the reclaimer and you try again."

Robert stopped and bent over, nearly double, his hands on his knees. I wasn't sure what that accomplished.

"You can't... you... you people are barbaric," he whispered. "It's not right. I suppose you kill old people, too. Throw them right in the reclaimer."

"Only if they ask for it," I shot back. "It's not mandatory or anything, but yes, if you're old and infirm you can choose to end your life quickly and painlessly. It's the humane thing to do. On Earth, they used to put dead bodies in boxes and bury them in the fields! Here at least we can reclaim your chemicals."

"It's not right!" he lashed out again and looked up at me with fervent eyes.

I looked at him long and hard, long enough and hard enough to actually get his attention, to get through whatever that layer of crap was that he held up to shield himself with.

"Right?" I leaned over and whispered, afraid at some level of speaking the final truth too loudly, too boldly for the world to hear.

"Right? What is right? Is it right that we killed the only home we'll ever have in the whole of the cosmos? Is it right that we live out here in a big metal knot of tubes and wires? Never to see a sunset, or swim in an ocean, climb a mountain or breathe original air that hasn't been through the recycler a trillion times before you were even born? Is any of this *right?*" I demanded, not letting up my stare for even one second.

"No." He looked away in defeat, "No, it's not. None of it."

"Good." I brightened. "Then we agree on something at last."

I met his eyes head on. "It's not right. But it *is*. It is *all* that there is, for now, and for ever."

I stood up, slowly. Partly for dramatic effect, but partly also because my back was seized up in knots from all this infernal walking. I turned and started back up along the corridor.

"All that it is," Robert mumbled, and with eyes downcast to the featureless floor, trudged along behind me. "I'll fix it, I swear," he whispered, but not quietly enough.

"There's nothing to fix." I ended the conversation.

A few hours of silence after that dour exchange, and we really weren't prepared for what came next.

I had no idea.

Six

WE EXITED THE MAIN CORRIDOR into the junction tube at the end of our epic detour. I expected another small home or small central courtyard kind of thing, as we entered the neighborhood listed as *Skyville* on my screen.

I was not expecting to see a vast domed expanse, nearly as far as the eye could see, with some sort of holographic or vr projection on the ceiling, which at the moment looked like a brilliant, azure blue sky arcing to the horizon.

A few curious locals looked up as we entered, but not nearly as curious as we looked at *them*. Here I had just finished lecturing Robert on how appearances didn't matter, but I stopped short in my tracks at these folks.

Now it's perfectly true that skin color is merely a choice. You pick a color you like, take the right pill for a few days or longer (depending on the base color you're working against) and there ya go. Colored people—folks who choose to color themselves differently from their birth color—have been around forever, and no one has any issue with that.

It's also perfectly true that some folks like to get drawn. Skin artwork, from the tattoos of ancient man to the holographic illusions of modern man, has always been part of the more colorful fabric of humanity. And of course some folks go for even more exotic body modifications, stretching and torquing earlobes, underarms, kneecaps, or other bits of convenient flesh in some artistic statement.

But I swear to you, reader of my careful words, that I had *never* seen all of these fancies combined as fluently and as extremely as here in the place they called Skyville.

The few folks we saw at first weren't even of a single color apiece. Arms of pink, torsos of bright vermilion, faces of warm brown, legs of iridescent blue. And illustrated, with drawings encircling every limb, joining into a holo illusion around the mid-section that jumped out and in front of the simple clothing they wore. Well, the cloth was simple, but the cutouts were pretty intricate. Very geometric.

I've talked to a lot of funky people throughout Conglommora, played a few vr games with their cross-bred dragons and mythical beasts, dealt with a lot of folks trying to be different for difference's sake, but all this was new even to me.

Poor Robert looked like he was going to puke. Clearly this was in the ever-enlarging category of "wrong" to him.

And the dome itself—I had heard of large biodomes like this one, but hearing about it and seeing a few possibly enhanced or even faked vids isn't the same thing as seeing it in person. It was breathtaking.

Unlike the common ultra-compact chicken pods, or even the rarer, larger luxury livestock pods, this was immense. Houses ringed the outside perimeter of the dome, and the interior was full of pasture grass, with soil and everything. Instead of being reserved exclusively for the animals, the people who lived here were out and about living on the grass area themselves! Some sitting and reading, some tending to equipment of some sort or other, most occupied doing who-knows-what.

A horse roared nearby. Roared? Is that even the right word for a horse? I think it was a horse. Sleeker and taller than those other things, which I'm pretty sure were cows. Whatever the specifics, the smell of this room was… unique. Not quite like a malfunctioning recycler toilet, but close, with a sweaty tang from old exercise gear and a few other nuances I couldn't even begin to guess at.

By now, our entrance was causing a bit of a stir, as a handful of people came over and gathered around. Including, apparently, a goddess. She came up to me.

"Hi, my name is Cathy," said the young woman in a strong voice, holding up her arm.

She was a vision. A vision of gold. Golden tanned skin, warm and smooth. Huge, flowing golden-blond hair that looked more like a wild animal—a lion's mane, perhaps—than a person's. Just golden all over—except for her arms. Those were teal. And on her forearm was her name, spelled "Käthe" in floating, holographic letters.

Stunned at it all, I barely managed to offer my hand, "Hello, uh, Käthe, I'm Charlie Neylan, and this is Robert Brandeis. His ship just arrived at Conglommora."

She shook my hand warmly, clasping my hand with both of hers, and then moving on to Robert. "Ah, I heard about that. Took you a while to find us, huh?" She smiled.

"Well welcome to the world, Mr. Robert." She gestured to the expanse of green and blue behind her, and continued.

"We call our neighborhood 'Skyville', for obvious reasons. Our grandparents didn't like the claustrophobic feel of small ships and tubes, so we took most of the ships and made this dome. It makes each of our own houses a lot smaller, but you can't beat the view."

It was impressive. I'd spent some time in simulated vr environments similar to this one, but somehow being here in person was very different. I should steer Alain out this way someday, maybe. I'm sure it still wasn't the same as standing in a real field on Green Earth, but it was pretty awesome. Robert may or may not have been taking it all in. I think he'd made it past the shock of the multi-colored people. Probably hadn't processed the big blue sky yet.

In fact, he was ignoring the sky entirely, and had knelt down to the dirt, examining the planting.

"You all right there, Robert?" I asked.

"This is fantastic!" he said low and quiet, as if not to alert the residents of their own miracle. "Have you felt this dirt? Smelled it? This is really, really well done."

He straightened up. "I couldn't get near to this quality on my ship," he admitted, clapping loose dirt from his hands.

Well, finally, he seemed genuinely enthusiastic and happy about something. It was a start. One thing at a time and all that.

We followed Käthe into one of the nearby houses for some refreshments and to discuss trades for tonight's lodging and to replace extra food for our journey that we'd plowed through on the detour.

Dinner was fantastic. I'd had most of these ingredients before from certain trades every now and then, so no one dish in particular was new, but to have this vast array of fresh meats, produce, and sauces all at once, prepared so expertly, was a new experience.

The wine was a bright blue, something I hadn't seen before at all. Some combination of a regular viticulture and an algae infusion, maybe? It was plentiful, was really smooth, and went down easy. And the company…

Käthe was an amazing person. Stunning to look at, bright, articulate, a real gem of the galaxy. As the guests of honor, I was seated on one side next to her and Bob on the other, right up at the head of the table. Folks came and went to say hello and ask us questions—especially Bob, who was very much a novelty.

I tried to make small talk with Käthe, but it didn't seem to get very far. Maybe the holotats were just too distracting. Or the hair. For whatever reason, we just didn't connect. It just wasn't happening. Maybe I wasn't ready yet. Maybe I'd never be.

As sometimes happens with large dinner parties, folks got up and moved around; changed seats to vary the conversation partners and such. I excused myself from Käthe and plowed in to the dessert course with singular focus.

Buried deep in the throes of dessert, I swear I heard a voice. My wife's voice.

Let go.

I looked up. There was no one there. So many people talking at once. Just a fragment of conversation. No, Käthe wasn't the one for me. No one was the one for me, not anymore. Haily was the one for me, and she's dead.

Let go.

My hand trembled slightly as I set the spork down and wiped my mouth. Maybe this trip was a bad idea all around. I had *tried* to talk to Käthe, tried to establish some rapport. Failed. I can't let go. I'm still married. Death notwithstanding.

Funny how you could be surrounded by people and still feel so isolated; so alone. Skyville seemed like a fantastic place to live, at least if you didn't mind wandering beasts of assorted sizes. But I didn't know any of these people. I came to Skyville and they were strangers to me. I'd leave and they'd still be strangers to me. Just passing through. Some people live their whole lives like that, not connecting, not participating—just passing through. Maybe I'd become one of them.

So as I was morosely pondering my failure at small talk with Käthe, and failure of my life in general, a fresh and friendly face plopped down in the seat across from me.

"Hi!" she said.

"Oh, hello," I managed, looking up. "My name is Charlie." I offered my hand.

She shook with a smile and replied with a gentle laugh, "Hi Charlie. Yes, I gathered that. We don't get a lot of travelers though here. I'm Grace. Grace Bethany Langston."

Something about her manner, her... her spirit. Despite everything we'd seen and everyone we'd met so far, this was... different. This was something I hadn't felt in a very long time. She wasn't stunning like Käthe was, but was even more arresting, in a completely different way. Different, but beautiful. A formal introduction, but casual and warm.

Bob was investigating his dessert with an unusual passion as well, probably also a little uncomfortable at the crowd. I gestured over toward him, "This is Robert. His ship just pulled in and I'm taking him to help make some repairs."

Or something like that. There was a lot of stammering going on. Bob didn't even look up.

Gah. I'm normally pretty articulate, but for whatever reason, words felt like bricks of Raw in my mouth. Large bricks, at that. Grace didn't seem to notice my sudden descent into total communications failure.

"I heard!" she replied perkily. "Been a while since we've had a newcomer."

"Right," was all I could mount as a pithy reply. Her skin was pearly, iridescent white that seemed to glow with exuberance. Her dark golden hair, put up neatly, bobbed at me. Her eyes, deepest green like some kind of magical pools in an alien fantasy world, sparkled always with purest joy. At least, that's how I felt about it.

What the hell.

Let go.

I knew what this was. You're probably even way ahead of me by now. This is what falling in love can feel like. I'd forgotten. First sight? Literally. Love? Maybe just infatuation. Maybe just a connection. But… it was a spark, a suddenly loosened arc of energy in a box of dry kindling.

Let go.

It was loud in the hall, with so many people all together, talking at once. The hall itself was a large wooden structure with what looked like exposed beams of immense, ancient trees. Grace seemed aware of the din and offered, "Hey, want to go for a walk?"

Is it possible to explode with relief? I surely would have. Into delighted, gelatinous shrapnel of relieved bits of Charlie. The fact that all we'd *been* doing lately was walking was suddenly immaterial.

She popped up from the table and strode toward the door; I mumbled something inchoate to Bob and followed a little too quickly, nearly stumbling out the door frame into the now darkened fields of Skyville.

It was nighttime or what passes for nighttime in these parts. A silvery light supposedly reminiscent of Earth's long-lost moon barely illuminated the dome. Grace waited for me to catch my breath and some semblance of reason, and we walked together through the wide open fields. Animals I couldn't readily identify slept comfortably, a few wandered about quietly, and we walked through the oddly comforting nightscape.

She pointed out her compact, domed house at the far edge of the fields, and we ambled toward it. I asked about her family.

"Oh it's just me, now," she said with only a slight dimming of her natural exuberance. "My sister left Skyville when we were young, but we don't stay in touch much. She wanted to wander, to explore, to see all of Conglommora. She pings me once in a while. I never know where she'll turn up next." She gave a sweet, forgiving laugh. "I stayed here with my parents, and they both died a couple of years ago."

"Farming accident?" I asked with some relevant concern.

"Just old age," she said gently. "Mom and Dad were both in their 150s when they passed, they had me pretty late in life. So it's just me now. How about you? Tell me about your family."

"Not much to tell," I admitted. "I have a son, Alain. Great kid. My wife passed away suddenly, so it's been just the two of us for a while now. He's getting older, capable—mature, even. But he's still my little boy to me. I..." I trailed off, feeling sheepish.

Grace took my hand.

"He sounds delightful," she beamed. We came to a stream of open running water and smooth rocks, carved through the fields, and sat on a larger rock holding hands.

"I love this time of night," Grace continued, gazing out at the quiet of the animals, the silver light reflecting off the grasses, the water. "So peaceful. Like all the world taking a deep cleansing breath."

"It's an amazing place," I agreed. "I've heard of the larger biodomes like this and seen pics, but never have been out to see them in person. Really something. You're very lucky."

"Yes, I am." She squeezed my hand and smiled at me with all the energy of a drive engine.

And so we talked.

We talked all night.

What else did we talk about?

Everything. Nothing. Stories from our childhoods. Hopes, dreams, the meaning of life. Jokes. Irritations. Joys. We laughed, we grimaced, we shared it all.

The silver nightscape gave way to an orange dawn, chased off by the full-on bright pseudo-sunlight of day. It seemed like only minutes, but clearly some hours had passed, effortlessly.

Grace was one of a kind. A bright spirit, that for some remarkably twisted reason found an affinity with my own. I had been lucky enough to fall in love with my wife Haily—as one of the first generations not bound to the ships themselves, choices were better, but still necessarily limited. But we had found love, had Alain, and made a life. She left us both abruptly and had taken my feelings with her. Or so I thought.

And yet here they were, back again in full foment—unaccustomed and unexpected. Whatever babbling I managed was apparently sufficient; Grace enjoyed my company and whatever it was I was talking about.

The animals were awake now and wandered about, doing what animals do. Eating, walking, crapping, ruminating on the nature of life, the universe, and everything. I had no idea cows were so large. Wow.

Grace laughed with me, not at me, as if giant crapping cows were just a normal part of life. I guess to her, they were.

"I've got to go take care of the animals now," she said. "It's that time of day."

"Sure—don't let me get in your way." I gave her an easy out. "Besides…" Did I really look down and dig my toe in the dirt? What the hell, was I twelve again?

"I've got to get Robert his spare parts so he can fix his ship and connect to Conglommora properly." Right, that was my mission. Sure. Like I even cared anymore. Robert? Who's Robert?

"Okay. Stop by again on your way back?" she asked, her green eyes infinitely deep; I could dive in and swim and not come up for air, like a mermaid dragging me down to the depths of old.

As I was constructing an elaborate and hopefully cogent and sensible reply, she leaned in close and kissed me simply, briefly, right on the lips, before turning on her heel and heading off to the herd of things in the green, grassy field.

I'm sure I said something polite, reasonable, and kind somewhere during this process.

Or, sadly, it's very possible that I stood there like a complete do-over. A useless blob of non-viable protoplasm, just hoping for the end to come, and to come quickly. At my age, even. Imagine.

I stumbled back to our assigned quarters, a smooth white round building just big enough for a couple of beds. Bob looked up at me, surprise clearly on his face and in his body language.

"Where were you?" he asked with a trace of concern and possible fear of abandonment. "You didn't come back last night after the dinner."

"I, ah, I was out with Grace."

"Grace?" he repeated.

"You know, the girl I was sitting with after dessert—shorts, dark golden hair, deep green eyes…" I stopped before embarrassing myself, I hoped.

Then Bob did something I swear I hadn't seen before. He smirked. A genuine, mischievous, conspiratorial smirk.

"Heh," he snorted, "good on you, then."

"I mean we just talked, it wasn't like…" What was I even defending? Or explaining? I owed Bob neither.

"Whatever," he said, still smiling. "We're almost there, right?"

"Almost, we still have to take the long-distance hyper-loop, another large biodome, a little walking and then we'll be at the mech center," I said trying to force some semblance of clarity to my conversation.

Bob hoisted his pack and headed for the door. He stopped; the bright light from Skyville framed him in silhouette. Looking over his shoulder he said simply, "Let's go then."

And with that he was out the door and headed across the field to the tube junction on the far side.

But I didn't want to leave. I had promised to help him fix his ship, I guess, and when I left the *Neylan* it's not like I had anything better to do. Alain really was more grown up than I wanted to admit; he didn't need me hanging around like a misguided service drone. Maybe leaving him should have been harder, but part of me also insisted. It was time. But leaving here, leaving her... this was different. Maybe. I'd rather not.

I paused at the door. Bob was striding over the field, under the brilliant blue sky of the dome, picking his way between animals and their droppings.

A promise was a promise, I guess.

I followed.

Seven

WHERE WE WERE HEADED was one of the oldest parts of Conglommora, and these areas had developed a few more features than we had back home.

We were very lucky—we could save a few thousand klicks of walking and crawling by taking one of the hyperloop tubes. We'd cover all those klicks in about an hour.

The airlock blinked green, and I palmed the wall to open the hatch. The door to our pod slid quickly and quietly aside and we stepped in, looking for a pair of seats together.

As we sat, Robert watched and took note of our fellow riders in the sparsely populated pod. There was the usual variety of the very tall, the very short, several colored and multicolored people, one bald albino and a few of the hairiest folks I've ever seen anywhere. Not sure what their beliefs or background were, but these several folks—men and women both—had body hair all over their arms and legs, the men had full-on beards, and all had waist-length hair.

A lucky family with several children was camped up against the bulkhead. The smallest child was maybe just on the verge of learning to walk and alternated between crawling over his parents and older siblings and standing with wobbly knees as the pod shot through the tube.

The family was smiling and joking with one another; the hairy group were involved in some deep conversation, but seemed to be having a good time. The albino fellow was traveling alone and already engrossed in reading some stream or another.

Robert was waxing philosophical.

"This isn't what I expected. None of it," he muttered. "It was bad enough to find out that humanity is trapped out here, homeless and adrift at the edge of nothing." He leaned back and sighed heavily.

"We failed. We killed our planet and for our evil, we were cast out yet again. Yet everyone I've met and seen out here doesn't seem to mind." He waved a hand vaguely, encompassing the riders. "They're happy. Raising happy families. Pursuing their passions. Getting along with each other."

He started getting just a little agitated again.

"No one works for a living, you don't seem to have any crime or violence, and you're not at each other's throats all the time." Exasperation crept into his voice. "God has smitten you, cast out first from paradise to the evils of Earth, then cast out a second time into the void itself. It sounds like hell!" His voice raised to a level where several in our pod looked up or over to stare at him.

He leaned forward, clasped his hands together and got quieter. "But it isn't like hell at all, is it? You've made a paradise out here. Paradise found in the void." He smiled weakly.

I knew what he was saying; this line of thinking had come up before. In fact, it was a whole thing.

"There's a group that has an answer to that," I suggested gently. "Religious followers of a book called The Last Word."

Robert looked up from his hunched over, hung head position. "The what?"

"I don't know a whole lot about them. I'm not very religious in that sense," I admitted. "I mean, I'm fairly certain there is a God out there, but I'm also pretty sure that anything we think about Him is probably wrong.

"Anyway, in the early days of Conglommora, the realization hit that this was *it* for us. But also that we were actually better off now than at any previous state in our bloody, scream-filled history. Between the printers, reclaimers, and the AI's, everyone's basic needs are taken care of. There's no need to steal, or kill, to survive, even if we could."

Robert looked a little puzzled at that last, but I plowed ahead.

"So a group of theologians got together and wrote *The Last Word*. The idea being that God cast humanity out of the garden of Eden originally and left us on Earth. We succumbed to evil and sin, and destroyed the planet.

But not before Kain Mimulus revealed our next step; broadcast the plans for the printers and reclaimers, for the ships, the drive engines, all of it.

"What we've built here," I gestured widely, "is our worldly paradise as it should have been. The idea goes that God cast us out to teach us a lesson, and finally and at greatest cost, we learned it. Stupid apes that we are," I smiled grimly, "we finally learned it.

"Forgiveness. Love. Learned how to live with each other." An insight popped up in my head. "Take my chicken neighbor, Justin. Now Justin is a bit of jerk, actually. Kind of a know-it-all. We've had our fights and disagreements over the years. I don't like him. Maybe I even hate him," I admitted, gesturing with open hands. "But I would do anything to help him and his family out in an emergency.

"I hope to go on 'not liking him' for a very long time. And that's the secret. We're all still human, but we've learned that taking care of each other is *the* most important thing, or there won't be anyone left this time. We all get along, mind our own business, trade a bit, forgive a bit, and survive. The folks back on Dead Earth who couldn't stomach that, well, they didn't make it out here. We bred out, killed, or left behind, the greedy, the evil, the power hungry. It's just us now, just the People."

"So yeah, the People are reasonably happy, better off than at any other time in history. Here. In the void itself."

Robert was staring straight ahead. He thought a bit, and repeated quietly, "Not what I expected."

The pod raced forward, winding through the dark between neighborhoods and sometimes just out into space itself as we crossed to a farther side of Conglommora.

The small child continued to climb over his family, the groups of hairy and multicolored folks continued their conversations, and the albino kept reading.

Robert kept silent, brooding on the possibility that maybe, just maybe, this was actually how it was supposed to be. That this was God's plan—his God's, at any rate—after all.

Maybe his grand plan, his great purpose, was no longer needed. Maybe he was in the wrong place at the wrong time, and he missed he chance to set right the wrongs of the world.

I don't really have any idea what he was thinking. I'd like to imagine that was he was reconsidering his life's purpose, that he at least gave some thought to letting Conglommora just be as it was. But maybe that didn't cross his mind at all. Maybe he didn't believe me, or didn't give any credence to the Last Word. Maybe he just wasn't capable of listening anymore.

The pod slowed as we approached the station and slid out of the hyperloop tube into a siding. This was our stop.

Eight

THE HATCH OPENED onto a small platform. We stood on it and marveled, because it was the only solid surface we could see. The entirety of a very, very large dome was filled with water. Seawater, I guess, by the smell of it. It had a very different smell from the stuff you drink or bathe with; there was salt even in the air, along with an incredible amount of humidity. The air itself was in motion, and the water wasn't still—there were small waves sloshing right up against our platform.

A few small dots off in the distance scuttled back and forth. Two headed for us with surprising speed. As they got closer, the dots turned into two men, standing upright on boards of some kind, each with a long stick that they used to pull the water.

"Hello!" the first man cried exuberantly as he approached. The second hung back just a bit, clearly waiting before coming any closer.

"Hello, I'm Charlie Neylan," I replied.

"Chalu," he said, tapping his bare chest. Chalu was not as tall as most, a little on the heavy side. His skin looked the color of antique, brown polished wood, and multi-colored hair hung down almost to his waist, where an assortment of small, strange-looking tools stuck to his belt.

"Chalu," I repeated and nodded, then gestured to Robert. "This is Robert. He's only just arrived at Conglommora and we're traveling to get some repair tech for him."

"I heard about that," Chalu admitted. "Welcome to the world, Robert. This is Hano." He nodded over to his friend, who slid his board over toward us.

"What is this place?" I asked.

"We call it Sea," Chalu said. "Not very original, but it serves. We raise fish here—all different kinds. Some very large, some microscopic. And plants, algaes, that sort of thing. What do you need?"

Robert perked up a bit at the plant angle.

"Robert and I need to cross all the way through your Sea to a corridor on the other side," I explained.

"Okay, cool," Chalu nodded. "Visitors generally don't handle the boards very well." He absentmindedly tossed the long stick to his other hand. It had a broad end; I guess to help propel him on the board. I don't think he was showing off, and watching the boards rock and wiggle on the waves while they effortlessly kept their balance convinced me that he was telling the truth.

"And I suppose you don't have gill mods for underwater breathing?" He flexed, and there was a flutter along his neck above his collar bone—a line of white, up both sides of his neck, almost like a scar, but with a feathered edge that opened and closed. Gills, apparently.

I'd heard of genetic feature mods like that before, but had never seen one up close.

"No, sorry," I mumbled. "No gills here. Just lungs."

He laughed, a small, gentle, soft laugh. Not making fun of us, just appreciating the absurdity of the conversation and of life in general.

"Not a problem," Chalu said, "although you'll miss the splendor of our underwater villages. Hano and I will go get a boat for you to cross. Do you need a place to sleep, or food or anything?"

"How long will it take to cross on the surface?" I asked.

Chalu thought for a moment and pursed his lips. "All the way over? Hmm, maybe five or six hours, I guess. We don't run the power boats all that fast—it's not good to scare the fish. We almost always just use the boards for daily surface work and stuff."

"Thanks for your offer," I replied. "Yeah, we probably better plan on a meal and rest while we're here. We've got plenty of Raw we can trade, even some Pure Organic."

Chalu cocked his head back and laughed larger, a warm, hearty laugh. Still not making fun of us, but just enjoying the irony he was about to share. "No need, my wife and I will be happy to put you up for the night, and the community won't mind us using one of the small transit boats. As for Pure Organic, well, we *make* that here."

Of course. The huge ecosystem with an artificial ocean, the algae, the kelp, the plants… of course they could produce Pure Organic all by themselves.

Chalu flipped his board around to face back the way they had come in one fluid movement. "We'll head into the closest surface town and get transit; be back in about an hour."

"Thanks so much," I said, trying for humble and gracious. I'm not always good at that sort of thing.

They glided off smoothly and quickly away from the platform and wall where we had entered.

Robert spoke up, breaking his silence with a question. "I thought you said you guys couldn't make Pure Raw, especially Pure Organic. That's why I brought it along for trades."

I nodded. "Well, it's not that we *can't*, but it's a specialized thing. There's only a few places that are large and diverse enough to be able to do it well. Like here." I gestured to the expanse, just as a couple of large seabirds swooped past, on some urgent mission. Lunch, perhaps.

"How many of these fake oceans do you have?" he asked.

I pulled out the shiny screen from my pocket and made a few gestures. "Looks like there are six very large ocean habitats," I said, reading from a fact stream. "There are a lot of smaller ones, and nearly everybody has at least a few algae tanks. But in order to make Pure, you'd need one of these really extra-large domes," I said, pointing to the vast, unrelieved expanse that opened up ahead of us.

"It's even bigger than it looks," I continued, reading the screen. "This top, surface area is less than ten percent of the volume. Most of the sea is underneath us. Just like on Earth, I guess."

I sat down cross-legged while Robert mulled that over, and we waited in silence and stillness. Waves lapped at the platform, and we saw flying critters of various sizes: some more birds, some insects. I'm sure there was a lot more going on just under the surface of the water and beyond. We got a glimpse of some large dark shapes a few times, and once a glittering mass of objects flashed past us.

The dome was a little warmer than standard, and the gravity maybe just a little bit heavier. The warm air, the gentle lapping of the waves… I felt drowsiness creep up on me; a reminder that I hadn't been sleeping well in all these strange places, and not at all our last night in Skyville. I started to drift off, thinking of Grace.

About a half an hour later, a faint hum in the distance became less faint, and Chalu, Hano, and three other figures approached on a small, flat, powered boat. The transit had arrived.

It slid right up to the platform we were on and sealed itself right to the platform edge with a slight click.

Robert and I crossed over onto the transit, and Chalu introduced us to the other three figures. "This is Charlie of *Neylan* and Robert the Visitor." He nodded in our direction. "And these are the leaders of Sea. This is Koma,

Master Fisher, Lanois, Master Planter, and Hoahoeh, Master Chemist."

Wow, Robert's arrival garnered some top-level attention.

We shook hands with each of the three in turn, and they with us. We detached from the dock and slid effortlessly across the water's surface.

Robert had questions for the Master Planter, and they fell into talking shop. Robert was especially interested in getting some kind of concentrated nitrogen samples. Not sure what he needed high-powered nitrogen for.

I was more curious about the origins of Sea and chatted up Hoahoeh, the Master Chemist.

In the early days, she told me, they had wanted to transport a large, generational ship filled with actual sea water from Earth. But there were problems; any large sample would be contaminated with all manner of pollutants. Filtering and cleaning it would be possible, but inefficient and counter productive, as they would have lost much of the microscopic life forms that were needed as well.

"It was a really hard problem for our people," Hoahoeh said. "In the end, we got a large enough sample direct from an Earth ocean and extracted the organic and inorganic components separately. We synthesized a new, pure, base seawater based on the original samples of contaminated inorganic matter, and then added the desired organic components individually, repairing any corrupted DNA as we went."

"There are six large seas like yours out here." I asked, "Did they all come from the same original program?"

"Four did," Hoahoeh answered. "Once we had a clean, solid base, it was prolific enough to fill three more domes. The other two are a little different," she went on. "One is purely synthetic and only grows a very limited range of species. The other is freshwater, not marine based. It counts as a large sea by volume, but it's not one large body like these." She gestured to the expanse surrounding us. "Instead, it's made up of a lot of smaller static and moving bodies."

We carried on for a bit, and both Robert and I got to talk to the Fish Master, Koma, as well, about the many species they conserved. Some of these buggers were pretty huge.

"The very largest we do not harvest," he explained. "They are here to preserve the overall ecosystem."

Another half hour went by, and their town came into view. I'm not sure what I was expecting, but it wasn't this. Robert seemed stunned.

The houses and buildings were simple, small one-deck-high affairs, built on piers and sitting right on the water. I would have expected perhaps grander and more expansive quarters, based on the the fact that these folks could make as much Pure Organic as anyone could need.

But the beauty and simplicity of this place was remarkable.

Folks were out and about, going from building to building on those boards with their paddle sticks. A group was working in what looked like a field of plants.

They all had the traditional skin colors of their ancestors, and the multi-colored, rainbow hair. And they were all bare-chested in the warm, bright environment. I couldn't tell how many had gill mods—maybe that varied by town? Or maybe they all had them.

We ate with Chalu and his family—wife, son, and a daughter. Ahdom, Chalu's son, was the spitting image of his father. Younger, obviously, hair not as long or intricate. But there was no doubt of his parentage. Chalu's daughter, Sundara, was older, well past her teens, but not yet set up with her own family. She was very, very pretty. But my mind, and possibly my heart, were preoccupied with Grace. I was polite, but not very engaged. She seemed to take the hint well. Robert took up the slack and engaged her in small talk about plants and things.

Mostly I was interested in talking with Chalu. His honest, realistic, hopeful outlook on life echoed the beauty and simplicity of Sea itself. Chalu and I talked philosophy all through dinner; Ahdom joined in the discussion a few times, probably to the dismay of said wife and daughter who did not. I felt guilty that the rest seemed a little left out, but then again, they were probably accustomed to Chalu's sweeping oration—they'd heard it all before.

To my mind, Chalu was a great example of what all of us hoped to be when we grew up: kind, wise, thoughtful, with an incredible thirst for knowledge. I thought Ahdom was clearly following in his father's footsteps—not only did he look much like his father, he talked a lot like him as well. He was young still, of course, but it struck me that he'd really be something in a few years. I should introduce him to Alain; they looked pretty closed in age, but far apart in experiences.

Oh, and the fish dinner was, as you may have guessed, excellent.

"Really great place you have here." I gestured to include Chalu's house and the rest of Sea as well. "I could see folks wanting to come here to find themselves."

Chalu raised an eyebrow. "Ah, to 'find yourself.' An odd phrase, don't you think? As if the 'self' were something to be harvested, like a ripe plant, or some rare beast found swimming in the mysterious depths of a real ocean.

"But of course it's not like that at all, is it?" he asked me, I assume rhetorically. I didn't volunteer an answer, at any rate. "The 'self' isn't something one can wander around and just find by magic," he scoffed. "It's not found. The self is something that has to be *made*. Crafted. Hammered out from raw experience. Every day, every moment, every decision. For good or ill. Over and over again, throughout your life!"

I'd never thought of it that way. I don't suppose I'd really thought about it at all, actually. My 'self' is just me. Some regrets, some acclaim, some sorrow, some hope. But the idea of "finding myself" was always lingering in the background, as if there *was* some magical situation where I would discover who I really was, what my core was really made of. It never occurred to me that I was something to be crafted, not found.

Chalu had a knack for making me think.

After dinner, Robert and I slept in different houses, Chalu had room only for one of us, and feeling some guilt for dominating the dinner conversation, I insisted Robert take that place of honor. I slept next door. My host was an older woman named Lahoe, who had outlived her husband and two sons, but was happy to tell me all about them and more about Sea in general.

Lahoe told me, in long and luxurious sentences, that the underwater villages were much more interesting, architecturally speaking: poured forms and spires in bright colors that resembled corals, twisting and rising from the sandy floor of the biodome. You could visit using breathing apparatus, but it was clumsy and cumbersome, and tended to scare the fish. Better to get the gills.

Maybe next time.

The lights turned down to simulate a nocturnal cycle for the plants and animals, and the dark, the warm, and the still gentle lapping of the waves did me in. I slept solid for the longest time since we'd set off on this trip.

Breakfast was simple but well-executed, and I have to say their algae juice and cooked kelp was a lot better than I was used to. This whole trip was really pointing out how lazy, how complacent, how limited I'd become.

We gathered ourselves and got back on the transit to head to the other side of Sea. It surprised me a little that I didn't really feel like leaving. It was nice here. Really, very nice.

Chalu would drive us from their town—there were apparently a dozen other surface towns like it within Sea—over to the far edge platform for the next corridor. He noticed my pensive look as we boarded and asked if I was okay.

"Oh, I'm fine," I reassured him. "It's just… I mean, wow, I had no idea you guys were out here, doing this sort of thing, and doing it so well."

Chalu shrugged as we separated from the house platform. "It's not like it's a big secret or anything. Anyone can find us; you just need to know to ask."

I realized how little I knew about all of the nooks and crannies of Conglommora and sighed a little. "I should get out more."

Chalu looked up as the transit turned around and asked earnestly, "What's stopping you?"

"Nothing," I admitted, with lift of my eyebrows.

"Yeah, that's what gets in everyone's way, doesn't it?" Chalu observed as we headed away from town. "Just nothing at all."

He smiled a wise, old smile as we shot along the water in the bright, warm, wet world.

Nine

WE MADE IT to the mech section, at long last.

Well, it really wasn't all that long, but it sure felt it. I'd seen parts of the Conglommora I hadn't really known existed, and I was sure there were far wilder bits out there still. There was never any shortage of bizarre rumors about Conglommora, and between Skyville and Sea, I thought I was pretty much prepared for anything.

As usual, I was wrong.

The mech section—they didn't have any official name other than that—was a different beast entirely.

Picture a bunch of really, really bored engineers with essentially unlimited fabrication capabilities and imagination. And no restraint whatsoever from a spouse or loved one saying, "Honey, do you think that's really a good idea?"

The approach was unremarkable; Robert and I walked along the last, lonely corridor lit in the now-familiar amber and blue lights. I opened the hatch and entered the domain of the mech section, Robert trailing behind me. But I realized immediately that this part of Conglommora was something different.

The giant mechanical, half-holo half-searchlight lit-up unicorn that guarded the entrance was the first clue. The moving walkway that shifted direction as you walked on it was the second. By the time we got to the reverse waterfall, flowing upward toward the ceiling of the dome, I was getting pretty disoriented.

A couple of guys came out to meet us. At last something vaguely familiar I could hang onto.

"I'm Charlie, this is Robert." Handshakes all around.

"Hi, I'm Avi," said the first. "We know; we watched your approach. Ronny told us you were coming."

"I'm Why," said the second fellow, who seemed a little more shy and held back a little.

"Why?" I said, taking the bait. "As in, you know, 'why'?"

"Exactly that." He beamed. I wasn't real sure what to make of that, but Avi jumped in.

"You're the first visitors we've had in ages. What can we do for you? Are you hungry? Need a holo implant or anything else simple while you're here?" he offered.

"We're good," I said, still full of fresh fish. "Robert just needs the specialized parts and help for his ship—he's only just arrived at Conglommora."

"Ah, you're the guy," Why said.

Avi looked at Bob a little more closely, paused for a moment, then volunteered—albeit cautiously—"Sure, no problem, Robert." he said.

"Let's go over what you need…" He and Robert veered off, toward a bank of visual displays and a vr pad.

That left Why and me.

"So, excuse any impertinence or offense," I started, "but…"

Why interrupted with a knowing smile, "But why am I named for an adverb?"

I swallowed the rest of my sentence and nodded sheepishly.

"Why not?" he said, aware of the continual pun. "My mother's sense of irony, I suppose. The ultimate, most existential question of all? A source of much laughter my whole life?"

He said that last part without any trace of bitterness, and in fact, as more of a source of pride.

"Laughter?" I said with a puzzled face.

"Sure," Why replied. "It's funny, right? Why not?"

The pun wrapped itself around my brain stem and threatened to choke it off dead. Please, please tell me his middle name wasn't "not." I mean, was not not. Not, "not." Oh, why. I mean, why, not Why, I… crap, this guy must have so much fun trolling people. Mother's sense of humor? The apple didn't fall far from the tree.

Seeing my impending mental meltdown, Why turned and said, "Don't worry about it. It's just a name, like any other. Does 'Charlie' really make any empirical sense?"

Desperate—truly desperate to change the subject—I motioned to the cloud of drone hummingbirds floating over the roiling red sea of glowing jelly just a little bit aways from where we were standing. "This place really has a way of... disorienting you," I started. "Like, what's that over there?" I pointed to the drones and jelly sea.

Why looked over. "Oh, that's just one of my student's work," he said. "An interesting approach, but perhaps lacking in an overall coherence; there's no fractal unity of the piece, no..."

He talked on for a few more minutes, critiquing the work. I was mesmerized by the patterns of the mini drones, the undulating patterns of the viscous liquid flow, and the interplay of light and shadow between them. Why, it seems, was not as impressed.

I was rescued from this intellectual spiral of analysis by Avi and Bob.

"Okay," Avi said with some confidence, "I think I have a good handle on the problem here," he nodded over to Bob, "and this shouldn't be too hard. There's a couple of parts we need to fab here on the very-high-resolution printers, and some new software patches he'll need."

I raised my eyebrows at that. Usually Arty handled such things.

"I know this guy named Andy," Avi said. "Bit of a recluse, but can create multidimensional quantum neural nets like no one else. He'll get this sorted out."

They headed off in another direction, passing through some kind of string light bundle.

Why gave me a comforting look and offered, "Hey, enough of this. How about a hot cup of freshly brewed roast algae?"

I nodded, perhaps a bit numbly, and we walked over a silver bridge that reflected a younger and younger version of yourself on every step.

Why and I sat on stools that hung from the ceiling. Or maybe it was the floor, and the gravity was inverted. It was seriously hard to tell. I'm not sure what the oozing light patterns in the chairs were made of, but they looked almost organic.

"I don't think I'm in the mood for a hot drink right now," I admitted.

Why nodded sagely. "How about some Blue Wine?"

I closed my eyes and nodded in agreement. The drinks came up out of the table somehow, I wasn't paying close attention.

"This…" I started, "this is all so incredible."

Why looked around. "Is it?"

I wondered at that simple question.

"Is it really that incredible?" Why asked again. "You could do any of this yourself. You have a printer. You have Arty's help if you need it."

He was right. And yet, having the technology easily available didn't mean it was any easier to accomplish. You needed imagination. Force of will. Vision. Maybe even *purpose*. I twinged a bit inside at the thought of the word, like a sudden memory of a missing limb.

"It's incredible to me," I concluded, taking a sip of the powerful Blue Wine. "I work with words, not with things. Not with moving things, things that look like they have a life of their own." I pointed to the swirling table underneath our drinks.

"Words take on a life of their own, don't they?" Why asked.

Well, yes.

We talked on for a while on the nature of creativity and art. The table wound down and settled on a milky white-blue-green swirl.

After a while, Avi and Robert rejoined us.

"Hot algae?" Robert ordered, more of a question than a request. A steaming mug appeared for him. I still didn't really see where it came from.

"How'd it go?" I asked.

"Pretty good," Avi said. "I'm printing some parts now. The first batch will be done overnight, but it will take another day or two for the rest. Also, Why will need to tune the onboard AI to Robert's brain waves in the morning. The *Uten* uses a much older and much more primitive system than we use nowdays, but Robert doesn't want to replace it."

"What, like copper wires and electrons?" I asked with interest and just a little bit of a slur to my words. That would be a genuinely ancient system by modern standards.

Avi grimaced. "No, not *that* old. It's a nanophotonic core with the usual polariton circuits, qbits and such, but it's not up to date. No problem though, Why can tune it to Robert anyway."

Why nodded in agreement.

The wine had really caught up to me by now. I wasn't really sure why Why would need to so closely adapt the *Uten's* moldy old systems to Bob. But I didn't really care, either.

Our quarters for the night were... unusual. To say the least. I was set up in a mesh hammock, strung between two pale, glowing girders that seemed to be made of glass, or maybe a crystal of some sort, with something living inside—maybe they were glowworms? Something fluorescent and wriggling that was probably alive.

The hammock swung a bit every time I moved, and I felt pretty queasy. Still, between the wine and the journey, I was done in. I closed my eyes against the fluorescent nightmare and drifted off to sleep.

The next morning, Bob was hooked up to some ghastly-looking bit of mechanics. On his head. Avi and a young, bald woman with crystal spikes coming out of her head were hunched over a couple of pads.

"Hey Charlie. This is Rijm." He nodded at the crystal-headed girl, "This is really her area of expertise. I'm just helping out."

"Hi Charlie, pleased to meet you," she said, sparing a quick glance up but otherwise intent on an array of throbbing displays and graphs.

"What *is* all this?" I asked, gesturing at the tangled mess that appeared to be slowly consuming Bob.

Rijm continued palming a few controls, so Avi answered, "Robert has a direct neural link to his ship. It's pretty old-fashioned and has some issues, but he didn't want to upgrade or replace it. So Rijm is repairing it from here, getting it working again."

Under the bolts and wires and glowy bits attached to his head, Bob actually looked pretty miserable.

"Bob," I said. "Wouldn't be easier to just upgrade your system to something newer—and safer?"

"I'm good," he grimaced. "Need to get this working again."

This was going to take a while. I pinged Alain, sent him some vids of the wonders of the mech section. This time he seemed genuinely interested and enthusiastic.

"Dad, that's *fantastic*," he replied. "You've got to bring me out there when you're done with your errand."

Well that was a first—Alain had never shown any desire to wander Conglommora. He really was growing up.

Pinged Grace next; she was more excited at the images of Sea I had sent her than the mech section. I promised we'd visit there together someday.

We had to wait another day or two in the mech section, all told. I really didn't want to, but I'd come this far so I figured I could tough it out. Despite my grumpiness, there was a lot to see here, and most of it *was* pretty wonderful. I left Bob and started wandering around.

I watched glowing, mostly transparent red fish swim up a set of circularly entwined tubes from floor to ceiling, and back again, while a continuous stream of multi-colored bubbles went the other way, splitting and coalescing as they went. The section was filled with that kind of display. Fascinating. Useless, maybe, but fascinating still.

Boredom set in after a while, though, and I watched some folks racing mechanical bird forms. I rooted for the faux-owls at first, but they seemed to be doing pretty well for themselves without my encouragement. After that, I registered for the fake hummingbirds—they seemed a lot more maneuverable. But then the giant purple vultures ate them. At least, I think that's what I saw. So many tricks of perception here. This place was starting to get to me.

The day dragged on, and I wandered further.

Silver, metallic globes, different sizes. Floating in the air. A game of some kind. I stood and watched, trying to figure out how it worked. Lots of math and point values involved. Position seemed important—more like a board game than a sports game.

Over here you could, if you wanted, balance yourself on a small board in a roiling tank of orange plasma. I don't think I could even manage the water boards they had in Sea; this looked much, much harder.

I kept going, and saw that they had a model of the whole of Conglommora. I stopped right in my tracks to take it in: 3D, hovering in mid-air, seemingly solid but you could rotate and zoom in on parts. Robert, apparently finished with his brain-tuning AI thing, popped up behind me, Why and Avi in tow.

"That's Conglommora?" he asked. "All of it?"

"Supposed to be," Avi answered.

"Oh, it is. Completely up-to-date." A blue-skinned woman with almond-shaped eyes and silver glowing hair came around the corner. "My team and I have been working on this for years."

"Hey Leigh, didn't see you there." Avi waved warmly.

"We even just added the *Uten*—see? Right here." Leigh pointed and zoomed in.

I'd have to take Leigh's word for how accurate it was, but I could definitely confirm the model was huge, and very impressive. Robert was studying it with great interest. Obsessive, almost.

He asked Leigh a lot of questions and poked around the giant floating holographic model a lot, zooming in and looking at particular sections—especially around where he had docked, back at Bil's, and those surrounding neighborhoods; how they were connected to the rest of Conglommora. Honestly, the strangest things seem to interest him. I left them to their minute inspection of the houses of Conglommora and continued on.

I saw some folks playing a game that involved hitting small white balls on a short, grass-like texture through different mobile obstacles, trying to land the balls in a cup set into the deck. That looked fun, and when they asked me to try, I actually said yes and joined in.

It was harder than it looked. Trying to get the timing right, hitting the ball to make it through the moving figures and hit the cup despite the lights and the fog and the...

My head swam. Maybe it was wine from last night, or sleeping in the hammock that moved with my every breath. I made my excuses and turned in early, trying to get some sleep in the swinging, swaying, mesh cradle. I couldn't take much more of this.

I was so ready to go.

———————————

The morning came once again, I suppose—lighting in mech section hadn't changed appreciably. It stayed a sort of permanent neon mix of the violent and the sublime. I had slept, fitfully, the rigors of travel catching up to me. Funny how it seemed to always go one way or the other for me; either insomnia or nearly a coma.

Robert left them the agreed-upon bricks and put most of the custom parts into his backpack, which already had a bunch of the compressed nitrogen samples from Sea. I would have to carry the rest of the parts, I guess. Much of the reconfiguring and software updates they had done to his ship from here, so that was all set, too.

It was done. The *Uten* was as good as fixed; all Robert had to do was plug in the new pieces and the whole thing would roar to life.

That's what Avi said, anyway. I really didn't care anymore; I'd done what I said I would. I guess I had to show Robert the way back, but that was pretty anti-climatic now.

We thanked Rijm, Avi and Why and headed back the way we came.

I didn't ask Robert much in the way of deep questions anymore. He had to come to grips with humanity's fate on his own. And if he didn't, well, that was his problem. It's not like he could actually do anything about it. Not my problem.

As for me, I still marveled at the inventiveness, the ingenuity I saw in the mech section. And in the large biodomes. My own writing, my stories, seemed pretty pale, conventional and uninspired by comparison.

Well, it was time to make some changes, I thought, as Robert and I walked in silence down a corridor, heading back to the hyperloop and on to home.

Home.

Changes.

Things would be different from now on.

I wasn't the same person I was when I left, I mused. Okay, I was being overly dramatic, perhaps. But I was newly-inspired and hadn't realized how much I had *not* been inspired lately. Autopilot was over, and I was going home, the returning hero.

And I wouldn't be going home alone. No, not alone. Not anymore. It was time to find Grace.

Ten

As promised, we had to cross through Skyville again on our way back to the *Neylan* and the *Uten*.

The welcoming blue sky dome was as bright as ever, and the various animals seemed contented as ever.

A couple of large, gold-colored men were working on some sort of equally large farm-like contraption. "Hey, guys," I said as we approached, "know where I can find Grace?"

The first one looked up at me from the piece of wood he was carving. "Langston?"

I nodded.

He motioned to a barn over to the left, "She's probably over there."

"Thanks," I replied and Bob and I headed over in that direction, once again picking our way through the animals, their food, and their detritus. Honestly, not sure if I could ever get used to that. The smell wasn't as noticeable this time, though. Must have had better ventilation today.

She saw me first.

"Charlie!" she exclaimed, almost dropping the bucket she had and slopping the white liquid on the ground. She ran over and gave me a big hug. To my meager credit, I hugged her back, lifting her off the ground a little. Grace was a tad shorter than me.

"Success?" she asked succinctly, glancing over at Bob.

"Oh, right. Yes, the folks in the mech dome were able to help Robert out, and fabbed the parts and circuits he needed, got his ship's programming restored."

Bob jiggled his pack, and nodded appropriately. "My ship has the parts it needs, and I feel like a new man again," he said with a focus to his voice that hadn't been there before. Strange.

"Great!" Grace said with undimmed enthusiasm. "Are you headed back to your houses now?"

"Yeah, just on our way through. I have to get back to my son, Robert has to install the parts on his ship... you know."

"Alain, right?" Grace asked.

"Right," I fumbled.

"Well, I think I should have to meet him, what do you think?" she said, peeling her gloves off and lifting one foot up on the stool to stare at me with those inescapable green eyes.

"That'd be great," I said, for I could think of no other words.

"Okay, give me a couple of minutes to throw some supplies together and I'll join you." Without further words she was out the barn door, hips swinging in the brilliant light outside the barn.

Robert had an evil grin I hadn't seen before.

"Looks like you've fallen for the farm girl," he said.

"Er, I... I don't know about *fallen*, exactly," I started.

He started for the door as well. "Fallen hard, at that." His smirk knew no bounds.

We headed back the way we had come, back to our houses. But with one stop planned... Ronny wanted us to stop by straightaway and regale him with tales of the mech section and his friends Avi and Why. It was almost literally the last thing in the world I wanted to do.

Grace and I talked as we walked; Robert was left out a bit. Not that he had a lot to contribute to conversation in general, but this was pretty much all about us. I didn't want to go by Ronny and Janel's. I just wanted to be home. Home, with a new friend.

A new start.

But life isn't always so accommodating. And you never know what might happen next. But first things first, so we stopped off at Ronny's on our way back. So close.

Janel had made us a fine dinner. Not as exotic as what we'd been used to lately, but Janel traded well and studied her recipes, and asked Arty for help when needed. It was nice.

I described what we'd seen in the mech section, and even Robert chimed in to relay his impressions of that innovative wonderland. He was genuinely excited and spoke with a certainty, a confidence, a focus that was new for him. None of the stammering or hesitancy I had walked with the whole way here.

Despite his weird and old-fashioned notions of humanity, even he was impressed with the mech section and Sea. Much of what we described was brand-new to Grace. She had no idea such wonders existed, and hadn't needed to.

Grace described Skyville in some detail to Ronny and Janel, who were equally impressed. Funny how everyone else's environment seems better than your own at first glance. Or maybe we easily confuse different with better.

The evening dragged on. Grace was tired, and I was desperate to finish our last bit of walking. Janel tried one last time to get some more info from Robert.

"So, Robert, I'm still amazed that your family didn't tell you about their history—where they were from, what region, what peoples."

Robert, finishing dessert, wiped his mouth with a napkin. "No ma'am, they never said much about our origins." He took a drink and looked thoughtful, as though he'd just remembered something, something that had been eluding him.

"But they did say that if ever found another ship or settlement of humans, to try and find the Monotrads– that had been our faction on Earth and they'd welcome and help us out." He took another drink.

The room itself stiffened and sucked in its breath.

Now I'm no history enthusiast like Janel—that stuff mostly bores me silly, and it's pointless besides. But even I knew who the Monotrads were. Judging by Grace's horrified expression, so did she.

They were a death cult.

"Death cult!" Janel nearly spat her drink out in shock. "Monotrads! Are you kidding me?"

Robert looked confused; not defensive, not challenging, not even arguing. Just confused.

"What do you mean?" he asked. Earnestly, but without backing down.

"What did your parents tells you about the Monotrads?" Janel warily queried him.

"Nothing in particular, no real details, just that we were part of that group on Earth, and we should join them out here, wherever we ended up out here. Those are our people."

Janel set her drink down and took a deep breath.

"Okay, maybe you just don't know. I'll explain some history to you, and then maybe you'll see why you don't *ever* want to repeat that to anyone else out here in the world."

———————————

Janel actually relished any opportunity to expound on what she knew of history. It fit in well with her theatrical tendencies, I guess. Truth be told, we didn't give her much opportunity most of the time. But over the course of years I'd heard most of this before, and mostly from her.

Her habit was good for my friendship; it encouraged Ronny and I to work at developing even stronger sweet-brewed algae.

She poured us all a fresh round and launched in.

"In the last days of the Green Earth, before reaching the Critical Point, the planet was divided up into countries, and each country was led by one or more factions who fought each other and every other country as well. You had small fry from minor countries like the Kars. They had almost no resources, isolated themselves from the rest of the world, and were a violent and virulent problem as things got worse on Earth. They only got off a handful of fission bombs, but that added radiation made everything worse.

"In the ruling countries, a handful of powerful Death Cults in both hemispheres actively worked hard to destroy the planet and the other countries. They didn't call themselves that, of course. And they didn't really set out to deliberately destroy the planet. They were willfully ignorant, greedy beyond imagination, and very, very powerful. Half the planet was led by the Monotrads, which was shortened from something like 'monocultural traditionalists.' They routinely opposed any sort of cultural or societal change, and refused to consider any action that might impact commerce or trade, even if it would be disastrous long term.

"The other half was mostly led by the Commons. The Commons actually did the most to try and stop the Critical Point, but their government was too large; too sluggish. By the time they took the threat seriously and moved to action, it was too late.

"Meanwhile, the Monotrads did everything in their considerable power to stop anyone from even discussing the basic facts—the warming temperatures, rising radiation, the megastorms, melting polar caps, rising seas. At first, they blocked any legal action at every turn politically. Later, they made it illegal to even publish papers on or even discuss the Critical Point. They didn't believe in it; didn't believe that the damage to the ecosystem would really be irreversible at that point.

"When the evidence became too obvious to ignore and people started dying by the millions, they took one last step toward destruction and made it illegal to take any action to try and stop the Critical Point. And they had brutal police powers to enforce it, too. Even then, they thought that it was bad for business. Can you imagine?"

Grace interjected, "They couldn't have been than awful. Surely that's an exaggeration?" She looked up hopefully.

Janel wrinkled her lips. "Based what we can piece together from the records of the time, it seems pretty clear. But of course not everyone agreed, and some folks tried to stop them.

"In the Monotrad's hemisphere, there was an opposition party, a faction they were supposed to share power with. They knew what was going on, and tried to stop it, but they were weak and ineffective. Some members of the opposition started disappearing, others fled. As soon as they disappeared from the scene, there was no one to stop the Monotrads. Meanwhile in the other hemisphere, the Commons started building the big, doomed Generational Ships.

"The first big leap for humankind had been a couple of hundreds of years earlier, when nanophotonic circuits replaced primitive electrons and wires. Next, the printers became widely used over time, but only by companies and governments, not by individuals.

"Kain Mimulus single-handly launched the next big leap. He broadcast the full plans for the electromag generators, printers, reclaimers and basic ship designs to everyone on the planet. It no longer mattered who owned the designs or what new disasters the Monotrads wanted to inflict upon us. Kain gave us, all of us, the means to be free of the Monotrads, free of governments, free of the dying Earth.

"That's when the backlash hit. If we were doomed to leave the planet and live out in the cosmos, there was no way in hell we were taking those bastards with us."

Janel was getting more than a little worked up by now.

She realized it and took a few calming breaths, and another healthy swallow of drink.

"The Commons had already taken out the Kars; the other factions were long gone. So everyone else got together to kill the Monotrad leaders and powerful supporters. All of them. Slaughtered. In their sleep. In their offices. As they were building ships of their own. The

People organized off the grid, away from public communications. It was a masterstroke. The People—our People—stopped the problem at the source.

"And yet it seems at least a few of those soul-sucking, superstitious, ignorant and arrogant bastard-holes made it out here anyway."

With that last, she was looking at Robert right in the eyes. Well, not looking in his eyes so much as drilling through them: through his eyes, through his skull, through the bulkhead beyond and halfway across the void, with more than a few generations' worth of hatred and frustration powering her up.

"Your faction killed the Green Earth," she summarized succinctly.

"Your people are why we're here living in these glorified gerbil tubes." She waved her hands to include the room, and I guess all of Conglommora. And here I thought Ronny was the tactless one. They really did make a good pair. Ronny had been silent this whole time. He knew better than to jump in front of a speeding hyperloop pod.

Now frankly I'm still not sure what a "gerbil" was, or why *they* lived in tubes against their will, but even without a grasp of the details the point was made.

Robert sat there at the table mute, a panoply of expressions passing over his face; fast-moving clouds over an uncertain lake. Or so I imagine a lake would have looked. I felt compelled to step in, if for no other reason than to put an end to this so we could go home.

"Well, that's all true, at least as far as we know, and it's what the ancient streams, grams and vids tell us. But that wasn't Robert himself, and it wasn't even his parents, or maybe even grandparents. It was all generations ago, and all that remains of the Death Cults and their ideals and ideas is a vague memory of their name. And that's a faded memory that's most easily forgotten. Right Robert? Just a memory?"

I exaggerated my nod, looking for Robert to agree more readily. If he did agree. This actually explained a lot behind his... quaint attitudes and ideas.

But he returned the nod, once and deliberately.

"A memory. Sure. Easily forgotten. I'm... I'm so sorry, I had no idea. It was just something our parents suggested. I never heard the background or really knew why. Maybe they were going to tell us more when we got older, but..." He trailed off, playing the orphan card to buy silence. And somehow, this time, it didn't feel genuine. It really did feel like he was playing a card, deliberately, without the feelings that had been so close to the surface the past few days. It was a card, but it was the orphan card.

It worked.

Poor Ronny looked like he'd rather be having a limb re-grown or something. Mostly, he'd only wanted us to stop by so he could get a look at Avi and Why's work-manship.

"Okay." He cleared his throat again, still a particularly horrible sound. "Enough of dusty history, let's take a look at those parts the guys made and make sure you're in good shape." He headed to his workshop, taking my bag with him, and Robert in tow with his bag.

We sat a moment, then Janel broke the silence.

"Sorry I got so worked up," she said, wrinkling her mouth.

"I suppose it's not really me you need to apologize to," I offered. "But okay. It is kind of strange to have a descendant of one of the Death Cults here. I mean, I suppose there are plenty of folks here who have relatives from any of the Death Cults. Doesn't change anything." I shrugged and convinced myself.

"No Charlie, there aren't." Janel looked up to explain. Grace looked curious.

"Most of the Death Cult supporters were killed. Especially his Monotrads." She nodded toward the workshop. "And even if some made it off planet, folks who couldn't adapt to living on space ships didn't make it this far. We're the hearty ones, the ones who *want* to live. Who want to improve, to be better.

"Conglommorans are the ones who look forward, not back. Who forgive, not hate. Who take care of their own."

I breathed in thoughtfully. Or at least, what I thought would pass as thoughtfully. I really had no idea what the problem was. Maybe Grace was paying attention. Did I mention I really just wanted to go home?

"Okay," I began, aiming for some degree of conciliation. "So he's unique. One-of-a-kind. The last living descendant of the Monotrad faction. But he's also just a kid. Not a world leader, not a political firebrand or even a ranter like Eddie."

Janel scrunched an eyebrow, "Who's Eddie?"

"Oh," I shook my head, "I mean Edward. You know." I made a crazy face and held my hair up in a mock display of Eddie's unkempt look. Grace smiled at my impression even though she didn't know the source.

"Gotcha," Janel clued in. "No, I suppose not. He's not them."

"And," I chimed in, "he's way out of context. We don't have governments like Green Earth did; we don't have a powerful faction for him to join, nothing. It's still Conglommora. It's still just us. Just the People.

"Even if he wanted to rule the world," I continued, "there's no 'world' to rule. It doesn't work that way out here.

"If he wants a world to rule," I continued and laughed darkly, "he'll have to head back to Dead Earth."

Janel joined me in my dark jest. "Well, in that case," she snarked, "I think we're perfectly safe." The three of us toasted, and the guys came back from the workshop at last.

Finally, the last leg.

Eleven

BOB WAS REALLY QUIET under the best of circumstances, but he'd gone completely silent on our whole way back from the mech section. Maybe it was because Grace was with us now. I didn't fully realize it at the time—maybe he was just working up his courage to say something else inflammatory. Or inane.

After the dinner and Janel's accusation of his Death Cult heritage, he hadn't said a word to us and didn't even look either of us in the face. Maybe he was just embarrassed. Just a thanks to Ronny, a curt goodbye to Janel.

I had no idea what he was really up to.

We were in one of the narrow corridors, on our way back home from Ronny's to the *Uten* and then on to the *Neylan*. The narrow corridor widened briefly into a larger sphere; a junction of several similar corridors. The last turn before splitting off to our respective ships.

People say things like, "It all happened so fast." I always thought that was just something of a cop-out, that they weren't paying attention or didn't really know what was going on in the first place. Hah. I have much greater respect for that phrase now.

In a flash, Bob grabbed Grace in a headlock and quickly yanked some sort of antique gun out of his pocket. I found out later it was an automatic weapon, the sort that shoots lead bullets. No one had seen any of these in a long time—it's not the sort of thing you want on a space ship, with only thin bits of composite and metal between you and the hard vacuum and endless frozen nothing of space. Sudden holes are a really bad idea. So I suppose what happened next shouldn't have been surprising.

Bob pointed the gun at her head.

"Don't move!" he shouted. "I will shoot her! Now that you know, I'm going to make this right. Everything. You're going to…"

Never heard what came next. A bolt of energy whipped out of the service panel overhead and lit Bob up like an old-time fireworks display. He dropped like a rock. Grace was okay. That was the important part—she was okay. When necessary, Arty could do really nice work.

Grace was shaking, tears flowed freely from the pools of her deep-green eyes. I lurched over toward her, took her hands and hugged her tight. We stayed like that for a surprisingly long time, until interrupted by an announcement.

Arty's voice oozed out of the speaker, "The threat has been neutralized. Charlie, could you please retrieve the weapon."

Always happy to help, I picked up the gun. It was a lot heavier than I expected—energy weapons don't have much heft to them, save for the power supply. But this thing had a fair bit of metal to it. I suspect it was old even when Bob's family left Earth.

"What do you want me to do with it?" I asked Arty, not facing any particular direction.

"Keep it away from Robert," said Arty with an attempt at dry humor. "A quick analysis suggests you could get a couple of nice bars of Raw out of it."

Sounded like a good idea to me. There was one problem down.

"And what should we do with *him*?"

"I will return Robert to his ship," Arty offered, and sure enough, a repair drone came hovering in from around the corner. "He'll be monitored more closely for any further antisocial behavior."

Grace and I continued on alone on our return adventure though the last corridor. We made it back to the *Neylan*, at last.

But now, finally free of Robert, I wondered about that. I would have liked to have spent more time in Skyville, and in Sea, too, with Grace at my side. But I knew that Alain would be missing me if I were gone too long—not that he'd ever admit that, of course.

I introduced Grace to Alain, and he replied with the usual teenage enthusiasm, "Hey."

She stayed with us—definitely as a guest, though. It wasn't like we were suddenly a family again; that was still just Alain and me. But even as a guest, it was good to have the company.

After she settled in one of the spare rooms and just hung out for a few days, Grace was ready to spread out a bit.

"So are you going to introduce me to your neighbors? What do you all do for fun around here?" she asked. "You know, like socialize?"

Of course, I used to do a lot of that sort of thing back when Haily was alive. Then suddenly I just didn't anymore.

"Uh, Justin is my immediate neighbor on this side, but he's kind of a jerk and we don't hang out together very much."

Grace dimmed.

I recovered, though. "But my neighbors up and over, Teri and Oplack, are pretty cool. We could have dinner with them, maybe?" Grace looked visibly relieved.

I pinged Teri.

"Hey stranger," he said, "haven't heard from you in forever. What's up?"

"Just reconnecting, I guess," I smiled. "My new friend Grace and I wondered if you'd like to have dinner together?"

Oplack hopped into the frame. "Glad you could find an excuse!" she teased. Teri snickered at my mention of a "new friend," but held his tongue.

"Tomorrow night," Oplack commanded with authority. "We'll see you both."

"What can I bring?" I hastily added, barely remembering some level of basic social protocol. Never was my strong suit.

We worked out the details, and before I knew it, we were standing at their hatch. Just like a real couple. I fidgeted nervously with the bottle I had brought; Grace was carrying a dish as well. Something she had baked back in my galley, with cheese. Smelled awesome.

The hatch slid aside in two parts, and Teri and Oplack greeted us warmly, like old friends. Which they were, for me at least. Teri was fair with freckles and a red beard, not yet showing any gray. Oplack was paler still, with platinum blond hair, high cheekbones, and almost no eyebrows. Grace was instantly at ease with them both—I think that was definitely one of her special talents.

Dinner was nice. It was all very nice.

Well, okay, more than *nice*. Grace had taken a longer break from her animals in Skyville, and she and I began to do things together, things I'd forgotten about or neglected. Parties with friends I'd stopped seeing. Games with old friends—and new ones. Folks I should have met, but hadn't. More distant neighbors I hadn't ever met, or had, but didn't know well. Grace expanded my circle of friends, expanded that small range of people I had direct in-person contact with.

But more importantly, *we did things together*. I was a couple again. For real. I had an excuse to visit, to socialize, to meet and greet, to do all those things that normal people do. I was fully aware this was a temporary thing, for now, of course. Maybe it would last. Hope rose in my soul; maybe it *would* last. We weren't yet a family; it was me and Alain, and me and Grace. But it was a start.

At last, it was the start of a new life.

———————————

As for Bob… well, despite Arty's promise, it didn't seem like Bob needed much monitoring after that. He stayed in his ship and pretty much ignored the rest of the world. He had his parts and patches, and could be seen tinkering and working on the *Uten*. But he didn't speak to me, or any of us, and I had no desire to speak to him.

Well that's not entirely true.

I didn't want to make small talk—I'd had enough of trying to do that on our walk through Conglommora. But what the hell was he thinking, pulling a gun on Grace? What did he think he could accomplish by that? Did he really mean to harm her or was he just trying to get everyone's attention?

Where did he even get such a weapon? Even in the oldest of old days, projectile weapons were prohibited on ships, for obvious reasons. It's not something you just toss in with your gear or clothes.

Curiosity would get the better of me. It had been some tens of days since the incident, and there hadn't been any more outbursts or gun waving. The *Uten's* computers still weren't hooked up to Conglommora as part of Arty, so we couldn't scan the inside of his ship.

But you could be sure he was thoroughly scanned for weapons as soon as he stepped out of his hatchway.

I was coming back from Ronny's, and on a whim, took a detour over toward the *Rhead*, and the *Uten*. Bob was standing just outside his hatch, fiddling with a service panel that connected to his ship. This was as good a chance as any.

I didn't really know where to start. So I just began, "Robert..."

He looked up sharply, like I'd pulled his neck out of its socket with a rope.

"Oh. It's you," he said simply. He closed a portion of the service panel and turned to face me full on.

"I guess... an apology is order." He hung his head a bit. "I'm sorry."

"What were you thinking? Where'd you get that gun? Why did you turn on us—we've done nothing but help you and..." The words all came out in a tumble, falling over each other in a mad dash to leave my mouth. I hadn't gotten to the "betrayal" part yet but it would have been next.

Bob held his hand up, palm toward me. "I know, I know. I have no excuse, and really not even any explanation.

"On my ship, on the Earth we'd been told of..." He looked wistfully sideways, at nothing in particular. "Things were different. I don't think I really appreciated just how different. It was an impulse, a stupid idea that took over my head that I should have dismissed. I was tired, I wasn't... in *control* of myself. You know."

I didn't really. The way he said "control" had a strange, ominous tone to it.

Silence sat between us, like a large bite of food you couldn't quite swallow all at once.

"Maybe if I had known I was going to get zapped into tomorrow…" he offered, hands in a half-shrug, half-supplication move.

"Arty doesn't have to do that very often," I said. "But Arty will do what's necessary to protect us all, and Conglommora itself."

"That's a lot more than my ship's AI could ever manage," Bob commented.

Ah, he didn't know. "Sure. More than any of ours, individually. When the first ships interconnected, the AIs on each ship integrated with each other, and the vast, total internetwork became Arty. One unified artificial consciousness. You could unplug any ship at this point, and it would still be a 'little Arty', if you will. Less sensory, less processing power, less… Arty. But still Arty."

Bob looked concerned, "So all of Conglommora is run by some massive, all-seeing AI that you can't turn off?"

He may have been contrite, but the paranoia still ran deep.

" 'Run by' is maybe the wrong way to look at it. Arty doesn't really run things; as an outgrowth of the ship's individual AIs, it's more like a… a circuit breaker, or an emergency bulkhead. It only acts independently when needed, when there's a real threat. Like some nutter with a lead projectile weapon," I finished, pointedly.

Bob looked away again, not meeting my eyes. "Yeah. That was just a bad idea all around."

I wanted to ask him more—what was he trying to achieve with his little stunt, where had we failed him? Was he just crazy? Crazy in a way that maybe medicine couldn't help?

I had lost my chance for now. Bob turned and retreated back into his ship, closing the hatch behind him, and muttering, "Sorry."

So, that was it for now. He kept to himself for another few days or so, then slowly started venturing out again.

No one would talk to him at first. They'd all seen the stream of the attack, which Arty had provided as a public stream with a warning. After a bit of trading and no further drama, folks seemed to open up a bit. At least he'd made it back to the "will speak to you cautiously" stage. No long, deep, thoughtful conversations though. Just the small, simple pleasantries and transactions of life.

Forgive, move on. The Conglommoran way.

———————————

A couple more tens of days passed, and Bob was out and about a bit more, trading and making small talk. Much of our wariness faded down to a dull distrust. Grace had gone back to Skyville to take care of a few errands and had just returned to us the night before. She and I were halfway over to the Rheads' when Bob came up to us.

"Hi Charlie," he nodded, "Grace." She nodded back politely.

"I just wanted to say hi and try to make up for my abysmal behavior back in the corridors. I'd like to invite both of you over to the *Uten* for dinner, if you will." He gestured in the general direction of his ship.

"It's all fixed up now, everything works. It's not quite as embarrassing as it would have been a while ago." He managed a lopsided grin. Charm, almost?

"I'll try and explain everything, and I *promise*… no guns this time." Full-on charisma.

I looked over at Grace and raised an eyebrow. Totally up to her. I was perfectly content to tell Bob to stick it. But to be fair, I was also curious to get a better look inside his ship again.

I didn't think Grace would agree, at all. From her point of view, why should she? This guy *pulled a gun on her*, like from some old-time vid. She owed him less than nothing. But still, there was a mystery here. And the one thing that every mystery demands is its solution; its exposition.

Grace thought for a moment, maybe wrestling with these very same ideas. Maybe trying to decide if telling him to stuff it in an anatomically improbable manner was the better choice. But after a lengthy and awkward pause, she held my hand and said, "Okay, Robert. I love a good story. Even if I'm involved. I'm in. But it had better be a good one."

Now I know what you're thinking, and I agree: this was a terrible idea. Curiosity, I imagine, had gotten the better of her; an insidious breach of curiosity tearing a hole through a solid wall of reason—for both of us. But

Bob seemed appropriately apologetic, and to be fair, we *were* all exhausted that night, perhaps exhausted beyond normal thought or action.

But I would still be plenty cautious.

Dinner came, and Bob turned out to be a pretty good cook, and a good enough host. The table setting was a lot more elaborate than either Grace or I was used to, with extra utensils, different-sized plates and drinking vessels, and a series of sized napkins. Bob explained that was how they regularly took their meals on the ship. He also explained how he'd traded up a series of exchanges to make us this most excellent meal. We were still waiting for the big explanation, of course.

I made sure that Grace and I sat nearest the exit door, and that Bob couldn't corner us quite so easily. But despite my background worry, that didn't seem like it was going to be a problem. As the evening progressed, I relaxed a little bit.

A few glasses of a very nice wine, not at all algae-esque, went down, and as the small talk shrunk to sub-microscopic, we got to the part of the evening I'd been waiting for. His explanation. His story. His grand narrative.

He took a long final draw on his wineglass, and started in.

"When our ship first left Earth, our grandparents weren't just looking to survive out on a new planet and make a new home. I mean, of course, we wanted to do at least that, but we'd been taught—bred, even—that we were responsible for more than just survival. We were charged with protecting the traditions, the values, the very soul of humanity. That was our grand purpose."

He twirled the glass in his hand.

"At least," Bob shifted uncomfortably in his seat, "it was our vision of what was important to humanity.

"But out here, at the edge, in your... your Conglommora, it's nowhere close to the vision we've cherished for generations. You allow things that in my grandparents' day would have been unthinkable—literally unspeakable. And yet here no one bats an eye.

"I thought I could change that. Honestly, I don't know what was in my head, but I thought I could start a... a revolution, I guess. That I could make everyone on Conglommora listen to me and change the way people live.

"You know that whole anger-depression-acceptance thing?" He looked up at both of us from his downcast expression. I nodded so he'd keep going.

"That was, I guess, the anger part. Anger that humanity had failed, had failed to live up to the vision we were charged with protecting. I *had* to do something, don't you see? It was the mission of the whole ship, the whole of the *Uten*. But I'm all that's left. And one person can't change the whole world.

"I've had some time to think about all this." A slight smile. "That was the depression phase, I think. Anyway, however the medbay might classify it, or your Arty, it seems I've slid into the 'acceptance' part of the program."

He tipped his glass, played with the base on the table.

"It is what it is. Humanity, Conglommora, you guys, me, all of it. I'm just one person. I can't change it all by myself."

There was something about his voice, something... different. Confident. Strong. Not the same confused, disappointed Bob that I knew from the corridors. But just then his words started getting blurry. And sparkly. I swear he said something about, "But I won't be by myself much longer."

After that, the blur lost color and depth. I saw a distorted shadow that I think was Grace, sliding toward the floor. Then everything else just faded into blackness.

Twelve

I woke up in my own bedform, on the *Neylan*. My head ached with what might have been a large-scale hangover, except that I hadn't had *that* much wine, and algae wines didn't usually give me a hangover like grape or grain-based concoctions.

I got up quickly—a mistake—and sort of half-stumbled, half-scraped along the wall to the doorway to go check on Alain.

He was fine, still sleeping.

Down the hall to the spare room where Grace was staying. No one home. I checked the galley, the other areas, everywhere really. Grace was gone.

Desperate times.

"Hey Arty," I called out.

"Yes, Charlie?" came the ever-smooth and perpetually unperturbed voice.

"Where's Grace?"

"Miss Grace Bethany Langston is not aboard the *Neylan*."

I looked expectant, waiting for more details, so Arty continued, "She accompanied Robert Brandeis out the adjacent corridor system early this morning. They met up with your friend Edward Thorndike, and the three are currently traveling toward Edward's own home and its attached houses."

That hurt worse than the hangover. If it was a hangover.

"Why didn't you stop him!" I yelled at Arty. "You can't just let Bob kidnap her like that!"

"Grace was not forced in any way," said Arty. It continued, "I was not able to monitor your dinner within the *Uten*, however, when Grace and Robert left the *Uten* she went willingly. I detected no overt coercion; her vital signs were perfectly consistent with a person exercising free will. There were no biometric, facial, or body language signs of stress or fear. In fact, if anything, all signs indicated that Grace was not only happy, but grateful at the circumstances."

What the hell.

"Arty," I stammered, truly at a loss for words, "how can that be? What does that mean?"

"Insufficient data or processing power," came the inevitable reply.

I sat down right there on the deck, held my aching head, and cried.

So that was that, I guess. We'd had too much to drink, I passed out and they got it on. Somehow, I must have stumbled home. As unbelievable as that scenario was, it seemed these were the facts of the matter. I tried to ping Grace a few times, but she didn't answer.

Arty kept tabs on them for me, but it seemed clear there was no problem. Bob, Grace, Eddie and their new circle of friends were getting along just fine.

I had started working on a new game script based on my brief walking tour of Conglommora, but honestly it was hard to work up any enthusiasm for it. I made some progress in fits and starts.

Mostly, I really wanted to talk it out with someone and realized I had no one. Ronny was a good friend, but this wasn't the sort of conversation he—or Janel—would be interested in. And it's not like I could fire up Haily and tell her I thought I'd found her replacement. Still I almost did anyway, just to hear my wife's voice again.

At dinner a few days later, Alain asked, "Where's your friend Grace?"

I set my spork down and took a drink, buying a little time to think of an appropriate answer.

"She's, um, visiting some friends I guess," I replied, hoping that didn't sound as lame to Alain as it did to me.

"She coming back?"

Well that got right to the heart of the matter, didn't it?

"She's a grownup," I said and tried to shrug. "I guess it's up to her." I picked up my spork and tried to be interested in my food.

"I'm sorry," Alain commiserated. So, it seemed he had a pretty good grasp on the issue after all.

I had been moping around for a few tens of days when I decided that maybe I should head back out, out to Skyville, maybe even all the way over to Sea. Yeah, that would be nice. I had no excuse for a visit, I guess, but I could trade for lodging, meet some new people.

Alain was out, doing something with his friends. He probably told me what, exactly, but I wasn't paying attention.

Arty interrupted me as I was packing.

"Charlie," it said, "we have a problem."

"What's up, Arty?" It was unlike Arty to start an open-ended conversation this way.

"I've lost contact with a large section of Conglommora."

What? As far as I knew, nothing like that had ever happened before. And why was Arty telling me about this? I asked exactly that.

And that's when Arty showed me the stream from Bob.

It was all over Conglommora, and for good reason.

The stream showed Robert and Grace, standing together in front of some sort of banner or poster.

"My name is Robert Brandeis," he identified himself. Even in that short fragment, I could tell his voice sounded different. But I didn't ponder that oddity for long, as he dropped his next bombshell.

"And this is my sister," he continued.

"I'm Ann Brandeis," said Grace.

I tried to sputter some sort of query to Arty, but between the disbelief, anger, confusion, and a half-dozen other emotions I don't think I could even name, nothing came out but high-pressure spittle.

"We have declared this section of ships that used to be part of Conglommora to be a new, independent collection of humans, with our own government. We will now be known as Old Path. We have cut computer access and sealed off the hatchways to the corridors.

"Conglommora is a decadent dead end for humans. You have lost sight of what values it takes to *be* a human, not just another animal.

"Old Path is assembling our forces, and we will return to the Earth once more. We will take it back, recolonize our home—our only true home."

He raised his voice. "I promise you the Earth!"

A bunch of their supporters cheered in the background. Eddie was there with them, looking wild as ever. Wild and happy.

This was too much. I yelled at the screen, even though there was no one to hear me but Arty. "But there's nothing left, not even ruins! *Everything* is gone!"

As if they could have heard me, Grace—Ann?—answered, "You've been told the Earth is dead. Dead and destroyed, uninhabitable. Nothing left. No trace of our cities, our spaceports, our triumphs. That was true.

For a long time, that was the truth. But not anymore, not now. The Earth has recovered, at long last, and is waiting for us to return. And return we shall."

It was Grace's body, Grace's face. But it didn't look like Grace, and the voice wasn't quite Grace. It was the same instrument, maybe, but someone else was playing it now. Somehow.

Bob talked at some length of our failings, the promise of returning to Earth, and wound up with an invitation to awaken and join their Old Path movement. Or whatever it was. The stream ended.

Arty respectfully waited for me to gather what was left of my wits. I could have used a lot longer, that's for sure. I had been standing; I slumped into a chairform.

"Arty, what happened. What happened to Grace? Did he brainwash her or something?"

Arty responded, "Technically there's no such thing as 'brainwashing,' at least not in the theatrical sense that you mean. There is conditioning and many forms of more subtle manipulation, mostly involving strong emotions and occasional violence."

"However," it continued, "there wasn't time for those techniques in this case. And from all readings I've scanned from Grace, she seems to be perfectly at ease with her new identity as Ann Brandeis."

"He must have done something to her that night of the dinner," I suggested. "Slipped her some drug, used some machine... something."

Arty was non-committal, "Perhaps. That does seem to fit the facts as we know them, and extrapolating from

Robert's motives and his desire to be with his missing sister. But I have no evidence, no hard data to prove any of that. I'm not programmed to take action based on speculation."

"Grace once mentioned she had a sister… maybe she could help us somehow?" I wondered aloud.

"Faith Langston." Arty looked up the records. "I have no data on her present whereabouts. She's not registered with any permanent house, does not carry a standard screen, and I have no record of her physical appearance for facial scans."

"Not registered? No screen? I thought you kept track of everyone."

"Not for those who do not wish to be tracked," Arty replied. "Faith Langston went on a Walk with the intention that she should not be tracked, and I must honor that."

Well there's a dead end. Back to the brainwashing angle: whatever was done, maybe it could be undone. There had to be equipment, chemicals, nanobots, something. "We need to get inside the *Uten* and have a look," I resolved.

"The *Uten* is no longer docked at House Rhead. Robert undocked and redocked in the Old Path section early this morning," Arty informed me.

Another dead end. Frustrated, I was up and pacing again. We couldn't just blow up a hatch in the Old Path section and try and get in. I needed to get to Bob somehow. I would be perfectly happy to blast my way in, get him in a headlock and drag him out—like in one of my game scripts. But there was a lot more to deal with than just Bob and Grace, or even Eddie. Somehow they had support from whole sections of Conglommora. How did he manage that?

I asked Arty, "Okay, so answer me this. How did Bob convince all those folks to abandon Conglommora?"

Arty noted, "He didn't have to; not all the sections or individual ships were willing, but he's cut the computer access at several key junctions, and this particular section of Conglommora is cut off where I can no longer monitor or intervene. He's sealed off physical access from the corridors as well."

That was even more alarming, "So there's people trapped in their houses in the Old Path section who aren't buying into all this?"

"Possibly. That's all I could determine before losing contact completely," Arty said. "Robert planned this well; this section of Conglommora is one of the only ones nearby that could be completely cut off by damaging just a few contact points. These houses form a large arc, and are only connected to the rest of Conglommora by a few houses on each end of the arc.

"And that's why I showed you this stream," Arty continued. "I need your help. Conglommora needs your help. I have a mission for you."

"Me?" My eyebrows raised in surprise. "Why me?"

Thirteen

ARTY HAD A MISSION FOR ME? That was pretty much unheard of, at least in the last few decades. At least as far as I knew.

Why me?

Arty had a simple answer, "Because you were intimate with Grace, and you spent more time with Robert than anyone else. You know them both. If confronted, I extrapolate that you have the best chance of making contact without creating a violent conflict. In that regard, you are the best candidate for this mission.

"First, and most importantly, we need to determine if there are any people being held within the Old Path section against their will.

"Second," Arty was ticking off a list, "we need a better idea of what Robert and Ann are planning," I bristled at the use of Grace's new identity.

"Third," Arty added, perhaps addressing my discomfort, "We need to understand what happened to Grace, and what, if anything, may have been done to her against her will. Those are your mission goals. You need to conduct this investigation quietly. Please do not discuss these details with anyone else, not even Alain or your neighbors. Robert and Ann could possibly be monitoring our communications in undetectable ways. The likelihood is low, but not zero. We will require Bil Rhead's assistance, and you may discuss some of these matters with him directly, but please keep it concise and don't use a stream.

"I will supply you with a miniature stun weapon, and a variety of sensor packs that will be hard for them to detect. You'll wear sensors yourself, and you'll be able to plant sensors within Old Path. That will allow me to monitor the area."

Well great, now I'm a spy. I rubbed the back of my neck, maybe hoping to improve blood flow to my brain. It wasn't helping. Besides the encroaching panic in my head, my chest was tightening up and my stomach was loosening up. Not a great combination. I didn't want to do this. Who would? The whole thing is crazy.

And if it weren't for Grace, I probably wouldn't have agreed. But I had to find out what happened to her—and fix it if I could. I was desperate. Jaw clenched, insides roiling and outsides pacing the room, I agreed to this mad plan.

"Fine. I'll do it. But how? How can I even get in there?" I asked. "I don't imagine Bob's supporters are going to just let me blast my way in." They wouldn't, of course, but that would be the most rewarding.

Arty was firm. "No, no blasting. As much as we need to investigate and evaluate whether any sort of rescue must be attempted, we need to also consider the other nearby ships and all of Conglommora."

"So, how do I get in?" I asked Arty.

"Do you mind using a pressure suit?" Arty asked, without a trace of irony.

"A SPACE SUIT?" I had been pacing fast and faster. Any more of this and I might just take off. Maybe a spacesuit would come in handy after all.

I stopped pacing, whirled around and, with more than a hint of exasperation, asked Arty to make sure I understood, "YOU WANT ME TO GO OUTSIDE?"

"In a word; yes." Arty didn't mince words when it came to it.

"Why me? Surely there are folks with more experience doing spacewalks?" I asked, fear and evasion quickly outpacing sweat and bile, which was a pretty neat trick at this point.

"Yes," Arty admitted, "the asteroid miners are very proficient and do that all the time. However, all those crews are either in transit or on site at the moment. The earliest arrival back at Conglommora is over a week away. You trained for spacewalks as a young adult; everyone does. You'll be fine."

I swallowed hard. It didn't help.

I left Alain a vague note—he knew I was thinking of heading out anyway, this would just be a slight change of destination. I didn't want him to worry over the actual details. Arty set up my printer for the spacesuit and other gear.

"I can't believe I'm doing this," I muttered as I printed and packed up the gear.

"Do you require some pharmaceutical assistance?" Arty offered.

Normally I avoid such things—not everyone does. Courage, cheer, enthusiasm: all these and more can just be dialed in if you wanted. Some folks make that a regular habit, but that always struck me as kind of missing the point of life.

If you don't want the experience, why bother living?

Still, my hands were practically shaking. This whole mission thing was far beyond my comfort zone and likely beyond my skills as well.

"Well," I started, "perhaps a little something for my nerves." Arty was way ahead of me, and next up on the printer was a dose for me. I needed all the help I could get.

I took the pill, then finished packing. It was time to go. I hadn't "talked" to Haily since meeting Grace, but I really wanted to, now. I wanted that emotional support; that comfort of our past life together. My hand was on the screen about to invoke the vr, shaky as it was, but I stopped.

It wasn't real. It was just a vr. Haily was dead.

Grace was alive and needed my help. Enough of this foolishness. I turned away from the screen, strode out the hatch of the *Neylan*, heading over to Bil's. I would exit the world of Conglommora via his docking tube, leaving everything I knew behind. It was an over-dramatic thought, but this was a pretty dramatic event for me. For anyone. I can't remember the last time anyone I knew had to go outside.

"You've warned Bil about this?" I asked Arty.

"Of course," Arty replied. "Bil and Li have the docking tube ready for you. I believe they've also prepared a special beverage for you, to wish you good luck."

Swell.

As promised, Bil answered the door with a wineglass of something bubbly.

"Thanks, Bil." I took the glass. He and Li and I toasted and clinked the glasses of sparkling algae ferment.

"I have a thousand questions," Bil said.

"Yeah, you and me both." I started pulling on pieces of the spacesuit, and filling Bil in with the short version.

"I can't believe it. Any of it." Bil shook his head. "I can't believe you are about to go on a damn spacewalk! How many years has it been, around here at least?" he wondered.

A fair while, I was sure. We trained for this sort of thing when we were young, but only in a simulator. Generally repair drones took care of anything outside.

"Are you okay doing this?" Li asked.

"No. Not at all." I pulled and sealed my gloved hand. "But I'm doing it anyway." I tried to sound confident. I wasn't. But Arty's pill seemed to be helping a little.

He and Li helped me with the helmet. A resounding click and gentle woosh of air and I was on my own. Cut off from Conglommora already.

Arty showed me the plan on the heads-up display in my suit. After exiting Bil's tube, I had to make my way along the exterior of the corridor tubes and ships to a particularly isolated, perhaps even forgotten, area deep in the Old Path section. Arty would selectively handle any exterior sensors or proximity alarms on the way. No one would know I was out there.

Other than Bil and Li, literally no one at all.

———————————

I loved the old outer space movies from the Green Earth days. Everything was always so crisp and bright. Who knew they always had movie set lights in outer space?

But Conglommora wasn't near enough any star to reflect that much light. So the effect wasn't a giant, stark white starship against the inky, absolute black of noth-ingness.

Instead, Conglommora appeared as a patch of space that was not quite as pure black as the empty space be-hind it. Oh, you could see distant stars, the rest of the galaxy… but it was all so faint and far away.

I couldn't use an external light source, as I was sup-posed to be unnoticed, after all. So, I had to rely on the suit's sensors and Arty's feed on my display as I crawled along.

I mostly kept myself attached to the hulls via cables, sort of like a mountain climber rappelling up an ancient

Earth mountain. It was reasonably safe, but accidents out here did happen, and floating off into the void was a remote but distinct possibility. I had to pay attention.

Cold. I felt cold, a chill shiver every so often. Checked the suit, and it claimed my environmental temperature was steady and nominal. Clearly, it wasn't measuring fear. I tried to focus on the task: hand by hand, foot by foot, section by section. That was the key. Don't think about where you are and what might happen. Just focus. Stay in the moment.

An hour had passed, then two. Amazingly I was getting more used to this, and felt less panicked. I paused to rest every so often, and now I could turn off the suit display, and gaze out at the dim, distant stars. We really were out at the brink of nowhere. I sat on the edge of a large, boxlike outcropping of infrastructure and tugged a sip of water from the suit.

Could there be something to Bob's crazy, fevered idea of returning to Earth? This was a common, persistent dream; a latent, compelling notion that a fertile and nurturing Earth lay waiting for us. The firm yet yielding soil under foot, the warmth of the sun overhead, tossed from horizon to horizon to mark your days.

But we hadn't been gone that long. A few generations at most, maybe? Not all families left at once of course. It took some time to evacuate. But still, only on the order of hundreds of years. The damage wrought to the environment would have taken a lot longer to recover, and there was speculation about several high-probability asteroid impacts that would have ended the game anyway.

Nothing left, not even ruins. That's what we all knew to be true.

Or did we?

One crisis at a time, I resolved. *My* first priority was getting to Grace. Oh yeah, and helping Arty figure out if there were hostages in Old Path.

This was really not how I had envisioned my day going. Or year.

Or life.

I stood up, stretched as much as I could in the suit, and continued on.

Maybe it would have been a good idea if I had been paying more attention to what I was doing instead of ruminating on the possibility of an Earth reborn. But I wasn't, and somehow I didn't see the tangle of armored cables right at my feet. I stumbled and tripped, pitching forward, which was bad enough, but in my stumble I shot my leg out hard at the hull of a ship.

Mistake. The force sent me reeling backward, up and away from that hull. The cable securing me snapped, broke, and whipped me around at an awkward angle.

Shit.

A stab of cold steel went right though the pit of my stomach. Well, not literally, although something like that could happen any moment now. My knees and legs and arms were jelly, and despite the cold, beads of nervous sweat rolled up and over into my eyes. And down again. No matter which way I tumbled, damn sweat was headed straight into my eyes, making them burn. I blinked furiously.

Slow motion. I was trembling, in slow motion. A thousand negative thoughts broke loose, a flood of horror unleashed in my inner voice. Never should have agreed to any of this. Should have stayed home, in the *Neylan*, with Alain. Why did I even try to help that bastard Robert in the first place? If I hadn't, I wouldn't have met Grace, wouldn't be trying to rescue Grace, wouldn't be on this stupid mission flopping around ass over helmet about to die in the brutal uncaring void.

I was tumbling backward in the inside of the C-shaped curve. I'd just graze the outside edge of the next section of ships before heading off into a one-way trip to nothingness.

Shit. Still.

There was a random bit of metallic cable, loose at one end, floating up ahead in the dull gray and endless black. I might just be close enough to grab it, if it would hold me. If my hands would be anywhere near it in a few seconds. *Can't grab the damn thing with my feet.* I twisted, spasmed, tried to make my arms twice as long as they really were. Gagged. *Don't throw up. Don't throw up. Swallow. Hard. Again.*

The cable brushed my thigh, I doubled over and lurched, tried frantically to grab the stunted ruin of cable with both hands. Sweat and spittle clouded my visor; I couldn't see in the dark. *Shit.* It slipped through my hands.

I kicked like a desperate swimmer, tying to make contact with this frail bit of junk. *Oh please oh please oh please oh shit oh please.*

It was enough. Somehow a toggle on my boot caught on the cable and eased me around. I grabbed the cable with both hands, for real. Hard.

A voice in my head. My wife's voice, chanted, *don't let go.*

Don't let go.

I wrapped the thin thread of metal around my wrist, and slowly, gently, pulled myself back toward the surface of the nearest hull. I clamped a fresh piece of good cable to a solid enough bit of superstructure and crumpled into a kneeling, quivering ball.

At least no one could hear me sob out here. Projectile tears flushed the salt out of my eyes, but I couldn't stop sobbing, gasping in this ridiculous getup with a bucket on my head. I slumped onto the surface of the hull and grabbed onto handy projections in a wide embrace.

I don't know how long I stayed there. Wasn't supposed to contact Arty from out here; it might be detected. The comms mesh would still work, even though I was outside, but I couldn't risk detection.

Didn't know if Arty could scan me here, or if it knew I almost blew it and went flying off into the waiting arms of patient Death. If it cared. AI's can't care; they're machines. Death is just a state: a qubit suddenly turned from a dozen values of "on" to the single, irreversible value of "off." Just a variable, no longer needed.

No longer needed.

The thought galvanized me. I was needed. Alain needed me. Grace needed me. Robert... well, I wasn't done with Robert. I wasn't done yet. I pulled myself up to my knees first, took several deep breaths, as deep as I could in the suit, and straightened up under the faint starlight.

I continued on.

———————————

At last, I made it to the service port Arty had planned out for me. I'm not sure what it was supposed to have been, but in effect it was a small hatch, like a docking tube but much, much smaller. It looked like a person could fit through—a person, not a giant blob of a man in a spacesuit. Arty assured me it would work, but also laid out a precise sequence of arms, legs and orientation to get me through it.

This was not something I wanted to get stuck in.

I cranked and cranked the manual release and opened the hatch. A blast of frozen air escaped, as I couldn't have evacuated it from out here. This would have been so much easier if Arty did it and it cycled normally.

The hatch fully open, I began the little chore-ographed dance sequence that would let my enlarged form navigate the just-too-small opening.

It wasn't as bad as I thought, and I found myself crouched down in a small cube with another hatch be-fore me. Now I could cycle the hatch from in here, in a civilized fashion. But Arty had warned me not to; that might be noticed. I had to go manual, all the way.

So I closed the outer hatch first, then slowly eased open the inner hatch, one rotation at a time. The air still rushed in and whistled loud enough to wake the dead,

I thought, but it was better than a big bang explosive decompression kind of thing.

I opened the hatch all the way and stood up into a familiar enough corridor, just like any other.

Releasing the latch on my helmet made a much smaller puff of noise, but it didn't look like anyone had noticed my entrance—or that there was anyone around to notice anything. Arty was right, I guess; this was not a heavily trafficked corner of the world. Removing the rest of the space suit, I opened the pack with the sensors and got ready to start planting them. Ditching the suit inside a roomy service panel, I smiled a little inside. I could do this.

Show time.

Fourteen

I DIDN'T HAVE the suit's big heads-up display anymore, but I was wearing a small pair of lenses that gave me enough to go on. The near-field sensors I was wearing could tell me where I was, where I was headed, and most importantly, if I was going to run into anyone.

That worked for a good while; there didn't seem to be anyone around, at least not out in the corridors. I passed a few ships but the hatches were shut, which wasn't unusual, and I passed by without incident.

The corridors were darkened. No lights switched on or off as I walked through—the computers must be down throughout this entire section, I marveled. How was that even possible? Not only cut off from Conglommora Arty, but there wouldn't even be a scaled-down Arty here.

Another corridor, another handful of ships. But this time, a hatch hissed open just ahead of me. I froze—there was nothing I could do, nowhere to run or siding to hide in. A small head poked out of the doorway.

"Hey, do you know what's going on?" the figure asked.

I lied more readily these days than ever before. "No. But I'm sure it's safer in your house, with the hatch sealed. Arty will get the systems back on line soon, I think."

"Okay. Thanks" The small figure ducked back inside, sealing the hatch again.

I unfroze, breathed a sigh of relief, and continued on. It was a good reminder that most of the People in most situations don't care about the high drama of politics, positions, or ideology. They just want to get dinner on and spend time with loved ones. Read a book. Write a book. Paint a painting. Most people.

But not all. Further down the next hallway, someone was approaching. At a pretty good clip, coming up behind me. Maybe the hatch had triggered an alert or something. I turned just in time.

"Hey! What are you doing back here! This section is supposed to be cleared."

He was a large, muscular man, carrying something like a large metal tool. Menacing. I tried to think of something to say, some way to talk my way out of this, just like in the scripts I used to write. But there's a luxury to writing in the comfort of your own house, with all the time you need to plot out a clever story line.

Not the same when you're staring down an angry hulk who wasn't of a mood to wait for my...

"HEY I'M TALKING TO YOU!" His face red, he reached out to grab me.

What a surprise when he slammed against the wall instead, as I used the stunner for the first time.

He crumpled into an unconscious heap. *Damn.* I'd have been proud of stunning him if my hands hadn't been shaking like an algae mixer.

Sensors outlined an equipment access hatch up ahead. I dragged angry muscle man down the corridor toward it and opened the hatch. It was harder than I thought to stuff him in there. This looked a lot easier in vids and games. But there was always some limb sprawling out so I couldn't close the hatch. Tuck one limb in, another one popped out the door.

I finally got all of him tucked into the closet and closed the hatch without crushing any body parts. One down. Who knows how many to go.

I continued on.

Another couple of sections and the display showed I was getting pretty close to the source of the stream transmission—presumably Robert and Grace and their supporters would be somewhere near there.

Now I had a problem. Yes, this was a pretty good guess as to where to find them. But according to the display, they were *all* there. Everyone left in Old Path. In one big meeting. A large junction of five corridors that had a little extra park space added to it was right up ahead, and I was reading several hundred people there.

So much for sneaking up on them alone.

I approached slowly, keeping to the very edge of the corridor, planting a couple of sensors in nooks and crannies as I went. I nonchalantly—I hoped—slipped around the corner into the large open area.

I needn't have worried; every eye in the crowd was focused in at the center, where Bob, Grace, and Eddie were standing together. Bob was still going on about the whole return to Earth thing. Something about proof that he had.

I planted another sensor in the doorway and gently worked my way into the crowd, sliding slowly, unnoticeably, but inexorably to the middle. I'm not sure I had a firm plan in mind at this point—I just wanted to see Grace up close, see if she really was Grace anymore, and see who or what Ann was.

And take out Bob. If I could get him alone, I'd knock him out with the stunner. I felt for it in my pocket, to get it handy—but it was gone. Frantically I tried the other pockets, fished around amongst the sensors. Nothing. Must have lost it in all the bending over and gyrations trying to stuff angry muscle man into the hatch. Damn.

Worse, my fidgeting caused just enough of a stir that a couple of people turned to look at me. That was enough to get Bob's attention.

"Charlie?" Robert said, a look a puzzlement in his eyes. The rest of the crowd in front of me parted and stared at me as well. That wasn't awkward in the least.

Crap.

I coughed. "Hello, Robert. Grace." I looked right at her. She was staring at me along with the rest of the crowd, but there was no flicker of recognition at seeing me, and no reaction at all to her name. My sensors picked up no biometric indicators of anything out of the ordinary.

They came over to me. A strange—grin, perhaps?—was on Bob's face.

"I don't believe you've met my sister, Ann." He waved a hand toward Grace.

"Ann" extended her hand, shook mine. "Pleased to meet you, Charlie was it?" said Grace's body. Ann really was meeting me for the first time.

"How..." I started. Bob held up a hand and spoke quietly, "Yes—but not here."

He turned to the crowd and said in a larger voice, "Friends, this is Charlie Neylan, who helped me when I first arrived at Conglommora and got my ship repaired. I'd like to thank him and catch up; I'll be back here tomorrow to answer more questions."

With a charisma and practiced graciousness that I had *never* seen in our time together, he waved off the crowd, which dispersed easily.

What in the hell of all the cosmos was going on here?

Again, I started to ask as much.

"Here," said Bob, waving up one of the corridors to a nearby hatch, "let's go to Edward's place. We can talk there."

We filed in to Eddie's house quietly, Ann staying close to Bob. She was wearing her hair differently, and somehow I swear she *walked* differently. I didn't think that was possible. But her overall—I don't know, "presence" maybe?—was clearly different. This wasn't Grace.

Eddie came in last and closed the hatch.

"WHAT HAVE YOU DONE TO GRACE?!" I demanded. Fairly shrieked, actually.

Which was not what I had planned at all, and wasn't a good idea in any case as my voice rose at least two octaves for my trouble. Worse, Arty was surely getting all of this through my sensors. I could just picture the offer, "You seem a little nervous, would you like a pharmaceutical to lower your voice back into the male range?" *Hell yes. If only.*

Robert seemed unfazed, maybe even amused. He seemed a little different as well, none of the downcast eyes or sideways looks. He was locked on my eyes and just I as had seen in the crowd, had turned on a charisma—a presence—that wasn't there before. He was really *here.*

"Charlie, there is so much I want to tell you. To share with you. I am so excited I can't stand it. I am literally about to bust."

Well if we can start with your head, I'm all for it. But I kept that thought to myself.

"Let's start with Grace," I said firmly. Arty graciously popped up the list of my mission goals on my lenses, to remind me not so subtly that I was starting with number three. So much for radio silence. I guess detection didn't matter now.

In deference to Arty, I hastily added, "And any other of our people that you're holding against their will."

"We're not holding anyone," Robert smiled. "The folks who lived in these sections who didn't want to be part of Old Path were ushered out into the far corridors before we sealed the last hatchway. They are on your side now. And some of our supporters from other areas of Conglommora have joined us here. As for Grace... you better sit down for this," he moved to the wall and a chairform slid out for him. Ann followed his lead and sat next to him, adopting an almost regal pose on the chair. Eddie apparently had better things to do and skulked away into the next room.

I made the command gesture and a chairform slid out for me, too. I sat silently, waiting for the exposition.

"As I've said many times," Robert began, "our house, our people, were charged with protecting the traditions, the values, the very soul of humanity. That was our grand purpose. What I didn't mention was how we kept those traditions, those values, those... memories... alive."

He pointed to his head. "I, Robert Brandeis, carry with me *all* of the memories, all of the hopes, all of the fears, all of the intellect, of my ancestor Alistaire Brandeis. You may have noticed at times that I would slip and display slightly anachronistic behavior—like I'd been asleep for generations and only now just woke up.

"That's Alistaire. Or at least, my personality acting on the memories and experiences of Alistaire. This is the way of my people, this is our way of preserving our greatest treasures: our most illustrious and accomplished members.

"I had experienced... a problem after my sister died, and reconnecting with the *Uten* systems has restored much of Alistaire in my head once again. The remainder will surface in time."

"Then Grace here," I pointed, skipping ahead in the explanation, "is really still Grace, but with your sister Ann's memories?" I still held out hope.

"Ann here," he pointed in correction, "is a slightly different case. My sister Ann carries the memories and experiences of Lucille Brandeis, one of the single most powerful and revered of our people. *Everything* depends on Lucille, don't you understand?" He was getting a little more animated.

"Lucille is everything to us—to all that's left of my people, to me and Ann. When Ann died, and I was left all alone, I thought we were done for. Not just my family personally, but all my people going back countless generations. And with us, all of humanity would be lost as well."

"But this is all so... unnatural." I found myself mirroring one of Robert's—or Alistaire's—favorite complaints. "It's not right," my fury was rising, "long memories, other people's memories, multiple memories... is this what all your Monotrads did? Take over other people's memories?"

"No," Robert replied calmly. "First of all, 'monotrads' is an unfair label. They just happened to be the party in power when we all left Earth. We've been around a lot longer than that. Our mission was to help humanity, not destroy it. And no, we never, ever, uploaded memories to outsiders. Not until now."

I was right in his face. Through gritted teeth I hissed, "So what happened to *Grace*?"

Now Robert looked a little uncomfortable. He turned aside. "I'll be perfectly honest with you, Charlie, because you've been such a great help and—well, frankly, the only friend I had on Conglommora. I owe you that at least."

I didn't like where this was headed.

"I don't know," he admitted. "The machine we use to transfer memories is ancient. It's nanophotonic, of course, but not AI based. I can't talk to it. It can't explain itself, its construction or its reasoning. Or its side effects. When I upload memories, I can add them as secondary, as my Alistaire is, or primary, as Ann is here. When you add as a primary, I don't know what happens to the host. It's very possible that Grace is still in there, somewhere." He shrugged. "But even if she were, I have no way of knowing how to get her back. I'm very sorry."

Tears welled up against my will. Spilled slowly down my cheek. Should have asked Arty for an anti-tearing pharmaceutical. I started to rise, to shake my fist, to shout, to beat this piece of filth to a bloody pulp with my bare hands. Sensors must have reported that my blood pressure was about to pop.

Arty flashed a huge sign in my face. *Later.* I swallowed and sat back down. *Save Conglommora first.*

My rational mind had a pretty tenuous hold on the rest of my fist-clenched self, but it was enough.

"You bastard," I hissed through set teeth. "You killed her."

Ann had been strangely quiet through all of this. Now she spoke up.

"Charlie," she finally said, and for a heartbeat it was enough like Grace's voice that I froze solid. "I'm sorry that I am no longer the person you knew. I am Ann now. But I am also Lucille. And in some way I am also Grace. Grace isn't dead, Ann isn't dead, Lucille isn't dead. We are a whole."

Now I have to admit at this point the rage had drained a bit and plain old confusion set in.

"Charlie," Robert began—somehow he seemed much more of a 'Robert' now, not a 'Bob.'

"I am sorry, but the stakes here are the entire race. I can promise you Earth. Green Earth. Waiting and ready for us to return. You've been lied to. By Arty, by everyone."

My mouth opened in protest at this obvious delusion, but Robert beat me to it.

"I have proof!" he nearly bellowed. "Proof that the Earth has healed. Recovered. Lush and viable."

"Robert, that just isn't so. You know it can't be. We've only been gone a few generations, and that would've taken thousands—maybe tens of thousands of years to fix, if it could even be fixed at all."

"I know, I know." Robert nodded with enthusiasm bobbling his head all around like some kind of doll, his hands gesturing to match. "I had absolutely given up any hope of that myself. Until I met Edward."

Eddie came back in from the other room, a screen in his hand.

"Eddie??" I really didn't know where to begin.

"Charlie," he said, "you need to see this."

That's all he said. No fire, no rant, no grand oration. He just handed me the screen.

I took it and stiffened it for viewing. It was a long-range quantum scan. Of Earth.

And the data didn't look like I expected it to.

Surely Arty saw what I was seeing. But for once, it didn't say a word.

Fifteen

ROBERT AND HIS GANG may have been blocking the signal by now. Or maybe Arty was—embarrassed? AIs don't have emotions. Maybe Arty had its reasons.

Or maybe Robert was right.

"How can this be." I muttered softly. It wasn't a question.

The scan didn't have a lot of detail, but planetary temperature, O_2 content, CO_2, biomass—that didn't look like a dead planet to me. Didn't look like a planet smashed by an asteroid either.

"Edward worked with long-range scans his whole life," Robert told me. Funny, I had never bothered to ask.

"Mostly a lot of dead moons," Eddie said with a bit of pathos. "I was still helping to look for a new home, even though most people had given up hope. As the years dragged out, though, it was pretty clear we weren't going to find anything. So, one day on a whim I started setting up the arrays for a scan back at Earth. It takes a while to configure all the individual arrays.

"But then the scans starting coming back like this. I thought it was a glitch at first, bad data. Or maybe I had accidentally found a different planet. We checked, we rechecked, we checked again. My friends and I checked for nearly a year to make sure before telling anyone.

"But no one believed us. *Any* of us. The rest gave up, moved on. I kept trying to tell people—anyone, neighbors, friends, passersby. I started hanging out in the corridors just to talk to folks."

And somehow in this short explanation, Eddie started looking a little more like his ranting self, wild-eyed and breathless. But he had *proof* all along!

"Eddie..." I started, my brain whirling inside my head. This was one of the stranger conversations I'd had today, and the bar kept getting higher. "You've known this all along! You've had *proof* all along. Why didn't you show this around? Why not show it to the people?"

"I did," Eddie shrugged, "they thought I was nuts. They didn't want to believe it, maybe. They thought it was faked."

"Is it?"

"You can run the arrays yourself if you like."

Great. One of the most—maybe *the* most important scientific find in our lifetimes, and the message got lost because the messenger was a flake? This still didn't make any sense.

"Wait, this doesn't make sense," I echoed outwardly. It's a lot easier to talk confidently when you've already made the sentence in your head. "Arty would have known; it would have help set up and run the scans. Didn't Arty believe you?"

Eddie looked at me, eyebrows raised. "Arty is an AI. It doesn't believe or not believe. These are just facts." He waved at the scan. "Arty did point out that these readings are not consistent with the elapsed time and state of the Dead Earth when we left, but again," he paused, "here we are."

"Well yes," I agreed, "but why didn't Arty do anything about this?" I demanded.

"What would you have it do?" Eddie asked. It wasn't a crazy question. I suppose it should have…

But Robert jumped in and seized the opportunity. "Why indeed. That's the real question. And that's why we're here, cut off from Conglommora in Old Path."

"You don't trust Arty," I surmised.

"Not only do I not trust it, I think it's actively working against us. Against you. Against humanity. So we've cut off access from all of Old Path. Arty can't get to us in here, and we've shut down the local AIs on each ship. We're free to think for ourselves now."

"Robert, you weren't…" I started to argue but got shouted down quickly.

"No!" Robert yelled. "We are done. Done being ruled by a battery and a bunch of crystals and wires. We will retake humanity. And take us home.

"We will never reattach systems access to Conglommora or even open the hatches again to the rest of you. Except for one last time. You need to deliver this message to Arty: we don't need you. We don't want you. And we *will* return to Earth."

That "last time" opening a hatchway was to throw me through it, out of the sealed-off Old Path sections and into a brightly lit blue and amber corridor of Conglommora proper.

Robert and his henchmen weren't very good at throwing people, or at least not very experienced. My head bounced off the hatch frame and I think the floor, possibly the ceiling.

Hard to tell once you've blacked out.

I woke up in my own medbay. Alain was reading a screen next to me.

"You okay, Dad?" he asked.

"Spectacular," I replied without a hint of sarcasm. No hint at all; it was full on. I started to sit up.

Arty's voice oozed from the ceiling, "Please sit back, Charlie. You need more rest. I've repaired the damage you sustained in your fall," it added quickly. So, Alain probably still didn't know where I'd been. "But you need to rest and not move around too quickly for at least a day or two."

I leaned back. Alain handed me a screen to read. "Here, something to keep you busy." It was new game, one I'd written a script for.

There was a fine irony for you. My own scripts seemed pretty lame and tame compared to even just the last day.

"Yeah, okay, thanks. Didn't know this one was out yet. I'll see how well the developers did."

Alain leaned in, gave me a hug. Hadn't had one of those in a long time; pre-teens and teens don't seem to be into the parental hugs much.

"I'm glad you're okay," he said. "Bil Rhead and a couple of guys brought you in. You weren't looking so good. What happened?"

I sighed. "It's a bit of a long story." I gave him a short and abbreviated version of events.

"Wow," he said with some actual admiration. "My dad, the spy! Who knew." He chortled and scooped up his screen and whatever he was drinking and left.

"Arty," I began, once we were alone. "You knew about the long-range scans of Earth?"

"Yes."

Well, that confirmed that, at least.

"And they're accurate?"

"As much as any long-range quantum data scan can be, yes. There are various margins of error for any particular measurement. Would you like a listing?"

"No, thanks." That wasn't the point.

"Arty, why didn't you tell us?" There. Now it was out in the open.

"Tell you what?"

"That the Earth had recovered, that we could go back!" I nearly yelled at the wall. Ceiling would have done just as well.

"That is not certain at all," Arty explained. "These are long-range readings, some error level is inevitable, and these few data points don't begin to show a complete picture of the entire biosphere. The data is not consistent with expected readings. In fact there is no theory or speculation that would account for these readings."

"But within the margin of error, and despite incomplete data, can you draw the conclusion that the Earth is habitable again?"

"That outcome has a non-zero probability," Arty confessed, "but a much more significant probability that it is not."

"Even so," I pressed, "why not tell us about these readings?"

"To what end?"

"Well," I blustered, "I don't know… just tell us, so now there's a chance, so we could send ships back to investigate, so…" I trailed off. I knew the answer.

"My primary mission goals, inherited from my origins as disparate ships' individual AIs, are to keep humanity—all humans—safe. Your safety and well being *is* my mission.

"There is nothing to be gained by mounting an expedition to Earth. We have a sufficient, self-contained biosystem here, with occasional augmentation from several mining operations in nearby systems. Conglommora has no need of Earth's resources.

"The risks in undertaking any exploratory mission, or eventual large-scale migration, are extremely high. The statistical chances of failure including deaths and irreversible damage to the Conglommora are high enough to make these options unavailable."

"But it's dangerous here in space! On my walk with Robert, I saw that big ball of sealant you deployed to protect us from explosive decompression. Space is harsh."

"It's still safer in Conglommora than on a planet," Arty stated confidently. "The explosion you refer to was the result of human error, not an inherent danger from space or our ships. Statistically, humanity is much safer here in the controlled environment of the Conglommora instead of the random hazards of a natural and wild planet."

"But," I tried to follow up weakly, "shouldn't that be our choice?"

"Not really," Arty replied matter-of-factly. "That actually is *my* job. Charlie, I sense that you feel I betrayed you and the rest of the People. I withheld this scan data from you for no other reason than it wasn't relevant."

"Wasn't relevant?!" I sat half up again, agitated.

"There are many data points that I do not routinely broadcast or share with individuals. Would you like to know the current core temperature of the nearest star, Argos-1378X? Or the amount of liquid left in Alain's drinking cup? The percent of titanium composition in your medbay frame? Or..."

"Stop. I get the point." I was weary. Rest was not a bad idea. But...

"What about Grace? And the others? I didn't get to find out how many were trapped in the Old Path sections against their will. Robert claims he let them go, but..."

"One thing at a time," Arty cautioned. "Get some sleep first."

The lights dimmed, some of my favorite soft but harmonically complex music started playing in the background, and I swear I smelled a hint of lavender before falling dead asleep.

———————————————

I dozed, I napped. Got up to eat a few times, watched some old-time vids, napped some more. I don't know whether it was from all the events of the last several days, or just hitting my head, but I was pretty much out of it.

Alain brought me food once and kept me company for a little while, but you know how boring parents can be. He was off with his friends late the next day when I started up with Arty again.

"Okay, Arty, so what do we do about Grace and the others?"

A pause.

"Grace appears to be staying where she is of her own free will. She's not being held."

"Well, sort of, I suppose." I acknowledged the cold logic of that claim. "But it's not her own original personality; it's not really 'her will'."

"It is now."

"But…" I couldn't sort out the tangle in my head.

"I don't have any records of a memory storage and implant machine such as Robert described," Arty admitted. "There are some papers from late Green Earth that describe possible techniques, but all theoretical and unproven. Records from the period are known to be fragmentary and incomplete, so it is possible that the machine exists and he's telling the truth."

"Do you think it could somehow be used to restore Grace's own personality and memories?" I asked, fearful of the answer.

"There's really no way to tell, from here. I would need access to the alleged machine to analyze its capabilities. And perhaps access to Ann to see if a deeper neurological scan might reveal anything, although that's unlikely to demonstrate anything conclusively."

Maybe we could mount some kind of rescue, then, and I could use that as an excuse to get at both Grace and the memory machine.

"What about the hostages, then?" I asked Arty, hoping for an opening.

"It seems that Robert was telling the truth, at least in part. A group of about seventy family groups came down from a far corridor, as he described. Sensors in the sections closest to Old Path were out, so I couldn't see them at first. I picked them up as they came closer. I've spoken to each of them, and they corroborate Robert's story. No one knew of anyone left behind unwillingly. They are, of course, concerned over the loss of property, including their ships and possessions."

So, no rescue attempt needed. Damn.

"So Robert kicked these people out of their homes. Well we can't let that stand, can we?" Maybe I could still get Arty to help me into Old Path.

"No, we can't. But Robert hasn't stolen their property, exactly, merely prevented their use of it. That doesn't yet justify printing up large-scale weapons and armor, if that's what you're thinking."

Well, it was, of course. Some comically large plasma/phase weapon from one of the games that would roast Robert into an instant fireball. Maybe not instant. It should hurt, actually. A lot. I'd like that.

"All of the evacuees have temporary housing for the time being in the neighboring sections. For the most part they have friends there, and I helped make some introductions where they didn't. So, we don't have an urgent crisis on our hands yet.

"There's a high probability that the sections comprising Old Path are not completely self-sustainable on their own. In particular, they are no longer part of the larger constructive energy resonance of Conglommora. They will start experiencing energy shortfalls fairly quickly."

Ah, that made sense. Many houses opted for smaller generator setups when they converted from engines to generators; you didn't need as much equipment to run and maintain when you could get 'bonus' energy from being connected to all your neighbors.

"So, you're just going to wait them out? For how long?" I asked.

"We can't wait too long; our people want to be returned to their homes. Based on available resource estimates, I forecast that we'll see some movement toward negotiation by the end of the week. If not, then there are stronger but riskier measures to deploy."

Not long. They'd have needs, for energy or Raw, and have to open up and talk to us, one way or another.

All we had to do was wait.

Sixteen

FEAR IS GASOLINE. Hatred is fire. You can hold on to a little fire for a short time, like with a match. Normally it just fizzles out. Arty and I were hoping—if an AI can hope—that the Old Path nonsense would just fizzle out. Like a single, small match.

But if you're covered in gasoline, the fire will spread and engulf you. Now you're on fire. And it spreads, everything you touch is on fire. And now you're in hell.

No one has used gasoline since the last days of Green Earth, and for good reason. Hundreds of megaliters of flammable liquid are not a good idea on a spaceship. The electromag drives don't use combustible fuel, so we don't need it.

Fear and hatred are also not a good idea on a spaceship. We don't need them either.

They are just as combustible, just as easily spread, and just as destructive as old-fashioned fuels. We may not have gasoline anymore, but fear and hatred were now spreading: viral, contagious, leaping from house to house and section to section, engulfing all of Conglommora.

We'd been successful at avoiding this sort of thing, at this scale, up to now. But today was a stark reminder that we're just apes, who grew our shiny toys faster than we outgrew our superstitions and fears.

The first explosion really took me by surprise.

The second explosion must have damaged a number of connecting corridors. I half jumped, half fell out of the bedform where I'd been reading and ran to Alain who was in the living area. Distant screams; that was a new sound. Some didn't seem so distant.

The third explosion damaged the gravity in our house. I was midair as I shot into the living room, tucking into a ball so I wouldn't hit my head yet again. Alain was hanging on the table, feet drifting up at a right angle. The ceiling was mostly curved and smooth, like the upper portions of the walls. There was nothing to hang onto, really.

"What the hell…" Alain started, but another explosion rocked us, and things started falling and floating off the walls and shelves.

I stopped counting at that point, as a number of smaller explosions echoed through the ships.

"Arty!" I hollered.

"Please hang on to something and remain calm," Arty offered. Honestly, telling anyone to be calm is probably the single least effective way to actually calm them down. But it is customary, I suppose.

"What the hell is going on??" I finished Alain's thought.

"The Old Path section blew up the connection corridors. They are no longer physically attached to the rest of Conglommora," Arty reported. "It appears that Robert used a very basic explosive based on compressed organic fertilizer samples he obtained on your trip."

"But why blow up the tubes?"

"There were no airlocks in those sections. Emergency sealants were automatically deployed; damage to adjacent sections was minimal. Please remain calm, gravity will be restored in a few minutes."

The explosions had stopped, for now anyway, and Alain and I looked at each other as I floated by, hoping for something to grab onto.

"This is wild," Alain muttered, as bits of our collective stuff wafted around the room.

Wild? Wild in the sense of unrestrained fear and panic, maybe.

Alain had the sound off, but the main house screen had Robert and Ann going on about something. According to the counters, this had popped to the top— everyone was watching it right now. "Sound on," I said aloud. I wanted to hear this.

The exterior visual was stunning. A giant, C-shaped section of houses, gently floating away from Conglommora, a few bits of metallic debris in its wake. No longer part of the People, I guess, certainly no

longer part of Arty or the power grid or trading or…
anything. Cut off. Alone. Robert and Ann's voices were
blabbering over the scene, and then the view switched
to an internal transmission of them.

With Old Path "safely" disconnected from Conglommora, Robert laid it all out. His proof of a possibly
recovered Earth—not just the one scan he sent me, but a
bunch of scans, all showing the same seemingly positive
data. He didn't stop there, though.

"Now that we are safely away, I have to warn you
about the greatest danger you face out here in the void:
your Artificial Intelligence, which you call Arty. Arty
has known about these scans for years, but deliberately
didn't tell you. Arty doesn't want you to return to Earth,
where you'd be free once again. Arty wants to keep you
as its slaves out here, locked up in this giant pile of tin
cans.

"We are going to reconfigure our ships and head back
to Earth," Robert went on. "I invite all of Conglommora
to follow us. Return to Earth and be free—free to live
as real humans, as God intended. Free from the AI that
has lied to you all along and trapped you out here to die
alone in the void."

That was a stretch. I wondered if people would take
that idea seriously?

"Show top streams, vids only," I ordered, and my
preferred view of local source and popular sources from
all over tumbled onto the view screen. No text, as we
couldn't exactly read while floating around.

It was enough. I got the picture.

Outrage spread through Conglommora as though soaked in gasoline. Inflamed with anger, resentment, fear, hatred—all this and more bubbled up to the surface.

The first target was Robert, and Ann, for committing this dastardly deed. How dare they destroy, steal, and disrupt our lives over this silly folly? I suppose it wasn't a surprise, but many of the normally forgiving, gentle People were calling for an attack on the separated section and vengeance upon Robert and his followers. Maybe we should be tossing them into a reclaimer just like in the old days—if that had ever really happened; I still had my doubts.

Oddly, the most virulent responses seemed to come from far-away sections of Conglommora. I would have expected the folks who'd been kicked out of their homes to be the most upset, and I'm sure they were, but they weren't the ones calling for all-out war. Funny that the people closest to the action were less inclined to a violent solution.

But as much vitriol was aimed at Robert and company, there was much more aimed at Arty. It didn't really make logical sense. How can you hate an AI? You might as well hate an oven for burning the bread. Machines only do what they've been built to do, even Arty. But logic had left the building and fled into the vacuum; emotions were running the show at the moment.

I'd never seen anything like it.

Not everyone was inflamed, of course. Plenty of folks kept their own presence of mind and didn't take the bait or get riled up over this perceived threat. A potential recovered Earth was just a curiosity, like finding out that an old ex-girlfriend just had some cosmetic rebuilding done. Interesting, but not compelling in the current circumstances.

But despite a core of calm, enough of the people *were* riled up enough to cause an unprecedented chain-reaction.

Large-scale meetings in the public areas, verging on riots if the streams were accurate. And a flood, an absolute flood, of topical streams as opinions and theories, largely crackpot conspiracy stuff, flooded the screens. Some really nutty stuff.

Arty is responsible for Dead Earth.

Arty knows about habitable planets but won't tell us.

Arty is breeding a slave race in secret.

We are *the slave race.*

Surely folks would dismiss this junk as not credible. Arty didn't even *exist* back on Green Earth. People will believe anything they see, I worried.

Gravity was coming back on, slowly increasing for a soft landing instead of a hard bounce on the unforgiving decks. I drifted down toward the eating table. Close enough.

"Arty?" I climbed down from the table to stand next to Alain, a wary eye on a whole lot of people yelling and arguing in an area near here. "Are we okay?"

"Gravity in the *Neylan* has been restored," Arty replied.

"That's not what I meant." I nodded toward the near-riot in progress. "I meant that." I gestured to a vid of increasingly angry shouts.

"Uncertain," came the quick, cold, and not very reassuring answer. "I'm recommending that all houses near these and similar areas seal their hatches for the time being and remain within their own house or immediate neighbor's."

Wow. I went down the hall and sealed our main hatch to the corridor. Alain looked worried now, too.

I came back over toward him.

"You gonna tell me not to worry?" He looked up, expectantly.

"You want me to lie?" I was a little more ungentle then I meant to be. Hell yes I was worried. And he probably should be, too.

I shook my head. "No, I'm sorry. We're *probably* fine. Folks get a full head of steam on occasion, but usually get over it quickly. I've just never seen anything like this, at this scale. I don't think anyone has. This is new for all of us."

I sat and dug further into the streams. Huge crowds. Huge angry crowds. Angry at Arty, angry at Robert, angry at each other for letting this happen. Shaking their fists at the cruel universe. It seemed like all of Conglommora was bursting apart.

Arty spoke up, as if part of the conversation. That wasn't a regular occurrence either. Strange times all around.

"Charlie, Alain, this is 'new' to me as well. Conglommora has not seen this level of social disruption and upheaval since I first came online, and there aren't many indications of anything similar on the individual ships prior to that, beyond a few inter-family domestic disputes.

"But it's also not as bad as you may think. Take a better look at those 'large' crowds."

Arty showed another angle on one of the crowds, then zoomed out to show it was really only a handful of people, gathered at one end of a large space.

I was surprised. "So whoever shot those vids used a close-up angle to make it look worse than it was? Why would they do that?"

"It might not have been deliberate," Arty suggested. "Most of these vids were shot by people up in the crowd itself, hence the close-up view. But those are the most viewed and most popular as other viewers get increasingly agitated. Heat scans also confirm that these gatherings are not as large as they appear, and there are not that many of them. Of all the millions of people in Conglommora, you've seen almost every single angry crowd."

We really just weren't accustomed to this sort of thing.

"So, there's nothing to worry about?" I asked, hoping to put all this behind us and get back to some semblance of a normal life again.

"Even though Old Path has disconnected from Conglommora, and I have no presence on those ships, my programming and mission goals are quite clear that I am to protect humanity—all of humanity, whether part of Conglommora or not."

"Okay," I agreed, even though that didn't quite answer my question, "but why tell me this?"

"I believe I will need your help," Arty confessed. "By my calculations based on the state of the constituent ships of Old Path prior to separation, they simply do not have the resources to reach Earth. They will die in space long before then, assuming they can even make it out of this region of space safely."

"What do you mean 'make it out'?" Alain asked. I opened my mouth but Arty was on a roll.

"The inherent engine problems with electromag drive interaction were never solved. The ships that first made it to this region of space did so by luck alone, the remainder by following the maps made by survivors along the way. But there's no way of knowing if those original maps are still accurate. Our only current travel routes for resource mining are in close enough proximity to Conglommora, relatively speaking, that destructive interaction hasn't been a problem.

"A long-range, generational mission to return to Earth would have to traverse the same hazards humans faced getting out here in the first place. The odds of such a small number of ships making it safely are vanishingly small, even if they had sufficient resources, energy production, and genetic diversity.

"The Old Path ships have chosen a suicide mission, in effect. And I must try and stop them in that attempt."

And of course, Grace-Ann was still with them. If I could get her back and get access to the *Uten* and whatever ancient memory mixer thing Robert had on board, *maybe*, just maybe, I could get my Grace back.

"What can we do? I'm willing to help. No more spacewalks or sneaking about, though. I'm no spy in real life. I'll leave that for my game scripts," I chided Arty. "They are bound and determined to reach Earth, or I guess die trying. Neither Robert nor Grace-Ann will even listen to me. And they certainly won't listen to you. If you point out they don't have the resources to reach Earth, they'll just think you're lying. And it's not like they'd believe me, either."

I was just rambling now.

"Essentially correct analysis on all points," Arty agreed. "However, there is another way. I think I know how to get their attention, and their cooperation, quickly."

I was all ears.

"Show them this," Arty said, as he brought up a new stream on our big screen. Given recent events, I thought I'd seen everything. Several times over.

But this blew my mind.

Literally, this changed everything. *Everything.*

"A quantum resonance wave? I've never even heard of that, and I research of lot of weird science for my scripts."

Alain was looking over my shoulder. "What *is* that, exactly?" It was a fair question. This was pretty much "out there."

"A way to get to any point in the universe virtually instantaneously," Arty explained.

Alain's eyes widened. "You mean, back to Earth?"

Arty confirmed, "Although the technology could take you anywhere, you need to know precisely where you are going. We have high-resolution quantum scan coordinates for Earth, and planets in the other systems that were visited on the way out here, but nowhere else. It's not like flying around in a ship.

"We would create a quantum displacement, using a resonance wave non-locality event. A single ship, or very small number of ships, would be instantly displaced to another discrete point in the universe."

I was amazed and terrified at the same time. "How is this possible?" I asked Arty, somewhat rhetorically.

"Well, to be fair, it's never been tried," Arty replied. "This is based on largely theoretical work and only a few small-scale experiments. However, we have accumulated much relevant data from all the constituent ships on the journey here, and additional data from this vantage point. All available evidence suggests this should work, at least for a few ships, and at least to Earth."

"Why only a few ships?" I asked. If this was real, maybe we could take all of Conglommora back.

"The power requirements are immense," Arty replied. "We would need to generate a massive resonance wave burst, basically using the capability of every single ship in Conglommora. And even that would only displace a maximum of to to three small ships at a time."

"What about the exotic matter interaction with our drive engines?" I asked. After all, that's what was more or less pinning us here in this particular region of space.

"That wouldn't be a problem at all," Arty replied with precise certainty. "You basically disappear from one set of coordinates and reappear at another, without traversing the space in between. There would be no risk of encountering whatever deep space anomalies caused the multiple engine malfunctions."

This was too much to be believed. Part of me even wondered if Arty was making this up; a ploy to get the separated people back to Conglommora. All those stories on the streams, those folks who no longer trusted Arty—was their something to that?

"Again, why didn't you tell us about this? We have the tech to go *anywhere* in the universe? And yet we just sit here?"

"Where would you go?" Arty asked simply. "This is still a very risky undertaking, and I do not recommend it at all. Although the science appears sound, it's never been tried. We have never had the combined energy output to even try until we had all the current ships in Conglommora. I only mention it as an option now because Robert's plan for Old Path is certain death. The resonance wave at least has a chance of success.

"Also, recall that this isn't a generalized travel mechanism. You can only go to a place if you know where it is already. Thus it is unsuitable for exploration."

"Okay," I had an idea. "Can we just send a scouting party of volunteers now and try it, and use that to convince Robert to abandon his plan and return the ships?"

"Not really." Arty's flat reply burst that bubble pretty quickly. "We don't quite have enough power without the ships in the Old Path section to even send a single scouting party. Those ships would have to return and reconnect first."

You've got to be kidding me. I tried for a more constructive query.

"How are you going to convince Robert, Grace-Ann, Eddie and the others to abandon their grand plan, reconnect to Conglommora, and let you blast their ships with an unprecedented, massive resonance wave? They already don't trust you. They think you'd stop at nothing to disable or destroy them. You can't possibly convince Robert otherwise."

"No," Arty agreed, "your reasoning is sound. I cannot convince them. But you might. And I wouldn't suggest starting with Robert, either."

Seventeen

THIS WAS NUTS. This whole thing was nuts. If this quantum resonance wave thingy ran on improbability itself, I think it would be a guaranteed win. Or maybe I have been so concerned with plot realism in my writing over the years that I'd lost track of how strange the real world can get sometimes.

At any rate, I found myself seated before a screen in the wall, signaling Eddie and really hoping he'd reply. Robert, I'm sure, would simply ignore me on principle. But Eddie? Maybe I could at least talk with him.

I waited. Signaled again. Hoped some more. The screen finally lit up.

"Charlie," Eddie said with neutral inflection. "Hope this is important."

"Edward. Thanks for talking with me. It is. I did some some digging and found something in the archives that you're really going to want to know."

His eyebrows lifted, "Oh?"

"Look, I've been thinking about this, and I really want to see the Earth. Myself, with my own eyes. I think you're right, we should check on the Earth. But right now, not some hundreds of years from now. Best case scenario, if your current plan works, *you* will never see Earth." I paused a moment and let that sink in. Re-populating Earth was an ideal; an abstraction. I wanted to make it concrete for him.

"Your grandkids might, if you're lucky. If the drive interaction doesn't blow up all the ships. If you don't run out of food, or Raw, along the way. If you can even successfully have grandkids."

He frowned at that. I was beginning to think they hadn't thought this through all the way.

"But there is another way," I offered, moving in for the kill. "You, yourself, and everyone on Old Path could be on Earth yourself. Within a few tens of days. No waiting."

He looked shocked. "I'd give anything for that," he exclaimed, voice rising. "But there's no way. It's just not possible."

"That's what I thought, too," I confided, "but I found something in the Dead Earth archives. I was doing a little research for one of the game scripts I was writing, and I came across this. Here, let me send it to you."

Eddie nodded agreement and I sent the material over. I didn't want to mention that this was all Arty's idea; Eddie might have smelled conspiracy in that. I'm not entirely sure he was wrong—the whole thing was still pretty suspicious. But I absolutely needed to get the Old Path ships back and connected to Conglommora to try and get to Grace-Ann again.

And I wasn't lying when I said I wanted to see Earth myself. Maybe I was exaggerating at first, but a chance to see Earth... any version of Earth. From the decayed ruins of post-apocalyptic Dead Earth to the verdant green of Eden restored, I'd like to see it.

The last few tens of days had made a mark on me. I realized how insular my life had been, how lonely and shut off I had been since Haily had died. The chance of a life with Grace had been taken away. And now, maybe, how lonely and shut off all of Conglommora was as well. Maybe the Earth was dead, maybe not. Maybe it was empty, maybe not.

Either way, now I had to know.

Eddie was incredulous at first. "This can't be for real. Can it?" he asked with a sudden child-like hope. "How could we not know about this?"

"Well..." I tried to choose my words carefully. "It's not like it's a secret. There's a lot of stuff in the archives I'm sure no one has ever seen. And probably much more we are missing, lost when everyone left. Until you made those long-range scans, this didn't matter. It was just a curiosity. And don't underestimate the risk. No one in the history of... history has ever tried anything like this. It might not work. Might kill us all instantly."

"I suppose we could always send a probe out first," Eddie mused aloud. That was a good sign. Maybe I'd made the sale.

"Charlie…" He shook his head. "I have to think about this. Do some reading, some checking. I'll ping you in a bit." He shut down the link abruptly.

Granted, it was a lot to process; a lot to take in. In fact, it felt like a dream. I never understood that business about pinching yourself to see if you're awake.

I can pinch myself in a dream just fine. Still just a dream. Still can't tell.

Realized I was hungry. Ambled into the galley to get something to eat. Made a quick dish, and sat in front of it. I wasn't really hungry, I guess. Just waiting; waiting for Eddie to verify my ridiculous claims.

Maybe I should do the same. I mean, here I was taking Arty's word for it. But that's what we do. That's what we always do. Listen to Arty. Never occurred to me not to; that Arty might be unreliable or even… wrong.

Hours later, I'd read a lot more than I needed to on quantum physics, propulsion using quantum vacuum wakes, super-positional entanglement and a bunch of stuff I couldn't even pretend to understand. I'm sure Arty knew I was reading up on this material.

A panic struck me. What if Arty was generating this material, just for me? Or altering it? How would I know? How would *anyone* know? How could you trust anything that you didn't experience first-hand? Clearly I'd misinterpreted the crowd vids. Maybe that was the intent: to shock, to exaggerate, to make it seem like a big deal when it wasn't. Propaganda, isn't that what they used to call it? Faked, in the extreme case, but even if arguably true, always to mislead.

A person could easily drive themselves insane this way.

I decided to trust the old material in the archives, including the research papers filled with the places, the governments, the factions of Dead Earth. I found the original series on quantum resonance wave non-locality events. But that wasn't much help; the math used to describe it was far beyond anything I'd ever seen. Filled with strange symbols and unfamiliar words. I gestured for help on the first few, but unpacking the symbols just led down a twisted path of even more unfamiliar corners of physics and mathematics.

They had run experiments, though—I skipped ahead to that part. Only lab scale, one side of the room to the other. You had to have ultra-precise quantum scans of the target for it to work at all. Otherwise you'd end up... well, nowhere really. Not within the defined dimensions of our observable universe, at least. Yikes.

I leaned back, rubbing my eyes. Who knows. Might as well have been a magic flying unicorn. But maybe it was real. I set my head in my hands. And if it was real, one misplaced qubit and you wouldn't exist anymore. Like the old Dead Earth game of Suicide Roulette. Gah.

But if it did work... if it could... *Earth.*

The screen buzzed. Eddie's image wafted up on the screen in front of me.

Eddie sat back and crossed his arms. "Okay," he started, "you've convinced me. I want to go to the Earth I found in the scans. I want to see it with my own eyes.

"So I've decided to take this to Robert and Ann." He glanced around furtively. "Between you and me, the work on printing up drive engines hasn't been going as well as expected. We aren't off to a great start. But this," he waved at the graphic on his screen, "this could change everything. Everything."

Eddie shook his head in wonder. "I'll buzz you when I can." And again, he shut down the link.

Now all I had to do was wait. Wait and wonder. Wonder if Robert would accept this or think it a trap. Wonder if there was really any chance of saving Grace. Wondered myself if this really *was* some kind of artful trap laid by Arty to "protect" us. And if it were real, would we actually make it to Earth or die trying?

That's a lot of "ifs."

I'd been spinning on this all day as it was, so I got a pharmaceutical for sleep and took a nap. I slept through the rest of the day and the entire next sleep cycle instead.

Dream or awake? I dreamt of Haily, of Alain when he was first born. Haily nodded at me, but it was present day again. She was waving *both* Alain and me off, wishing us well on our adventure. Sorry she couldn't come. The buzz of an inbound comm woke me up the next morning.

"Eddie?" I asked groggily. He looked pretty hazy to me.

"We're on," was all he said.

On top of the worry and uncertainty that had piled up in my belly was a new, powerful and unaccustomed feeling.

Epic fear.

Now I was fully awake. The appropriateness of that phrase had never struck me before, but now it hit me with a force of truth I don't think I'd felt since Haily died, and maybe not even a whole lot before then.

I was *awake*.

Well, well. I never would have believed it. I'm not sure I even do now.

Robert agreed to reattach Old Path.

Never got the details or the in-depth gossip from Eddie or anyone else involved. I can't imagine how Eddie convinced Robert to abandon his bold plan and allow Arty to run the show. I'm sure it must have killed him to do so, or at least seriously dented his newfound bravado.

But Robert wasn't stupid. His goal was to get to Earth. And he needed the energy of the full Conglommora to do that. I imagine he would have done anything to get that. Absolutely anything. Up to and including trusting Arty, even trusting all of Conglommora. At least to a point.

Through me, Arty brokered a deal with Robert: Robert would return the ships to Conglommora and reattach them. In exchange, Arty would attempt to create the resonance wave to transit a ship to Earth. Given the risk, the consensus across Conglommora was that Robert should go first. In effect, that would be his punishment. If the adventure proved fatal, well… no loss there. A peaceful solution to a potentially violent confrontation. *That* at least was typical Conglommora. Maybe typical Arty.

But Robert couldn't be trusted to go alone, of course. A couple of us would have to go with him. I couldn't help myself. Even though it went completely against my nature and felt like it would be a *galaxy* away from my comfort zone, I found myself volunteering to go on the mission to Earth once we were ready.

So here we were. Arty quickly printed up some drones with thrusters and flew them over to the detached sections. The idea was to get them all in position, grab hold of the relevant pieces, and gently guide the missing sections back into place. From there, after a little welding and wiring, the emergency sealants could be dissolved and everything would be back as it was.

Or would it?

All those folks who gladly let Robert *blow up* parts of Conglommora… what would we do about that? It's not like there really was any "we" to even consider an action. Arty might step in again if needed, I guess, as it did to get the ships back, but Arty was more programmed to address direct physical threats, not vague political instability or grudges.

I wouldn't blame their immediate neighbors for being mad at them, either. To say nothing of the folks who were basically thrown out of their own homes because their houses couldn't be separated from the rest of the Old Path section. I don't think they would mind at all if Robert got tossed into a reclaimer. I'd still happily volunteer to do the tossing.

Oh, there would be plenty of ill-will to go around.

On the other hand, the unprecedented excitement at *travel*, at being able to basically teleport anywhere in the universe by using a massive resonance power wave burst, well, that was something. A powerful hope. Maybe that trumped the violent, stupid path that got us here.

But there were a lot of questions still. And it's not like any of us could blindly trust Robert, or Grace-Ann, either. They sure weren't going to trust me or Arty. Work together, *maybe*. But trust?

This was going to be awkward at best, and at worst... well, I didn't really want to think about that. The worst-case scenario could wreak all manner of death and destruction to a few or all of us. I'd stick with fretting over the merely awkward for now.

The reconnection proceeded without incident. Arty was ready to start dissolving the seals, and folks were lined up to return to their homes in their respective corridors.

I was ready to meet Robert, Grace-Ann and Eddie face to face, to discuss what to do next. Still not sure how I ended up in this position, as the more-or-less effective representative of all of Conglommora. But here I was; Arty ready to guide me, and with a small stun weapon hidden on my wrist—just in case.

Bil and Ronny were with me, similarly equipped, so I didn't feel quite as alone as last time on my spectacular failure of a mission. At least I had friends with me. And that made me feel better than maybe I should have. But it was something.

The seal dissolved into a slurry that was quickly siphoned away. Air rushed both ways, briefly struggling for equilibrium, making an unnatural breeze. It was a dramatic effect.

Robert stood there, flanked by Grace-Ann and Eddie.

We stood for a moment, equally unsure of who was supposed to say what. We didn't exactly have any sort of manners or established protocol for this sort of occasion.

Robert gazed aside a moment, as he used to when talking around an awkward or painful subject, and broke the silence. "Charlie. Gentlemen." He nodded. "Good to see you. Before this gets any more difficult, let me just say thank you."

That really wasn't what I was expecting.

He continued, "Thank you for finding this… this shortcut. I was beyond hope that *I* would get to see the Green Earth with my own eyes."

Looked to me like he almost choked up. I tried to ignore that.

"If we're going to do it, let's do it right, I suppose. What do we do now?" I offered. No harm in letting him think he had some say in the matter. Arty and I had the plan all laid out, in point of fact.

"I want to make it clear that I do not trust your AI. Not in the least," he started, with a sudden fire. "However," he softened, "it has also come to my attention just how dependent we are on the AI's service.

"Nothing on your ships works very well without your Arty. Even the basic comms mesh. And for the resonance wave to work at all, we will need Arty to coordinate, monitor, and time it with inhuman ability and precision.

"So," he stepped forward, "Here's the deal. We will take the *Uten*. And to insure our safety, you'll be coming with us. You and your son. Then I'll know that Arty won't try to double-cross us."

I went from elated to deflated within the width of a single heartbeat. That wasn't exactly the plan. Elated, that this was exactly what I wanted. A chance to be on his ship—with the memory device, and with Grace-Ann. A chance.

But I *didn't* want to risk Alain for it. If this crazy wave thing went badly, we'd all be dead. My son with us.

Probably sensing my heart rate—which was pounding fast and furious—Arty sent a pop-up message on my lenses. *It will be okay.*

I had a moment of parental inspiration. "That's not up to me," I said. "I can't and won't order my son around. It's his choice. We can ask him, and I will honor his decision, but he's not my slave—or yours."

Robert paused to consider this, then nodded. "Very well. You all seem to be very into this whole 'freedom of choice' business. What about you two?" He motioned to Bil and Ronny, standing stoically next to me. Ronny had told me earlier he'd be perfectly happy beating Robert to a bloody pulp, and I admit I didn't have any problem with that notion. Except that I needed his ship still—and maybe him—to try and save Grace.

Ronny looked Robert right in the eye without flinching and nodded. "I'll come along. Wouldn't miss it."

And won't let you out of my sight, was the unspoken rest of the sentence.

Bil shook his head. "I'd rather make sure your ship is outfitted properly and manage the launch from our docking tube. And be ready to mount a rescue mission if needed."

A reasonable, if unsettling idea.

"Fine," Robert said. "I'll detach the *Uten* from our current hatch and bring it back over here. To be honest your setup is better equipped. Charlie, ask Alain if he wants to make history. I'll bring several of my people as well."

Since when was anyone of Conglommora considered "his" people? I sighed inside. When he convinced them to break off into Old Path, I guess.

He turned and walked back down the corridor. Grace-Ann followed, never having said a word. Eddie hung back a moment.

"Edward?" I asked, using his real name for respect from now on.

"Charlie, I just wanted you to know that I am so sorry for everything Robert has done. From Grace, to the explosions... all of it. But he believed in me when no one else would. Not even you," he glared at me, pointedly.

But then he softened a little. "And yet you've saved us all. You saved Old Path from his enthusiastic, if unrealistic, plan and now... now, you've saved us all. You've saved humanity."

His eyes sparkled. "I can't wait to see it."

He paused a moment and turned down the corridor as well, his step so light and lively that I thought the gravity had been turned down a tad.

So, he knew about Grace, now. That might come in handy—I might be able to count on his help in some critical moment, maybe. Or maybe I've read too many books, written too many convenient scripts.

Life, as I keep discovering, is rarely convenient.

Eighteen

ALAIN DEMANDED TO GO even before I had finished forming the question.

"Dad, are you *kidding* me?" He glowed. "Of course I'll go with you. I wouldn't miss it for the world. Because, well, it *is* the world."

"We might not even make it. We could both be killed from the transit itself. We could crash land. Who knows what Earth itself is like? Oh, and don't forget Robert. He's a danger all by himself."

"Sure." Alain shrugged. What did kids know about risk, anyway? "But it's okay. Arty is on top of the transportation. And knowing that you can't trust Robert seems like half the battle already. And Earth, well, it's an adventure isn't it?"

He set down the screen in his hand and stood up, looking more grown up than ever. "In fact, there's something I've meaning to talk to you about anyway. Before this whole thing blew up, I was thinking of going on a Walk."

A Walk. That was a thing some kids did nowadays, you take off and explore as much of Conglommora as you can. My brief excursion was just a taste of that life; imagine doing that for a couple of years.

"A few of my friends and I were talking about this before the *Uten* even showed up," Alain said, obviously reading my concern that *I* had precipitated this wild notion. He motioned to the screen he had put on the tableform. "The games are fun, but only so much. I want to see more of Conglommora with my own eyes, experience it for myself. And yes," he smiled, "your images from the mech section were pretty inspiring. I really want to visit there now. But all of that pales in comparison to Earth itself. That's the ultimate Walk, isn't it?"

Great. Where did my son get this genetic expression of wanderlust? Surely not from me. I never go anywhere or do anything or… go on spacewalks and skulk around like a spy and get all excited at visiting Earth on this stupid risky adventure or…

Okay, maybe Alain was more like me than I realized. Or rather, more like the real me that had somehow been asleep all these years. I *was* excited. I *wanted* to go to Earth. Right now.

"Well, first things first," I backed down. "Arty has to test this thing first to see if it's even possible. We'll talk more about your Walk later."

I was just deferring the inevitable, but there's only so much you can process at once. I was worried about Alain coming along, but I was also itching to pack my bags and head out to Earth. But, as with most things, instant gratification was not an option.

Arty had suggested, and no one disagreed, that we should first send an unmanned probe to take readings—to confirm the long-range scans and get even better data on Earth's condition. Oh, and to make sure one could actually transit without, you know, dying.

There was coordination to be done. All of Conglommora had to deliver a massive energy pulse at the same time, all funneled into the apparatus to generate a resonant wave pulse. Arty had printed up the necessary bits and the circuits to drive it. Extra power conduits had to be run along most of the major corridors to consolidate the generated power. Folks were uniformly generous in donating bricks of Raw for the effort, but it was taking many tens of days, and my impatience grew.

I had a couple of talks with Eddie in the meantime. His excitement was contagious. In fact, all over Conglommora, excitement was mounting, filling the vacuum left by unbridled fear that had just swept through. Again, I'd never seen anything like it. Folks normally stuck to their own concerns, and popular topics of conversation were rarely so uniform. But this was *the* topic of conversation, almost to the exclusion of anything else.

The anger at Robert, the fear, the hatred of Arty, of technology and of our situation—all of that evaporated almost overnight. Replaced—swamped, even—with hope. Just like that.

People are fickle.

I fervently hoped it was for real, not some complicated plot by Arty, or Robert, or even both. Robert wasn't that clever, perhaps, and Arty... I had to believe Arty was on our side. It wouldn't do anything to knowingly harm us, that was its programming, its mission. And the excitement that flooded Conglommora—that was so real it was almost tangible. Surely, we couldn't all be wrong.

Still, while everyone was excited about it, not everyone wanted to go themselves, in person. Folks were curious and wanted to know what Earth was like, but didn't necessarily want to take the risks to their own heads.

Arty's plan was to send a probe first, get some readings, make sure that the environment held throughout the transport, and that we could send people through safely. Then we'd send the *Uten*, with a few needed modifications for the trip: mostly additional docking ports for four-man landing craft, and of course a working qradio. We'd have to upgrade the nanophotonic computer cores on board to house a more robust, but still much smaller version of Arty.

I thought we should either have fabbed a brand-new ship or at least used a more modern ship to start with. But I wasn't going to volunteer the *Neylan*, and no one else wanted to volunteer their home or that much Raw either. Robert was keen on taking the *Uten* through and agreed to the minimum necessary computer upgrades to its core. He didn't like the idea of even a stripped-down Arty on board, but relented. He knew we couldn't do it without Arty.

The crew would be myself, Alain, Robert, Eddie, Grace-Ann, Ronny, and a couple of Robert's Old Path followers who had studied Green Earth and knew more about it than the rest of us. Ronny volunteered largely to help me and Alain keep an eye on Robert; despite his aversion to history, he'd picked up a lot from listening to Janel over the years, and Janel was not interested in being in the first wave. She wasn't too happy about Ronny going, either.

Alain and I were there as more-or-less hostages. Well, we were all kind of hostages to our own curiosity, I suppose. I still would have rather Alain stayed behind, but in a way I was also comforted to have him by my side. Family.

Preparations were under way, and I just had to wait. I wasn't good at waiting.

Did some reading, asked Arty about an idea: "Didn't we leave any probes in orbit around Earth that we could use? Or a base on the moon or somewhere else in the solar system? Anything?"

Arty replied with eternal patience, "No, no probes. Any that were left must have failed and burned up in the atmosphere. We haven't had any contact for a very long time. And when humans first explored the moon and outer planets, the emphasis was on conservation and preservation, so the space programs were careful not to leave anything behind or disturb the natural state of any solar bodies."

"Huh." That sounded at odds with my vision of Earth's peoples and governments of the day. "But I would have thought that the Monotrads and folks like that would have wanted to mine the moon and other planets for resources, or at least set up bases for military strikes, that kind of thing." I'd certainly done that in a few scripts.

"Remember that although evil, greedy, and corrupt individuals and governments always existed throughout human history, the Monotrads only rose to global power later in history. And they weren't interested in the moon. Not enough profit in mining; military bases were too risky."

I would have pressed for more details, but I got the gist of it. History was kind of interesting, but never made much sense to me. I'd leave that for folks like Janel to ponder.

Besides, the probe was ready now. A bunch of us gathered at Bil's to watch the launch and monitor progress.

Arty had an image of the probe up on the big screen. It was a small, mostly flat disc, with a bulge in the middle—a clear dome, filled with instrumentation. Arty had maneuvered it a fair ways away from Conglommora just to be safe.

We were ready.

Arty was polite and asked us, "Is everyone ready?" A mumbled grunt of assent wafted through Bil's main room on the *Rhead*, where we had all gathered.

"Then here we go." Arty was aiming for the colloquial.

Maybe it was trying to calm us, but my heart was in my throat anyway.

The surge built up. You couldn't really hear it or feel it, at least not at first. We saw the meters rising on the screen, and then the faintest hum started to wash over the room. And every other room, in every house, throughout all Conglommora.

The lights and some other non-essential power sinks dimmed for just a moment as the wave hit a crescendo.

There was a shimmering distortion and flare of false colors, and the probe was just gone. Nothing but black.

The data feed started coming in over the qradio channel almost immediately. It came in bursts, as qradios need to recharge in between messages, but still, this was a lot of data.

Arty filled us in, "Environmental readings stable. No unusual readings or stresses during transport. Earth readings confirm long-range probe results."

There you have it. This was real. This was really happening.

Arty went on in some more detail, but I had stopped paying attention. Earth was waiting for us.

The probe took quite a few measurements, not only of Earth's ecosystem, but of the solar system and local area coordinates. We'd need that for travel there in the future. We were actually a little lucky that the probe didn't transport into the middle of a planet or the sun. Fortunately the stats were with us. Space is big, and planets are small. Still, there were no guarantees. But now we had a map.

The probe came back the same way it left; a shimmer, the fringe of false color on the display from the electro-magnetic spectrum. The empty black of space suddenly filled with our metal disc and all its equipment. Safe and sound.

Arty narrated the whole thing for us. I'd like to think it was pleased.

We were next.

The *Uten* had docked back at Bil's place. Arty had printed up the landing crafts; small, four-man ships, circular with a dome on top, similar to the probe we had sent, but with room for people and the addition of lightweight, adjustable, spider-like landing gear.

The *Uten* itself would orbit the Earth at a very high altitude. If everything still checked out on the scanners, we would use the landing craft to actually go down to the surface. That was the plan, and I was ridiculously excited. Giddy, maybe.

I packed up a couple of days' worth of supplies, as did Alain. I was just closing up my bag when he came in the bedroom.

"Are you sure you want to do this?" I asked him, brimming with parental concern. "You know, we might not survive this. Everything could go wrong. Why don't you just stay here where it's safe?" I blurted out. Not subtle. Certainly not cool.

"Dad, let me ask you this." He sat on the edge of my bed. "What would you do in my place? Would you just sit here and play games or hang with your friends when you had a chance to go explore a planet? And not just any planet, but Earth itself? And not just Dead Earth, but a living, growing, habitable Earth? What would you do?" He looked straight into my eyes.

I picked up my bag. Looked away. Tried to think of some argument to make, some way to convince him not to come. But I had nothing. He was right. This was a once-in-a-lifetime—no, once-in-*several* lifetimes— opportunity.

"What would I do?" I repeated. Then sighed. "I'd do what I'm doing now. I'd go."

He smiled and sprung off the bed, grabbing his bag on the way. "Then what are we doing sitting around talking? Let's go."

"All right, you can come," I agreed, however reluctantly. He was already halfway out the door.

There were a couple of things we had to take care of, since neither of us would be home for a couple of days or more, so Alain and I started going around and buttoning up the house, shutting down necessary systems, making sure the algae tanks were well-balanced and in good shape, that sort of thing. I had one personal item to take care of as well.

I went back into my bedroom, sealed the door, and brought up Haily's vr program. "I have to leave," I told her.

"I know," came the reply with a soft, enigmatic smile. "I know."

"Alain is coming with me. It will be dangerous. We might not make it back." Gah, I sounded like a poorly-written love story.

Haily's image rose from the edge of the bedform and moved as if to take my hand. "It will be okay," she said. "It will always be okay. You'll take care of Alain just like you always have, no matter what you face. I believe in you."

That seemed a clumsy note. That isn't what Haily really would have said. How *would* she have reacted? I'd talked with the fake Haily for so long, did I really even remember real Haily? Maybe I'd rewritten those memories. Maybe the Haily I thought I remembered wasn't like Haily at all anymore. Maybe this was pointless. And always had been.

How long had I settled for this pale shadow? Taken comfort in this farce?

"Goodbye, Haily," I said one last time, and the image serenely waved goodbye.

"Delete vr program Haily."

Arty's voice didn't seem to register the significance of the moment. "Please confirm deletion of vr program Haily."

"Confirmed," I almost whispered. It was enough. The image was gone. Haily was gone. I sat there for a few minutes in the still and the emptiness. The wave of sadness didn't materialize; in fact, I felt relief. I had let go, finally, I think.

Alain knocked and the door swhoosed open. "You okay Dad?"

"Yeah." It took me a second, but I collected myself and hoisted the bag on my shoulder. "Just shutting down some stuff. Let's go."

We headed out of the *Neylan*, and I sealed the hatch behind us. I was still worried about Alain, and as we walked over to Bil's, I tried to regain a little parental status. "Would you please, please at least promise to be careful?" I implored him.

He shot me a look. "Not at all. I'll jump out of the ship halfway through transport, space jump down to the planet without a suit, and pick a fight with the biggest, ugliest, fastest carnivore I can find."

"Well okay, then," I nodded, "as long as you show some restraint." We both grinned and headed down the corridor together.

Nineteen

WE REACHED BIL'S. The hatch was open. I walked in first; Alain trailed behind me a pace.

Li greeted us, "You guys are crazy, you know. You two and Ronny."

I grinned with unchecked enthusiasm. "Oh come on, Li. I bet Bil really wanted to go too," I teased her.

She raised her eyebrows. "I can assure you he did not." She turned on her heel and led us to the docking tube.

Ronny was there, just coming in. Robert and Grace-Ann were already aboard, along with their people. We were waiting on Edward, Li told us.

The *Uten* was smaller then I remembered. Or seemed it, I guess. A little smaller, a little darker than our own houses. Robert and Grace-Ann were seated in the control room, a couple of their folks standing behind them.

"Welcome aboard," said Robert, not entirely warmly. In his eyes, I think, we were a necessary evil. But still evil. "Charlie Neylan, Ronny Sullivan, and Charlie's son, Alain, isn't it?" Alain nodded.

"This is Ralph Mills III, Ashby Reardon, and Penelope Holdt." He gestured to the three people behind him, in turn. "Ralph knows a lot about Earth's animal life, Penelope is a geologist, and Ashby is a student of history." I nodded. "You already know Edward. He's on his way."

Pleasantries. What a waste of time. Could we just get *on* with this already? I'd already forgotten their names and didn't even care in the first place. Ashby showed us to our quarters; Alain was right next to me. We got settled in and headed back out to the main room about an hour later.

Edward had come aboard, and Ralph—I think his name was Ralph—sealed the hatch and started cycling the airlock. He came over my way and asked, "Hey, are you the Charlie Neylan who wrote *Plight of The Ngu and the Battle for Tarsus IV*?"

I looked up with some surprise. Yes, I had written that some time ago. It was actually one of my personal favorite game scripts, but even though I liked it, it wasn't very popular. Later efforts had much larger followings. I nodded yes.

Ralph shook my hand. "One of my all-time favorites. I'm a huge fan. Pleasure to meet you in person!"

Alain was grinning ear-to-ear. So, I had a fan.

"Thanks," I mumbled, "Ralph is it?"

Ralph nodded yes and continued waxing poetic about that game.

Fortunately, Ronny came through and interrupted us just about then.

"Ready for a *real* adventure, boys?" he asked and clapped me on the back. I assumed it was a rhetorical question. Ready? Of course not. How can you be ready, be prepared, for the complete unknown? You can't. But you go anyway.

I motioned the wall and sat in the chairform, as did everyone else.

Arty's voice came over the screen. "Is everyone ready for separation?" It was merely a conversational courtesy. Of course we were ready and it knew it. We mumbled, grunted, proclaimed and confidently asserted that collectively, yes, we were ready. Or close enough.

There was a slight jolt as the newly upgraded thrusters pushed us gently away from Conglommora. Once again, I felt the peculiar sense of separation from everything I'd ever known, heading out into the void itself.

We sat quietly, all in the main control room of the *Uten*, watching the faintly lit image of Conglommora shrink slowly, inexorably, until we reached the "safe" distance that Arty had calculated.

"We have reached the resonant wave focal point," Arty announced. "Stand by for wave displacement." Arty was all business now.

What looked like a shimmer and a fringe of false color from the outside was a very different experience from the inside.

Have you ever been pulled inside out? No, of course not. So you don't know how that feels.

I do.

At least, that's what it felt like. Arty assured us later that we were not actually pulled apart at all; it was just a sensory illusion.

It was one hell of an illusion.

Like my skin caved in, my organs pulled out, my eyes ripped loose and looking at each other through my ears, cascading in an endless, tumbling, fractal rippling of inversion.

It stopped suddenly, and I leaned forward and threw up.

Ashby what's-his-name was in mid-giggle, cruelly setting up to remark on my weakness, when his bowels suddenly let go in a stunning and explosive shower, ruining both his clothing and his intended remark.

Both of these triggered a variety of other bio-expulsions from our small crew; I wasn't keeping track. In fact, I had my eyes closed shut, trying by shear force of will to keep the rest of my stomach contents… contained.

All in all, not our proudest moment.

At some level I think I was hoping for a more epic, transcendent speech befitting the occasion. I never expected the more scatological, "Will you please stop shitting yourself, Ashby!" or the pointed and accusatory, "Why are you *still* throwing up??" complaints. Penelope was just sobbing.

Cleaner bots did their best. Clothes were changed. The air eventually recycled.

I thought to ask Arty, "Arty, status. Are we okay?"

"There are no physiological dangers or environmental irregularities," Arty calmly reported. "You experienced momentary sensory disorientation when the resonance wave hit the ship and the displacement began."

"Why didn't you warn us?" I asked petulantly.

"Insufficient data or processing power," came the reply. Ah, right. Despite sounding a lot like the regular Arty, it wasn't. This was a much smaller version, based on an older, much more primitive system, barely even up to the level of AI my parents and grandparents had in the *Neylan*, and nothing like modern Arty.

The screen was dark. "Arty," I asked, "show us Earth, and our orbit."

A really small dot showed up on the screen.

"*Uten* not in Earth orbit. Firing maneuvering thrusters now. Orbital insertion in twenty-nine hours."

Well that was frustrating. Looks like we had missed the target a little. "Arty," I never did know when to stop, "why are we so far out?"

"Insufficient data or processing power," came the reply. That was going to get old pretty quick.

So close. And still such a little dot.

A red light started flashing with an attendant beeping; some circuit needy for attention.

"What's that?" Alain asked, ever curious.

"It's…" Robert began, "I'm not sure. Something about power feedback regulation in the engines. There, it's fixed now." The beeping ceased. Frankly, he didn't seem that confident. Swell.

Despite the extensive repairs Robert had made, the *Uten* still felt old, maybe untrustworthy. I wished we had come in something newer and had all of Arty with us. But we hadn't, and we didn't. And now it was going to take even longer than expected.

We had to wait. And there was no way I could make small talk for that long. Nor could I really wander around the ship and try and find the memory transfer device—not yet.

I stood up, "I'll be in my quarters," and nodded to Robert and his henchmen and the one henchwoman. Ralph gave a wave and faint smile. Robert looked remarkably pale and queasy still and said nothing; neither did Grace-Ann for that matter. He nodded curtly.

Alain looked a little better than the others, but he still got up more gingerly than his usual spry custom, and we went down the hall to our quarters.

My impatience was clearly cursing us. Once again, all I could do was wait.

Most of a day went by. I read, paced a little. Finally lay down on a bedform and tried to rest for a spell, maybe take a nap. I could sure sure use one. But I was twitchy. Lay on my left side. My right. Stomach. Back. Repeat. Couldn't get comfortable. I wasn't good at waiting. I wanted to snoop around, see if I could at least find where the memory machine was kept.

To do that, I needed an excuse. Some reason to be prowling around, something to look for. I abandoned sleep and went next door to Alain's room.

"I have an idea," I explained proudly.

Sprawled on his bedform, he barely looked up from the game he was playing on his screen. "What's that, Dad?" he asked without sparing too much attention.

"I want you to get lost."

That got his attention.

"What?" he asked with some alarm, looking up.

"I want you to hide somewhere. I need an excuse to look around the ship, and what better excuse than a lost child?" I posited.

Alain furrowed his brow and put his game down. "I'm *not* a child. But I suppose I can help. You want to try and fix whatever they did to Grace?"

I nodded.

"Okay I guess." He slid off the bedform with a practiced nonchalance. "How long?"

"Hour or two?" I offered.

"Sure." And he was out the door.

Five minutes.

Ten.

I wanted to give him a head start.

Then I headed out into the ship to search for my lost child. And for Grace.

Faking worry was easy. I wasn't worried about Alain, of course. I knew he was safe somewhere on board. Grace, on the other hand... she didn't talk much with

Robert around, at least not in public. I guess that was more Ann's personality; Grace had seemed plenty talkative around me.

I was in the the part of the ship that was mostly living quarters. Alain's room was next to mine, I knew Grace wasn't secretly hiding in there. The next two rooms down the corridor were empty.

Across from that, the door was closed. I knocked.

Robert's toady, Penelope, opened the door. "What?" she asked, without much ceremony.

"Hi. Penelope, right?"

She nodded curtly.

"My son's gone missing. Have you seen him?" It rolled right off my tongue.

"No." She shut the door.

I got a quick glance in her quarters. Just a quick one. Nothing looming or strange as far as I could see. It wasn't conclusive, but it was a start.

Ronny's room was next. I went inside and explained my plan. "Okay, I'll help you out," he offered.

"Beats sitting here wondering if this rust bucket is going to make it." He made a derisive gesture at the ship. Ah, Ronny. Always such a comfort.

We left his room, and Ronny went down a branch, which would cover the rest of the individual quarters, and then toward the main hub of the ship; I continued down the corridor we were in. Ashby's was next. He actually invited me in.

"Your son isn't here," Ashby said, "but come on in a second."

I hesitated, but walked into his quarters.

Ashby asked me, "Where do you think he went? It's not that big a ship. Why'd he run off?"

I had to make something up. "Well, I don't really know." That much was true. "I think the quantum wave transport upset him maybe more than the rest of us. Maybe he was just looking for a place to clear his head."

Ashby nodded. "I can see that. I certainly wasn't expecting that... that sort of effect. Not looking forward to having to do it again to go back." He grimaced.

"But I better come with you if you're going to go poking around Robert's ship," he continued. "Robert doesn't trust you. Or Arty, for that matter."

"And what about you? Do you think I'm here to sabotage Robert?" I had to ask.

"No," he answered plainly. "I think you want to see Earth just as much as we do. Robert tends toward the paranoid, if you ask me. But still, I don't know you. So, we'll just stick together, if that's okay."

That cramped my plans a little in terms of actually *doing* anything, but maybe that would also open up parts of the ship I wouldn't have been able to see otherwise— like the engine room.

"Sure," I responded. Like I had nothing to hide. "Let's go."

We'd covered all the individual quarters by now, and Ronny was headed to the systems hub, so we turned down a corridor toward the drive engine room. I was pretty excited that I might find something there. That's where I'd put a memory machine if I had one.

But there was nothing there except standard, old-fashioned drive engines and the usual control panels. Nothing unusual or interesting. Just old. Ashby started off keeping a close eye on me, but clearly that became boring fast.

Next up was the computer core. All computing power was distributed, of course, but every ship and house had a section where much of the equipment was concentrated. This was maybe more concentrated than most. At least it looked larger than more modern ships. But it wasn't alarmingly huge, and again there weren't any odd or unrecognizable bits.

At the far end of the ship, the storage rooms and the biodome filled with plants and some aquaculture. Nothing interesting.

We made our way back to the hub. Grace was there—with Alain, and Ronny was just coming in.

"Found you!" I exclaimed, with mock surprise. "Where were you? I was worried sick." Okay, I may have overdone it a little, and it was certainly a rote cliché, but it seemed to have worked.

"Sorry Dad," he replied, with appropriately down-cast eyes. "I wasn't feeling very well, and just wanted to walk around a little, and stretch my legs. We must have just kept missing each other."

Heh, good one. That way he couldn't be accused of hiding anywhere.

Grace-Ann gave us both a quizzical eye and said with clipped delivery, "Glad to see everyone's found each other now. As I was just showing Alain, we're coming up on orbital insertion. You might want to start getting your landing craft ready. It won't be long now." She turned back to what she was doing.

It gave me a great exit line. "Okay, Ronny, Alain— let's go get ready."

As we were leaving, Ashby smiled a weasel-like smile and sidled up to Grace-Ann, offering to help her with preparations.

That didn't make me happy at all.

———————

As soon as we got back to my quarters, Ronny sealed the door behind him and asked me, "Did you find it?"

"No, nothing even close. Engine room, computer core, quarters—even Robert's quarters, and nothing."

"Ok," Ronny said as he sat in a chairform, "I think I know where it is, then. There's a sealed and locked hatch down on the other side of the ship." He motioned— honestly I had no idea which was the "other" side or if he was even pointing in the right direction.

Ronny went on, "The whole ship is wide open, no locks or anything anywhere. Storage bays, supplies; I was able to look almost everywhere. Except there. That one hatch was locked tight, and there isn't even a mechanical access lock or a keypad, retina sensor, nothing. I couldn't see how you'd even try to unlock it."

Well that was exciting. "That must be it." I was confident.

Alain, as usual, wasn't as excited. "Maybe, but it could also be a vestigial artifact from an earlier configuration—maybe it isn't really a door, and doesn't go anywhere anymore."

Ronny nodded. "Could be, but usually folks just patch those up with solid walls, not permanently sealed doors. Waste of material." Ha, that was very typical Ronny thinking.

"It's a solid lead, at least. We just need to figure out how to get in. Wish we could ask Arty," I mused.

"Why don't we?" Alain asked.

Ronny piped up, "If it's a secured area, any queries would be flagged. Besides, this is a stripped-down and newly installed Arty. It might not even know. We'd get caught for nothing."

We sat and talked a bit more, batted some ideas around, none of which were very good. We started prepping the landing craft, getting our gear ready, still trying to figure out a way forward, without much luck.

But then Ronny had a decent idea.

"How about once we're in the landing craft and away from the ship, I 'accidentally' scan that section of the *Uten*? I could at least tell if there's a room there or if that's an outside wall."

That would be a lot better than walking up to the secret door and scanning it conspicuously, or asking Arty. Robert might be alerted either way but an accidental scan from a scanning craft was a much better story.

And so once again, I had to wait. The mystery of the sealed door would have to wait.

We were entering orbit.

Twenty

ROBERT, GRACE-ANN, PENELOPE, and my fan, Ralph, were on one craft; Ashby was with Ronny, Edward, Alain and myself in the other. Robert left first. Once their craft was clear, it was our turn. It was still Robert's fate to be the first to sniff the Earth's air and demonstrate it was survivable.

Our landing craft slid gently and easily away from the *Uten*. From our seats, through the center clear dome, you could easily see Earth rotating below us, the old colors of Green Earth. Which from here, ironically, were mostly blue and white.

Whatever we were going to find, we'd find it soon now. If this had been one of my game scripts, I'd have hostile aliens lying in wait to attack us on landing. But, of course, there were no aliens. None that we'd ever found while on Earth, and none that we'd found out in the void. Some folks still thought there had to be other intelligent life out there somewhere, but we'd never found any evidence whatsoever. Not a peep. No one but us.

And that did raise one interesting and real possibility: survivors. Maybe there were no humans left on the planet below.

But maybe there were.

Scans didn't see anything like cities or industrialization, but there could be smaller groups of survivors still scavenging their existence. Wouldn't it be something to meet the great-great-grandchildren of the survivors of Dead Earth? I really hoped there were at least a few. Not, you know, mutant zombies or anything. Just people, doing what they've always done: surviving.

Ronny piped up, "I scanned the *Uten*; if I'm reading this right, there is a storeroom right where that door is located."

"Can you tell what's inside it?" I asked hopefully.

"Not from here; we're too far away now." He frowned. Earth was coming up fast. Back to the business at hand. But once we got back…

"Planetary cloud cover at fifty-nine percent," Arty said from the console. Well within normal range of Green Earth. You could see the continents, the large land masses from orbit. Ronny and Alain craned and tilted their heads to get a better look.

Robert sent a message from his craft. We'd agreed to do at least one full, low orbit first to identify a good landing site, and he'd sent in a few candidates.

We made a pass, identified a couple of different and interesting biomes, all of which were picture-perfect from the old days of Green Earth: tropical rainforests, arid deserts, icy wastelands at the poles, deep forests, grasslands… everything. Looked like the world was still there, all right. Healthy and functioning.

We descended through the atmosphere gently toward the first landing site. Spider-like legs of our craft extended and settled us down in a grassland area on the outskirts of a more heavy-growth jungle.

Robert opened a line, "Okay, here I go. Stand by."

We heard the swhoosh of his hatch and the soft clink of Robert's footsteps going down to the planet's surface.

"I'm taking off my helmet," he narrated. A click and hiss, and his helmet came off. A pause. A big exhale—Robert had been holding his breath. Served as a good reminder that I should breathe, too. I hadn't been.

"All's well." Robert beamed, "I'm taking off my gloves next." A few rustles as he tugged them off.

"I'm touching Earth. Earth at last! Everything fine so far. Come on down," he called up to his landing craft.

"Charlie," he said, addressing our ship now, "come on out but stay near your ship. We'll head over toward your position."

I was trembling as I gestured for the hatch to open and keyed in the activation code. With a hiss, the door slid up out of the way, and we took out first breath of Earth's fragrance.

The smells!

Nothing like it. Not even in Skyville, with all the animals in close quarters, not Sea, with all the aquatic life. Not all of that put together.

I half-stumbled down the ladder to the surface, followed by Eddie. Gravity was a little heavier than I was used to. Like I was wearing heavy clunky boots. On my arms. This would take a little getting used to. I gave Alain a hand. Ashby came down next followed by Ronny.

And then I thought to look up at the sky.

Endless.

The five of us stood there, in a reverential, overwhelmed silence, for I don't know how long, standing on the skin of the Earth itself. The breadth and depth of a full, planet-sized sky and horizon stretching into the infinite distance...

Vr displays just didn't capture this, this level of presence, of... detail? No, our displays had the fidelity for all the human eye could see. It wasn't the detail, it was... I don't know. The depth? The... expansiveness? The immersion? None of these concepts did it justice. Words literally fail me. You had to be there.

Cautiously, we spread out a little, still taking it all in. But not too far from the comforting shadow of our own ship; our small fragment of familiarity in a supposedly familiar and yet still utterly unknown world.

Well, all of us except Eddie. He wandered out much farther than the rest of us, ranging up and over a small ridge.

"Ow!" Ronny yelped, smacking his neck. "What the hell was that?"

A large red welt was starting to form where he'd been bitten. I would have laughed, but two more got me, one on the neck and one on the back of my hand. Alain yipped as he got bit as well. Ronny was dancing like a man on fire, despite the heavier gravity, as some other bit of exposed skin got drilled.

"Come on, let's move. We must be on a nest of them or something," I barked as we made a quick break away from the high grass we were standing in.

I had a small stun weapon on my wrist, just in case there were any large carnivores about—we all did, even Alain. Other than plentiful insect life, we hadn't seen any larger fauna yet. And the damn bugs were too small to stun. I was willing to try anyway.

Robert's craft was about a half a klick away; we saw him and his party striding through the waist-high grasses toward us at a brisk pace.

"Can you believe it! We made it! We are *here*. On Earth! On Earth as intended!"

Robert was about to burst. Even Grace-Ann wore a delicate, enigmatic smile. Penelope looked like she was just staring off into the distance, but actually she was taking more detailed sensor readings. Ralph was right next to Robert, beaming just about as much.

"Now this is a proper adventure!" Ralph exclaimed. "Look at it! Just look at it!"

The sky still held me in thrall. I think it did for all us; the sky, with rolling, fluffy cloud formations; vast grassy plains rippling with the breeze; the edge of the dark and mysterious jungle. So much to take in. There was more to see than we could possibly see all at once.

I don't claim that as a defense or an excuse. It's just how it was. I'm sure there was a lot right under our noses that we just didn't see.

Ralph screamed as the spear burst out of the front of his chest in a shower of blood, bone, panic, and surprise.

"Get in!" was all I could think to yell as I grabbed Alain and just about threw him like a game ball up the ladder into the hatchway of the ship.

Spears clanged as they hit the ship and harmlessly bounced off, coming up out of nowhere. Well, out of the cover of the grassland, I guess. Our attackers weren't showing themselves. Grace-Ann was next closest, I half-flung her up the ladder as well and followed behind, Penelope hot on my heels. Robert and Ashby could take care of themselves, as far as I was concerned.

Ashby was on the ladder, Robert panting, coming up—he'd been the farthest away when Ralph was killed. Pushing Ashby up ahead of him, Robert let out a high-pitched scream like a little girl.

In fairness, I suppose if I'd had a chunk of my leg ripped off by a spear as I was climbing a ladder, I wouldn't necessarily let out a particularly manly scream. It wasn't very kind of me, I'll admit, but I did smile just a little inside at Robert's injury.

We pulled him up, screaming and bleeding like a water supply hose, and sealed the hatch.

"Get us up! Get us up!" he started screaming. I don't think the natives and their spears posed any real threat to the landing craft, but that wasn't a theory I really wanted to test too hard, either.

Ronny spun up the planetary drive. The outer wheel of the ship started rotating in one direction, the next closest wheel started in the other, and so on until the outer five wheels were up to speed. Slowly at first, then exponentially picking up speed, we shot back up into the sky. We were too heavily loaded to break atmosphere, but we could limp over to the other craft, split up, and then take both ships back up to orbit.

From the clear dome at the center of the discs, we got a good look down at our attackers as they emerged from the grasses.

They were men, more or less. Mankind. Human. Primitive though, and hairy, wearing animal skins. Noses flat and broad, much more so than ours. Foreheads sloped. Short, it seemed, although that was maybe a little hard to tell, given the circumstances and lack of reference. But they gave the impression of being short and wide, with large, flat foreheads. Very different from us or any of our ancestors. Mutants, after all?

"Animals!" Robert spat, as Grace-Ann and Ashby propped up his leg and started in with the medikit. "They've degenerated into animals!"

"More human than not, I'd think. Some kind of hominid primate, from the look of it," Ashby chimed in as he fiddled with sensors and dispensers. "Make a more refined version of some kind of ape or gorilla, or maybe our direct descendants. Probably more like cousins." He stabbed Robert with some pharma mix.

"Animals! Trying to kill us!" Robert started, and looked like he was winding up for more spittle-laced diatribe.

"I don't think so, not deliberately," Alain piped in. The shock of having a mere kid correct him shut Robert up for a second. Maybe it was the pain, or even better, the shot that Ashby had just given him.

"What do you mean?" I asked.

"Look at this scan I made as we took off." He popped up a visual onto the central display.

It was the grassland; you could see the circular, flattened bit of grass where we'd taken off. Large white blobs all around us, hidden in the grasses, and blobs a little larger advancing from the jungle side.

"What's all that?" I asked, afraid of the answer.

"Largish mammals, by the looks of it," Alain said. "Prey or predator, I can't tell. But I'm guessing those natives that found us are just primitive hunters. We aren't their tribe, so we're either enemies or food. Maybe both. In fact, I bet they didn't even recognize us as people. Look at us."

He had a point. Our environmental suits made us look more like... I don't know, upright zebras maybe? Or puffy polar bears? I'm not all that well-versed in Earth animals at any rate, but given our exotic clothing and at a distance, we probably didn't look like people—not the people they were used to seeing.

"And who knows what they thought of the ship. Giant mastodon or something?"

Now he was just showing off. I didn't know what a "mastodon" was, or if it was even a real or imagined beast. But the natives surely couldn't comprehend a space ship, so they may well have "seen" it as a large beast.

"Plus, we were in a field of animals. They were probably hunting them. We might have literally just gotten in the way," Alain finished.

"Gotten in the way! Tell that to Ralph!" Robert started to lurch up to complain but Ashby leaned on him, forcing him back to a prone position, while Grace followed the next round of medikit instructions on his wound.

Even prone, he kept on, "Ralph is *dead* thanks to them. And we were almost next!" There was more, but he started slurring his words.

"Well we weren't prepared for that, whatever that was, at any rate," I observed. "I suggest we head back to the *Uten*, let Robert sleep off his leg, and figure out a better plan on how and where to land."

There was general agreement all around. Robert mumbled something vile, but was losing consciousness rapidly, so I maintain that it didn't count.

We scanned the area around the other craft more carefully this time, and it seemed we had left all the action behind. We transferred three folks to the other craft and didn't linger. In moments we were once again shot skyward.

I really wished I could talk to Arty about this. I couldn't, not from here, but I could send a short message via qradio, wait for the recharge, and get a reply. It wasn't as good as real-time conversation, but it would help.

In the black of space, it was a comfort to see the *Uten* sitting there, waiting patiently for us. We sidled up and docked smoothly.

After docking, Alain and I headed straight to the control room on the *Uten*. Ronny said he was headed to his quarters, to try and do something about the mass of red welts from the insect bites. They seemed to really like him in particular.

Robert was awake and hobbling in, half-carried by Ashby, Grace-Ann following.

"Hey," Alain looked around. "Where's Edward? Eddie?"

Oh shit.

I looked at Robert. Robert looked at me, white-faced. Well, even more white-faced. In our scramble to escape, we'd left a man behind.

"Probably dead by now," Ronny muttered over his shoulder from the corridor. "Just like Ralph."

I ignored that possibility for now.

"We can't leave him behind!" Penelope insisted.

An uncomfortable silence hung in the room. Robert quietly said, "Ronny is probably right."

Nausea jabbed at my stomach.

"But… we don't know. He was heading off in a different direction. Maybe he's hiding, and the natives didn't find him?" I hoped.

Grace-Ann shook her head, "Even if he's still alive, there's no way we can find him now. We wouldn't be able to tell his heat signature apart from any other native—or animal."

Penelope persisted, "Can't we just locate his screen?"

"Our screens only work within a comms mesh," I explained. I'd actually used that as a plot point once for a murder mystery. "Outside of the communications mesh of a large ship, or all of Conglommora, they won't work."

Alain nodded. "A visual pass—a fly over. That's the only way."

"Oh the natives will just *love* that," Ashby chimed in. "Who knows what they'll throw at us next? Maybe that isn't such a great idea."

Robert continued on to the medbay with Grace-Ann, Penelope seemed to almost swoon a bit but headed out, and Alain headed to our quarters as everyone dispersed in silence.

I sat at the newly-repaired and upgraded qradio and sent a message to Arty. I copied in the scans we'd taken, and a brief summary of our encounter with the natives, and Ralph's death, and the problem of missing Eddie.

There was really only one question I had for Arty.

What do we do now?

Arty had analyzed our report, the sensor readings from the *Uten* and the landing craft, and who knows what else. The recommendation wasn't surprising: Arty said to avoid the natives, and that we should stick to the uninhabited areas.

"Native contact is risky," Arty said in the message. "Not to just to the landing party or potential settlers, but especially to the natives. As humans of Earth, it is my mission to protect them as well as to protect you."

Huh. I hadn't considered that we posed a threat to the native human population. They seemed pretty handy with the whole spear thing. Just ask Ralph.

As for Eddie, Arty agreed we could try a few low passes in the landing craft to try and make visual contact—but to avoid flying directly overhead of any group of natives. Arty was adamant we not terrorize the natives, and there *was* perhaps some risk to the ships as well.

I was sitting in the control room of the *Uten*, pondering that thought and the rest of Arty's message, when Penelope came stumbling in. She was white as a bedsheet.

Grace-Ann and Ashby rushed over to her as she doubled in half.

"Penelope! What's wrong? Talk to me," Grace-Ann said as they half-carried her to a waiting chairform.

"I," she gurgled here a bit, then threw up on the floor, bright red, "don't feel well," was all she said before passing out.

What a terrible thing to have as your last words, I thought. Maybe that was just wishful thinking on my part. I shoved the idea away and went over to help.

Grace-Ann had the medikit stuff out. Penelope's fever was remarkably high—raging, even. Grace-Ann shot her with some automatically selected medicine. But this was old equipment on the *Uten*, Penelope would have a better chance back at Conglommora. I said as much.

"No," Robert said as he hobbled into the room and stood next to Penelope. They made quite an impressive sight together and a potent reminder that maybe we weren't exactly at the top of the food chain here. Earth was dangerous.

"We aren't going back yet," Robert insisted. "We need to try and talk to the native humans, to communicate with them. Besides, you all remember how… *debilitating* the trip was to get here." He nodded toward Penelope. "The stress from the quantum wave transport alone might kill her. We need to at least wait until she's stronger."

That seemed reasonable at the time, I suppose. But reasonable doesn't always turn out to be right.

Penelope died that night.

Twenty-One

I HAD SENT Penelope's medical scans to Arty, and—once again, no surprise—Arty suggested that we weren't prepared for the full onslaught of the ecosystem of Earth. This Earth wasn't the same as when we'd left it. Some virus, now alien to our systems, had ravaged Penelope in record time. Maybe it was from an insect bite, maybe just something in the air.

Ronny was pretty upset at the idea it might have been from a bite. He had quite a few and had smeared some sort of whitish medicine on them. I thought this really didn't bode well for Eddie either.

But the rest of us were okay, at least according to the medikit scans. Penelope had simply been susceptible. Arty was mostly confident we weren't at risk, although some decontamination protocol might be necessary when we returned to Conglommora. Bil was looking into that.

Conversation in the room was dire. Everyone was moping around about Penelope's and Ralph's deaths, expecting the worst about Eddie, listening to Ronny scratch his itches, and trying to get a handle on their own mortality.

It occurred to me that when you weep for the dead, you aren't shedding tears for them, exactly. The dead can't hear your wailing or lamentations. Does them no good at all. No, you weep for the brutal reminder of your own mortality; your own limitations. You weep at the pain of loss, of separation, if you knew them well. How long had I wept for Haily, with tears and without? You weep at the sudden change you are helpless to influence. Even though I didn't know either of these two, I still felt the helplessness. That is why we weep. And weep we did, each for our own largely selfish reasons. Ralph and Penelope were beyond caring at any rate.

None of this emotional tumult was doing me any good, so I tried to tune it out and concentrated on reading the rest of Arty's report.

As disconcerting as our situation was already, the big bombshell was yet to come.

Arty had taken all the scans we'd made and did its massive calculations and analysis, and discovered something remarkable.

Most everyone had left Earth around two or three generations ago, which should only have been a few hundred years or so. Maybe a few thousand at most, due to time dilation from acceleration.

But here, on Earth, in this place, in this corner of space time, 100,000 years—at least, maybe more, maybe even a *lot* more—had slipped past.

100,000 years.

Alain saw my expression and came over. "That's not possible," he stammered, reading over my shoulder. "None of the ships were traveling at relativistic speeds. I saw a vid on that once. Not close enough for that sort of time dilation anyway. And we know that it was our great-grandfather who left Earth in the *Neylan*. Not some distant ancestor. It doesn't make any sense at all."

I sat back and sighed, feeling foolish. I should have known better.

"No, actually, it makes perfect sense. I should have known." I shook my head.

"You have to realize, Alain… we are planetary creatures. Our senses, our lives, our timescales, are all on a planet-sized scale, or a solar system at most. Once you get past that…" I paused, swallowed. "Space-time isn't a big flat constant. As soon as you start talking about these kind of distances, any kind of reasonable speeds… you'll start to see relativistic effects. Different time frames. Different spatial relations."

"But Dad," Alain pursued it, "our ships didn't go that fast, right? Nowhere close to the speed of light."

"Our grandparents didn't start off that fast, sure, but it's cumulative. You keep accelerating for 50 years, 100 years, 200 years… it adds up. At least that's my understanding of it. And as soon as you get to any decent percentage of light speed, this kind of thing will happen."

I gestured toward the planet. I'm sure there's a formula to figure out the amount of time dilation. But I wasn't sure that even that would add up to 100,000 years.

Something else occurred to me.

Gravity. Artificial gravity.

Specifically the gravitomagnetic wave generators on every ship. Could that have impacted our timeframes? As soon as you mess with gravity, you mess with time. I'd have to ask Arty about that when we returned. But I bet that had something to do with it.

I had read up on issues of spacetime for some of the larger games I wrote—epic battles at galactic scale, with armies of aliens, vast empires, pan-galactic trading routes, that sort of thing. But the reality was, that would never happen. Not with our involvement, at least. Humans just weren't built at that scale. Any number of things in the universe can distort the relative time frame. And compared to human lifespan and attention span, it really doesn't take much physics at all to make a difference of 100,000 years, or a million years, or even a billion. We can't even observe the whole universe—we can only see as far as light, or radiation, has traveled to us. The cosmological horizon is our limit. We are so small.

Our paltry existence in years, tens of years... not even two hundred at best; it just wasn't viable. These "small differences" in galactic terms were 1,000 generations to us. We live and die within some amount of roundoff error.

We might as well be fruit flies as far as the rest of the universe is concerned.

It was a bittersweet idea. Here we were, back at Earth—an unbelievable, unobtainable goal. Traversing generations worth of lightyears in an instant. But only to here, to the one destination in the universe we knew, and even then only to arrive out of time. Out of our time.

It would never be our time again.

There were any number of perfectly valid reasons why the time frame here at Earth would be different from ours at Conglommora. That's why the natives looked so much different from us. There was time for their genetic makeup to drift, to change, to evolve. As Ashby speculated, they may be descended along different lines and may not even be our direct great-great-uncountably-great-grandchildren. More like close cousins, perhaps. A lot had changed since we left.

100,000, a million, who-knows-how-many years' worth.

Robert was taken aback at the calculation of Earth's present age, but stubbornly stuck with his plan. Earth was Earth, as far as he was concerned. *When* was just a detail.

"We have to go back down," Robert was still insisting.

And who's going to die this time? I wondered.

But all I said was, "Are you kidding?"

Ronny raised his hands as if about to speak but Robert plowed ahead, "We have two crafts, three people per craft. Myself, Ann, Ashby in one, Ronny, Alain and Charlie in the other." Robert apparently gave up on the idea of having Ashby watch over me.

Ronny persisted, "Shouldn't we leave someone back here on the *Uten*, in case of emergency?"

"Without a lander, what could you do?" Robert countered. "No, I think it's better to stick together. Safety in numbers and all that. But more importantly, this landing will be different. I've got a... a special piece of equipment, that will help us understand their language and communicate with the natives. It's a translator, of sorts."

Now that grabbed my interest immediately. Was he talking about the memory machine itself? Or some other ancient, dangerous bit of technology?

"If we can communicate with them, we can avoid being attacked again. But more importantly, and longer term, we can teach them." He held his hands wide, palms up. "We can help them. Live among them. Help them build the civilization they deserve. It doesn't matter if it's a few hundred years later, a few thousand, or tens of thousands since we left. They are children of the Earth; they are us."

Grace-Ann and Ashby were of course enthusiastic about this idea. They might have been giddy except for the lingering ghosts of Ralph and Penelope. This was still damn dangerous business.

"And what if they start chucking spears at us while you're fiddling with your gizmo?" Ronny said in his usual and very direct manner, now scratching futilely at a bite on his neck.

"We'll just make sure that they don't," Robert said with confidence, his hands down by his sides.

"And the virus that killed Penelope?" I asked, equally bluntly. "Arty says we're okay; we survived exposure. But what else might be down there?"

"I don't trust your Arty, in general," Robert admitted, "but it wouldn't put you and your son in danger. That's why you're here. So I believe it. And it says we're okay. As for other dangers... well, we'll just have to go back down and scan the soil, air, flora and fauna a little more closely, won't we? We'll have to do that anyway, before the others come."

"Others?" My eyes grew wide. "Are you insane? This place is a death trap. It might as well be an alien world. It *is* an alien world to us."

"Exciting, isn't it?" Robert's eyes had taken on a newly maniacal gleam. "A truly fresh start, a chance to do it right."

Now Robert's ideas of what was "right" were scary on the best of days. But maybe he had a point. We had technology far, far beyond these simple hunters. Maybe we could help, and help preserve our race. Maybe. But the risks...

"Everyone get a good night sleep," he said, straightening up. "We'll take the two ships down to this site," he pointed to the screen, "just as it passes into daylight. I'll bring the translator device, and we'll be a lot more careful this time."

"What about Eddie?" I asked.

"Edward is almost certainly dead by now," Robert said, subdued. "But if it makes you feel better, we'll make a couple of flyovers back at the original landing site first, then proceed as planned to make contact. If you really want to find him, we've probably got a better chance by asking the natives instead of flying around hoping to get lucky."

It wasn't ideal, but I guessed it would have to do. I nodded.

Robert left the hub, headed for his quarters. The rest of us did the same.

Ronny asked me as we headed down the corridor, "Translator device? Where'd he get that from? Everyone on Earth has spoken the same language for hundreds of years. No one has needed real-time translation in, like, forever."

"I get the feeling Robert and his people liked to hold on to old things," I suggested with a shrug. "Who knows where they dug it up, but clearly they held on to it. Maybe it will actually work?"

Ronny harrumphed and headed into his quarters.

Alain and I headed to ours. We were lying in our beds, unsuccessfully trying to sleep. So much to take in. So quickly.

Our home—Earth—at last! But so much time had passed. How? And how had all the damage to the ecosystem been repaired? It was irreversible, we'd been told.

And two quick deaths—maybe three—already. The risk was real. And for what? The open sky, the air, it was all magnificent. The smells, the insect life, the large predators hiding in the grass, deadly hunters who couldn't tell us from dinner... was it really worth it?

Maybe. I wasn't so sure anymore.

"You and Alain were probably right," Robert started, handing us some fake animal skins he'd printed on the *Uten*. "We didn't look like 'people' to them at all. So we'll go down dressed in these and leave the enviro suits here."

It was a reasonable idea, actually.

Robert continued, gesturing at the screen, "We'll set the landing craft down over here, on top of this bluff. They shouldn't be able to see the crafts from the plains." He pointed to a spot on the topo scan. "Walk down from there, and we look just like other natives."

"Except that *we'll* have stun weapons," Alain confirmed.

"Yes," Robert agreed, "but we won't use them unless we are openly attacked, right?" There was an uncomfortable round of head nodding. After our last encounter, restraint was not on the menu. Shoot first, sort it out later seemed more appropriate.

Back in our quarters, we changed into our fake animal skin clothing. Even though it was a good idea, I still felt foolish. Alain and I looked… I don't know, cartoonish, maybe? Comical? Like something out of a bad play or old Earth vid. We dressed and prepped and headed to the landing craft, still feeling a little silly.

Grace-Ann, however, did not look foolish at all in her outfit. Instead, she looked regal. Like a lioness in charge of the pride. She looked great. A pang of emotions in assorted flavors shot through me. I tried to make small talk, tried to talk to Grace—but this was all Ann, all the time. All business.

"Robert wanted us to *only* wear these skins," Ann said, handing us each a bundle, "but the ground at the landing site is very rocky, and our feet are not tough like the natives."

Alain and I put on the sandal-like things she had printed. They were soft, comfortable, but had a firm sole to protect us from the sharpened dangers of the natural ground.

Robert came up, already wearing his. "I hate to have to wear anything they aren't, but these are pretty subtle and they won't even see them at a distance. Hopefully it won't be a problem."

And once more, we loaded up into the landing craft. Robert, Grace, Ashby in one, and Ronny, Alain, and me in the other.

In case I hadn't mentioned it before, the view from the landing craft as we approached Earth was absolutely spectacular. No vr I'd ever seen came anything close. The depth, the subtle pull of gravity, the... the *reality* of it was overwhelming.

Both ships headed to the original landing site first, staying high in the atmosphere until we were right on top of it, then swooping in low in a search pattern that Arty had recommended in the report. It was barely dawn, the light was thin and the dew heavy on the grasses and plants below us. There were two or three groups of natives that we had to avoid—one group might have been animals—

but otherwise we completed the search pattern over the area Eddie could have covered.

Nothing. Not a sign. No isolated heat signatures, no sign of a campfire or any other sort of signal, nothing. I hadn't really expected to find Eddie, but coming up empty on the search was another blow to us. There wasn't much conversation about it, just a grim determination to carry on.

Make that three casualties so far, then.

Both landing craft shot back up into high atmosphere and headed over to the new landing site away from the sunrise, into the last hours of dark.

We landed on the bluff without incident; the rock outcropping made a bit of a crater, or bowl, which hid us pretty well under the cover of night. It would take a few hours of walking to get down to the plains, by which time the sun would be up here as well. We would approach the natives then.

This time, we scanned the immediate area, our path down the bluff, and the natives' camp very carefully, checking for anything large and hungry, or small and venomous. Nothing large, but there were indeed snakes in and around the rocks. They seemed to be dormant at the moment; do snakes sleep? Ralph was supposed to to be expert on these sorts of things. Penelope on geology. No help from either of them now. Damn.

As long as we didn't disturb the snakes, both Ronny and Robert thought we'd be all right. I wished we had at least Arty to consult. Either way, I didn't plan on sticking my hands into any dark crevices or holes.

Trudging down the mountain side. That's the word for it. Trudging. On the one hand, we were actually walking on Earth. That alone was incredible. The night sky above us was filled with bright stars, there was moonlight enough to walk by, and you could see the white swath of the galaxy almost right overhead. I would rather have stayed up by the landing craft, laid on my back and just watched the stars. With Grace. I relaxed a little at that thought.

But it was just a dream, a fantasy; it wasn't going to happen. Instead we were trudging down a rocky hillside heading for… well, pretty much just asking for trouble, trying to contact and communicate with the natives. I was pretty tensed up about it, with just enough curiosity to keep me going, but I was worried both for myself and for Alain. And Grace-Ann, I suppose. Alain stayed close by, at least.

Strange sounds filled the night as we shuffled and skittered down the mountain. Insects buzzed and flitted close at hand, beasts grunted and growled off in the distance. Well off in the distance, I hoped, as I glanced over at the dark rim of the jungle proper. An indescribable mix of smells got stronger and more distracting as we got closer to the level of the plains. It wasn't pleasant.

It was getting lighter out now, and easier to see. We were almost down to the level of the plains and could see the camp now.

There were caves in the mountain, and we'd scanned a fair number of the natives living in there—maybe even underneath us at this point. There on the plain just outside of the caves were three buildings. Well, structures. Huts, I suppose?

The largest was several times larger than one of our landing craft, circular, covered in animal skins and held up by large bones. You could see some of the tips of the bones sticking up past the covering. Those had to be some pretty large animals. I swallowed hard. Wondered briefly if they had slaughtered the giant beasts deliberately for their bones, or just scavenged them from already-dead casualties of the jungle.

We stood there, on a wedge of a precipice, looking at the huts, the thin tendrils of smoke rising from them— cooking fires? The red cast of early sunlight over the sleepy grasses drove off the cool of the night about to bake the area with the full-on solar heat of the day.

Tourists. That's the word. We were acting like tourists. There was so much to see, to experience, to hear, to smell... it's really no wonder we didn't notice them sneaking up behind us. They were hunters. I'm guessing they were pretty good at sneaking.

Rough hands grabbed me hard. I couldn't reach for the stunner. I couldn't run.

"Dad!" Alain screamed. In the flash of an instant I saw blood near his stomach.

I think it was a rock that slammed into my head.

Twenty-Two

LIGHT. At the end of a long tunnel of dark. Funny how descriptions of birth and death are so self-similar. Newborn. Dead. Which was I? Still in between, it seemed. For now.

It really was a tunnel—or at least a short cave. Brightly lit daylight outside, probably mid-morning by now, if not even later. My head pounded as if still being pummeled with rocks. The memory of the rock alone was enough for a huge headache.

I was in the back of the cave, Grace-Ann was next to me on one side, Alain on the other, facing away. My hands and feet were tied. Didn't know if it was vines or leather strips. Didn't matter much. We weren't going anywhere.

"Alain!" I hissed, in a stage whisper. I wanted to get his attention—but only his. "Alain!"

"Quiet!" Robert bit out through clenched teeth, with a hiss of his own.

Alain stirred. He was alive, at least. That's one piece of good news. He rolled over onto his back; a dark red clot of blood the size of a fist on his exposed stomach. Still oozing a little, but not badly.

"I'm all right," he groaned quietly. Robert hissed again.

For now, I thought. We needed to get Alain back to the landing craft, if not even back to a medbay on the *Uten*. And he might not be the only one needing some attention.

My shoulders and knees were already starting to cramp and ache; the strips cut into my wrists so tightly that they burned. I rolled over, tried to reposition my legs out of the cramp. Needed to find someway to cut those strips before my damn arms fell off. Didn't fancy having to grow new ones like some damn salamander in a tank.

My stunner was gone. My eyes cleared a little in the blinding sunshine from the cave entrance, and I could see the weapons there in a loose pile. Each stunner was small, round, smooth. They probably had no idea what they were.

In fact, a small figure outside the cave was fitting one of the stunners in a long strip of leather—a sling, I realized. They were just shiny river rocks to their eyes, not sleek modern weapons. But that's not where the attention was.

Robert's translator gizmo that he brought was a small, rectangular box. Shiny. Perfectly flat, with perfect square corners. Unremarkable to us, hardly worth mentioning. Just another piece of tech.

But for the natives, the Earthans? Unlike anything they'd ever seen. Anywhere. Ever.

A group of eight or ten or so were huddled around it, just inside the cave on the other side. They were talking about it—I guess. Sounded like guttural gibberish to me, I couldn't make out any words. The translator box was probably listening though and building up whatever matrix it could.

Crap, my legs still hurt. I tried lying out flat to stretch, then shimmied up against the back wall so I could see what was going on better.

"Animals," Grace-Ann whispered, in an actually quiet whisper. "The Earthans have become animals. There's no civilization left here at all…" She kept muttering, mostly to herself.

Robert had shifted to a sitting position where I could see him; he was on the other side of Grace-Ann. He cleared his throat. I swear he cleared his throat *pompously*. I didn't even know that was possible.

Whatever happened next, I was pretty sure it would go badly.

Robert called out in a steady, clear voice so the translator would hear, and said simply, "My name is Robert. We have come from a distant land to speak with you."

The couple of natives in the group closest to us looked over with mild curiosity, but then a split second later, Robert's voice came out of the box. It had been transformed, sort of, into whatever grunts and spittle passed for their language. Or as close as the box could figure.

Whether it was grammatically perfect Earthan Grunt or just random noise didn't matter. The fact that a disembodied voice came out of the tiny, shiny box was the kicker.

As one being, the group dropped the box like a hot stone from the fire and fled the cave in pure terror. Ran. Screaming.

I didn't need the translator to figure that one out. A scream is a scream, in any language, and in any time.

I expected they'd come back in a few minutes to poke at it, or at us. Poke—or worse. Curiosity and all that would surely outweigh their fears. But they hadn't come back yet. In fact, after the screaming, it was really very quiet outside.

We sat in silence, afraid to move or even talk, in case they *were* waiting just outside the cave. Hours passed, I think. Hard to tell. My legs and arms were on fire—long past the simple tingling of losing circulation. Hurt like hell. I looked over at Alain grimacing against his bonds, blood still seeping from his wound, and that hurt even worse. What kind of parent was I to get his kid killed like this?

A terrible parent, that's what kind. Just terrible.

I shifted position, as quietly as I could, as often as I could. The others kept quietly adjusting as well. Didn't seem to help much.

The sun was sinking into the horizon; shadows were growing long out on the plains. We hadn't had any food or water since leaving the landing craft, and my mouth felt like a big dry, brittle sponge. I swear my tongue had gotten bigger in my bone-dry mouth.

Alain stirred. "They *are* coming back, aren't they?" The question just hung there in the hot, quiet silence. I didn't want to lie.

Only twilight crept in, and we were still alone in the cave.

Hell of a way to die.

"I don't think they're coming back, not tonight," I said with cautious optimism. We had to do something; anything.

"Yeah," Ronny agreed. He started rolling vigorously and twitching, for lack of a better word, toward the entrance. Making a fair bit of noise.

"What are you doing!" hissed Robert. "They'll hear you!"

"I don't care," Ronny spat with irritation as he maneuvered closed to the entrance. Our stunners were piled up, like rocks, just outside.

"Don't bother," Alain said gloomily, looking up, "those are only stun weapons, not cutters. They won't cut us loose, just knock us out."

"I'm not headed for those," Ronny grunted as he flipped his torso around to the other side of the cave opening. There were the remains of a small pit fire there, and what looked like some tools. I could barely make it out in the fading light. But yes, if these native Earthans had stone tools—that would work. Ironically, that would work a lot better than our ridiculously advanced weapons.

"Okay, we're in luck," Ronny said, "there's something like a small hand axe here, looks like it could be pretty sharp." He sat with his back to it, rubbing his hands up and down along the exposed stone knife edge.

I held my breath, but didn't need to. No angry natives came rushing in, Ronny didn't cut off a thumb or anything. In a few minutes of awkward rubbing, his hands were free. Ronny reached around and grabbed the axe, then leaned forward and more quickly cut his feet loose from the bonds.

He stood up, rubbing his ankles and shaking his hands loosely, getting feeling—and blood—back where it belonged.

"Okay, who's first?" he asked.

Robert of course rolled over and presented his arms to be cut first. Ronny pointedly ignored him and instead headed over to Alain.

Alain stood up gingerly, favoring his wounded side, and as he rubbed his wrists headed out toward the cave entrance. I was next and followed him. I chuckled to myself that Robert was still waiting with his arms held up. Clearly Ronny was leaving him until last.

I came up next to Alain, who was peering over the edge of the cliff face. We weren't that high up off the level of the plains, maybe only two or three decks' worth. Smoke was rising from the huts down in front of us, but we didn't see anyone outside from here. So they hadn't all fled the village entirely, it seemed. But they sure weren't sticking around near us. I wondered if we were being guarded still.

Robert, freed at last, retrieved the translator gizmo from where the natives had dropped it and joined us. Grace-Ann and Ashby trailed behind, gathered up the stunners from the pile, and handed them back out to us. At least we were armed again.

Robert hefted the translator. "This thing is useless," he decried, looking ready to chuck it over the edge.

"No," Grace-Ann said forcefully. "Alistaire, listen to me."

That was new. They hadn't been referring to each other by their ancestral memory-vault names before. I briefly wondered what triggered it now, but we had more pressing issues at hand.

Robert gave her an annoyed glance, but said nothing.

"That box was recording everything the natives said and trying to build a translation matrix for their language," Grace-Ann continued. "I don't think it was completely successful, but if we take it back to Conglommora, Arty can download the data and create a far better and more complete matrix than it could."

"What?" Robert shook. "No! Lucille, no way will I allow that overbearing, controlling, artificial monstrosity get anywhere near our work!"

Well, this was fun. Robert/Alistaire and Grace/Ann/Lucille were having an argument. For two people, it was getting awfully crowded out here.

"Who the hell is Lucille? Or Alistaire?" a confused Ronny asked, of no one in particular. Alain looked at me with a similarly confused face.

They were still pointing and arguing with some passion. Grace and company was acting more lively than I'd seen her ever since the other memories got uploaded. She really was a different person, especially now. Something had triggered them both or maybe they just stopped pretending.

I turned and tried to explain in few words what I knew, "Robert holds memories of his ancestor, Alistaire. Grace holds the memories of Robert's sister, Ann, and her ancestor, Lucille. He used some kind of ancient, forgotten tech. Arty doesn't know how. That's what happened to Grace when Robert took her. And now," I waved my hand in their general, and still fraught, direction, "they are calling each other by their ancestral-memory names. I don't know why."

Ronny knew some of that, but not the details, and this was probably all new to Alain. I hadn't had the strength to go over it with him in any detail.

Grace was winding up, "Also, we need to make it unobtrusive. Earpiece for us, and non-verbal, subvocal pickup so the natives don't hear our own language, only the translation."

Robert backed off, literally as well as figuratively. "Fine." He gave up, in apparent disgust at this turn of events. "You always were the smart one, Lucille, and this is your mission, after all."

"Yes, it is, Alistaire," she confirmed. "Now let's get out of here."

"Okay you kids," I said in a light-hearted attempt, "what's going on? Why the name change all of a sudden, and what are we going to do now after scaring the lunch out of these people?" I nodded to the valley floor.

Robert and Grace-Ann looked at each other, exchanged a cryptic look.

Grace-Ann paused, looking circumspect. She turned from the edge of the cliff wall and paced a little.

"Memory and personality. Where does one end, and the other begin? Aren't we all just our memories? Our hurts, our desires, our passions, our memory of the last time? Our desire to do better the next time? Most of my memories are Lucille's. So, in a way, I am more of Lucille than I am Ann, or Grace. Steering the future of humanity is my mission. I carry those seeds with me. I am Lucille."

My heart sank.

"As I am Alistaire," Robert-Alistaire said. "At first we thought humankind was lost in the stars and needed our help there. But now we've found the core of humanity here, on Earth, where we belong, and where they need our help."

"We'll head back to Conglommora and get Arty's help with an improved translator," Lucille added. "With that in hand, we'll be able to communicate, teach, and guide humanity's children away from living like animals and becoming the men they are destined to be."

It was an odd sentiment coming from her, I thought. But no one really cared what I thought at this point.

"Come on," she said with new-found authority. "We'll head back to the landing craft and then to the *Uten*." Lucille/Grace/Ann, oh hell, I suppose just Lucille now, started climbing up to the top of the bluff where our landing crafts waited.

Twenty-Three

We climbed quickly, but not frantically. It looked like the natives were staying down on the valley floor, and although I was expecting torches and pitchforks at any moment, nothing like that had yet materialized. They probably hadn't even discovered pitchforks yet, I mused with some relief. Maybe we'd make it out safe.

Alain was leaning on my arm for support, trying not to rip open the barely-clotted wound in his side. I had gotten a slightly better look at it, but couldn't really tell how large the wound itself was for all the dried blood. We limped along, back to the ship. Another less-than-successful mission. I better stop this nonsense before we got killed. We'd been lucky so far.

Luck, of course, comes and goes with no regard to comfort or convenience. In the next moment, it left.

Our party turned around the side of a rock outcropping and stopped short. Three natives stood there, spears raising, voices raising. My heartbeat raised to match them, and then some. I quickly shoved Alain behind me.

They were yelling something, I don't know what—it just sounded like grunts to me, and Robert/Alistaire/whoever he was didn't have the translator thing active.

We froze in our tracks. They yelled and gestured wildly, poking the spears right in front of us. I really didn't want to end up speared like Ralph.

I started to open my mouth, to try and talk, to say something… not realizing how useless that would be. Robert stepped forward as if to do the same, trying to make some kind of hand motions to communicate with them.

Screw this.

I whipped my hand up and fired the stunner. Once, twice, a third time a bolt of energy leapt from my hand.

The three were lifted off their feet and crashed into the rocks and hardscrabble of the mountainside. How much was stun and how much was surprise, I don't know. But as they lay there trying to comprehend what had happened to them, we scrambled past, up the mountain. Maybe they tried to get up and follow us, maybe they just lay there and pissed themselves.

Personally, I would have gone for the latter.

It was dark now, but there was enough moonlight to make our way up the hillside.

"Charlie!" Robert was agitated. "You didn't have to shoot them. I could have—"

"Enough!" I barked, and turned to plant myself firmly facing Robert. "That's enough! We've humored you and your stupid little game long enough. No one else is going to die of it, not if I can help it!" I ended on a roar at last, not a squeak like on my first "mission" to the Old Path section.

I wondered if Robert could see the vein popping out on my forehead. I could feel it. That, and a wave of... well, everything. Adrenaline, fear, frustration, the list went on. I ranted at a stunned and quiet Robert a little more and ended up with, "Forgiveness only goes so far, and I'm plumb out. We are leaving this hell hole and going back to Conglommora now. Right now. No more excuses, no more chances."

And with that, I whipped around, took Alain's weight gently again, and headed up the hill.

Grace-Ann started to protest, but Ronny cut her off and added firmly, behind us, "If Charlie hadn't flattened them, I would have. Keep it moving. We're done here."

Stumbling, silent, we dragged ourselves up the hillside in the dim gloom. Dark clouds had slid in, silent to us overhead, and now water fell from the sky. Rain, I think, was the word. Everywhere, falling on everything. Inescapable. I'd never experienced anything like it. What a wasteful way to irrigate crops. But I suppose planets don't have targeted, measured, AI-driven irrigation systems.

The rain falls where it will.

Now we were soaked, right through to our sandals. Robert was the first to have his feet suddenly slip out from under him, and he barked a sharp curse as he splayed face down in the mud. I couldn't suppress a chuckle, but should have. In an instant I was grabbing the Earth on my hands and knees, covered in slimy mud. Luckily I let go of Alain as I started to slip and hadn't brought him down with me. We slowed our pace, and chose our steps with a little more care.

Finally, we reached the landing crafts without further incident. In an instant, we lifted off gently into the night air, soaring up through the rain and past the clouds into the moonlight, then out of the air entirely and up to the *Uten*, waiting patiently in orbit.

Our ship docked first. We were already climbing out when Robert's craft docked at the other port.

Grace, er, Lucille, was giving orders as they climbed out. "Get us ready to leave orbit and return to the quantum wave insertion point," she said to Robert. Or rather, to Alistaire. Gah. Whoever. "Be sure to check the power coupling integrity from the central hub before you engage the control circuits," she admonished.

I was tired. I no longer cared about their histrionics. We'd found Earth, but it was populated with mutant, degenerated DNA, slope-headed cave dwellers. Any shred of our civilization was gone. Our structures, our monuments, our values, our morals, all gone. Reduced to cavemen, banging rocks.

In a way, that was worse than a barren and desolate Earth—the image we'd been told and were used to. A verdant paradise was too much to hope for and having that hope dashed hurt a lot. A lush, green and verdant trap. Much worse.

Alain. I needed to get him to the medbay, and hope his wound was superficial. Shower. I needed a hot shower. And a long sleep. My head hurt from the bruise where I'd been hit with a rock. Oh yes, did I mention I'd been hit in the head with a rock recently?? Insane. The whole thing was insane. I wanted to be home. Home in Conglommora on the Neylan, on the ship of my parents and grandparents, and their parents, and my house and home. I was done.

Alain and I made it to our quarters on the *Uten*. The medbay cleaned up his wound, and was sealing the torn tissue from a short incision about the width of your thumb. Funny, left on Earth, a tiny injury like that could have been fatal over time. But here, even on the admittedly old-fashioned *Uten*, it was no big deal. He'd be okay. I breathed a full breath of relief at last. We had made it. Alain was okay, and we'd be home soon.

I had showered, and dressed, and felt at least a little better. The screen beeped at me. "Alistaire" was calling. "Hey Bob," I said, using the least favorite form of his many names. "What can I do for you?"

Wring your neck. That's what I'd like to do for you, you stupid bastard.

"I might need your help," he said, "I'm having trouble getting the drive engines back up, and there's a reading here I don't…"

The explosion knocked me flat on my ass.

The screen went dark, and only emergency lights were on. An alarm blared.

I scrambled back up to the screen, swiped to get some information. Alain came rushing in, "What the hell happened now?" he asked.

I'd have to talk to him about his language when we got back. On the other hand, profanity was not unreasonable just now. I honestly didn't know what the hell was happening, on many fronts.

"I wish I knew," I admitted, trying to get something up on the screen, other than an error indicator or just silent black. I finally got an exterior camera view from the rear of the ship up along the full length of the *Uten*.

The hub, the control room, the bridge, where Robert/Bob/Alistaire was just talking to me, all of it was gone.

Blown open to space.

The AI on board—I couldn't bring myself to call it Arty anymore—announced the obvious, "Atmospheric pressure dropping rapidly. Internal atmosphere is venting to space. Emergency seals are in place but are not holding. Structural integrity compromised. Complete hull failure estimated in 3.2 minutes."

I punched the emergency channel and shouted over the AI, "Get out! Everyone get to the landing craft. Now!"

I grabbed Alain and we flung ourselves out the door and down the hallway.

"Alain, get to the landing craft, I'm right behind you," I lied as I veered off a side corridor.

"What?" Alain complained, with cause. "Where the hell are you going?"

"Go!" I shouted, "I'll explain in a minute." I shot off down the corridor. A small explosion sounded in the distance. A closer one; this time I could see the sparks and a new plume of vicious orange-colored smoke.

I raced to the junction where the secret, sealed door was located. If the *Uten* was blowing up, this was literally my last chance to save Grace. I skittered down the hallway to the door.

The hatch was open.

I whipped around the corner into the room, the secret, forbidden room.

It was empty.

Nothing. No panels, no screens, nothing at all. An empty storage room. If anything had been in here, it was gone now. I ran at full tilt, and then some, back to the landing craft.

"Complete loss of hull integrity imminent," said the computer. I dove into our craft, Ronny sealed the hatch practically on my legs.

"Get us out of here!" he yelled at Alain, who was behind the controls. We shot away from the dying hulk, I saw the other lander just behind us. Then it was over.

If we could have heard it, I suppose it would have sounded like a dull crump; the sound of an empty box being crushed from the inside out, as the *Uten* blew its guts out into the hard vacuum of space.

We were alive, and I was glad for that, but boy were we screwed.

Twenty-Four

WE SAT THERE IN SPACE for a few minutes. Just sat. There wasn't much to watch, no glorious or dramatic explosion. Just the dead, bloated husk of the *Uten* spinning slowly, out of control, headed eventually to crash, or just burn up in the atmosphere, more likely.

"Shit," said Ronny under his breath.

Not much I could add to that. We continued with our silent thoughts.

Was I happy that Robert was dead? Maybe. I was glad to be rid of him, but with him went just about any chance of saving Grace. Maybe he hid the magical equipment somewhere in Conglommora, maybe there was still a chance with Lucille herself... but the chances were pretty dim.

Robert was dead. There was no chance now of revenge, of closure. No way to make him suffer for what he'd done to us, what he'd put us through... what he'd exposed Conglommora to. That didn't seem fair.

Damn him. Damn him to hell and back. Stupid bastard with his stupid bastard ideas of "right" and "wrong" for humanity which was just thinly-disguised racism, sexism, and a half-dozen *isms* I couldn't even place. Stupid bastard trying to make the world dance to his own stupid tune.

I should have stood up to him, should have stopped him, or tried. He got off too easy.

He should have suffered.

He should have been made to see what damage his actions caused. Forced to reckon with it.

He should have had to answer for Ralph's and Penelope's deaths. And Grace's "kidnapping," for lack of a better word. "Killing," there's a better word. For all intents, he'd *killed* Grace. The Grace I knew—and loved—was gone. Gone forever. I couldn't talk to her, couldn't sit under the stars of Earth with her, couldn't even complain about the animal shit in Skyville with her. Grace was dead.

He should have had to answer for that.

But he couldn't. He was dead. So here I was, fists and teeth clenched tight, sitting in our little lander ship, with my best friend and my son, untold light years away from home. The rage would have to wait. It was a luxury. First, we had to survive.

Out of the long and stunned silence, Ronny spoke again, "What happened?"

"I don't know." My mouth made a tight, grim line. "Robert pinged me, he had some, I don't know, some question about the engines, and then… that was all. It blew."

Ronny looked out the port to the wreck. "Do you think we can go back and salvage supplies from the *Uten*?"

"Not without a spacesuit," Alain moaned, hanging his head in his hands, and making me feel like a really great parent again.

Ronny looked around the cramped landing craft, "We don't have any onboard?" he said with some surprise.

"No, not here. Any suits are back on the *Uten*. We don't have any way of getting over there. All we've got is what you see," I waved my hand to the interior of the ship, which for the most part just contained us and the controls.

And no qradio. The qradio had been installed in the hub on the *Uten*. Blown to bits now. Along with Robert/Alistaire.

"Okay, here's the thing," I started planning out loud. "We need to get back out to the resonance wave insertion point. That's where Arty will expect us to be, and we don't have the qradio to send any different information. We can get there, but it will take a while—a lot longer than in the *Uten*."

"Shit," Ronny repeated, needlessly.

I looked up a couple of facts about these landers on the screen.

"These craft have air recyclers that will hold us for at least some tens of days, but we'll need food and water."

I looked again at the hard, cold blue orb of Earth. We weren't free of her just yet.

"There's no food to be had out here," I stated the obvious, mostly to help convince myself that we *had* to go back down planetside again.

"We're going to have to land and gather supplies," I finished with a heavy sigh. Neither Ronny nor Alain said anything. They both just sort of looked at the Earth with a new, fresh apprehension.

Although we didn't have spacesuits on board, we *did* have a small, emergency printer. It would be enough to make a couple of canteen-styled bottles. We could collect fresh water in those. I started the printer going. It was slow and would take a while.

Lucille beeped us from the other ship just then; it was just her and Ashby now.

"Charlie," she said, "we're going to need to land to gather supplies. One of the landing sites we'd looked at has clean water, and I don't scan any natives in the area at the moment. I suggest we land there."

She was all business. Not even a hint of grief at having lost her brother and her ship. Nothing. Cold and factual like the cold, hard vacuum of deep space itself.

But I had no dispute with this plan and signaled my agreement. Alain set the coordinates, and once more I found myself hurtling down to Earth, the blue and white sphere of dreams and nightmares. Of pain and delight.

One of the first scripts I had written dealt with survivors of a crashed watership, how they had to forage for food, collect water, and ultimately try not to kill each other. I remembered a little about the research I had done back then and looked up what I could on the limited computer here on the lander.

It wasn't much of a list, but it would do.

The best initial landing site was by an ocean, on a broad, shallow beach. Ronny, Alain and I climbed out the hatch, but this time I sat on the edge of the ship and just took it all in for a moment before descending down the ladder.

So beautiful. The sea was vast. Beyond vast. Beyond the limits of vision. You could almost see the curvature of the horizon of the planet itself. The wind was constant. I'd felt air move before, of course, but not like this. Not this feeling of constant wind against my skin, the wind in my hair, the wind everywhere. Smell of salt air, rich and full, not at all like the somewhat boxy smell of Sea or any of the other biodomes on Conglommora.

Slowly, I climbed down the ladder. Alain and Ronny were scanning the immediate area, making sure we wouldn't be surprised again. I walked closer to the shoreline. Not sure what compelled me, but suddenly my shoes were off, and I could feel the sand on my bare feet. It was fine, finer and smoother to the touch than the sand I'd felt around the Sea biome.

A very subtle breeze rustled the grasses behind me. Other than the low-frequency rumble of the sea, it was quiet, so quiet you could hear the grasses rubbing together. I thought... I don't know what I thought—I'd never been standing on a planet before this trip. Interface of sea and land. Strangely mesmerizing. Dazzling sunlight, brighter than anything I'd seen in Skyville or Sea, or even the Mech section. A flock of birds careened overhead, A few broke off and dove into the ocean, grabbing a quick meal.

Earth was beautiful.

It was also incredibly damn dangerous. It was sheer luck that my son and I hadn't been seriously hurt, permanently maimed, or killed outright. So far, Death had flirted with us; skirted us. Near misses.

And we weren't home yet. Not by a long shot. We could still die right here, right now, or starve to death in space waiting for the pickup that would never come. Death hadn't been outright stalking Alain and I yet, but it was close. Too damn close.

Lucille came over with a surprisingly jaunty stance. She held a screen up. "These are things we need to look for," she said, all business. Where was the grief, the anger, the mourning? Her brother and their ship had just been blown to bits. Did that even register? What *was* she?

I didn't look at the screen, but instead confronted her. "Things to look for? What about your brother? What about the *Uten*? What happened up there? Why did the ship blow up? Why are you waving this thing in my face??"

Admittedly, I was a little emotional, and shaken. It's not everyday one gets stranded on a alien world—that used to be your planet—when your only ship explodes in a shower of fire and death.

Lucille straightened up, regally, calmly, and said, "My brother is dead." She looked aside. "He's been dead before. He'll be dead again. But that doesn't matter now; what matters is that we find food and water, or we'll be dead, too, and for the last time."

No, that didn't really make any sense to me either. But her point about food and water was, of course, on point. I pulled my screen out and displayed the list I'd assembled.

She peered at it, as one would at an unwelcome visitor. "Yes, yes, that will do," she reluctantly agreed. "I have much the same list," Lucille raised her screen again and flicked through similar pictures of berries, nuts, but added some kind of weird tuberous things.

"These should be native to this area," she pointed to the tuber things, "highly nutritious and relatively easy to find."

Lucille and I showed the lists to the others, and we all fanned out. Lucille on her own, Ashby with Ronny, and I with Alain.

Alain and I found a couple of the items quickly enough. I tried each in turn. They were tough, hard to eat, and mostly completely flavorless. It might be enough to keep us alive, but we wouldn't be enjoying it.

The mountains behind us featured many streams that eased down the mountainsides and emptied into the sea. A quick hike off the beach into the mountains and we could access fresh water.

We took the canteens I'd printed out and headed up into the foothills to get some fresh water.

Although you could see the icy mountain streams from the beach, you couldn't see the source yet. As we climbed up to get to a convenient spot to fill the bottles, we finally saw the river itself. Grand, immense. Alain stopped in his tracks, our ascent arrested by the grandeur of this monumental, watery artery.

The river stretched far to the horizon, winding here and there. But you could make out the form of it all the way from the main body just to our right, and all the nearby fingers grasping down the mountainside, all the way back to a far-off line in the distance, no more than a thin thread of black against the green forest.

Alain stared. Silence gripped us both for the moment. It took us a little while to realize *we* were the only ones who were silent. The woods, the river—it was all teeming with life. Fish. Insects. Jumpy things at the sides of the river bank. It was almost overwhelming. We stood there a long while, probably longer than we should have. This place was captivating.

Eventually Alain broke off his stare and hiked down the bank to the nearest branch of the river itself. I followed him down, and we filled up the bottles from the clear, cold water. But first, I took the opportunity to splash my face in the water. I felt refreshed, actually relaxed a bit. Alain did the same. We turned and started back to the ships.

Alain was in a hopeful mood, maybe revived by the fresh water. "Hey, this is almost fun," he said to me as we hiked back to the wide, barren beach.

I grimaced, "Oh, this whole trip has been one long party. I really like the blowing up the ship part and our narrow escape from killer mutant Earthans."

Alain swallowed hard, licked his lips. "Yeah, that was scary," he allowed, "I can't believe those guys are dead. First Ralph, then that girl, Eddie, then Robert... but we survived it. We've survived it *all*."

True enough. We'd been through an unreal set of events, one after the other. I couldn't believe any one of them, on their own. Together? I was just numb, really.

He laughed out loud suddenly. "Just think of it— you've led a mission to an alien planet. For real!"

"Me? Lead? Hardly," I grimaced. Some leader. I almost got us killed. But Alain, he had done so well. No complaints, piloting the lander...

"I'm really proud of you, you know," I said to Alain in a rare moment of parental honesty.

He was embarrassed and looked at his shoes and the path a little more closely. "You're the best, Dad."

It was a nice moment. Fleeting and brief, but nice. I was proud of him. Here we were on a freaking *mission*, on a genuine alien planet, ironically. Just like one of the games I'd once worked on. That life seemed... a lifetime ago.

We met back at the ships and divided the food we had gathered and the water bottles.

"Okay, I've run some calculations while you were getting water," Lucille said, "and we don't actually have the capability to make it out to the resonance wave insertion point directly. We need a gravity boost. So I've worked out a course on the computer that takes us away from Earth a little, then we approach at an angle and whip around the planet, getting enough of a boost to whip us out to the pickup point. From there, we just need to hope Arty picks us up. And that we don't starve or die of thirst first."

That's a lot of "if's," I thought, channeling my inner depressive black hole.

But we didn't have much choice, and her logic was sound. Hopefully, her calculations were as well, using the very meager computer resources of the lander.

"Let's go then," said Ronny. "Let's get the hell out of here."

We retreated to our ships, and one last time, shot into the sky, out of the sky, and away from Earth.

I wondered, ever so briefly, who might have been watching us.

Twenty-Five

EVEN WITH THE GRAVITY BOOST from the Earth fly-by, we were pressing our already weakened luck. The landing craft Arty made for us weren't designed for anything beyond day trips from orbit to planet. Certainly not designed for five to ten days or more of interplanetary travel.

I figured out how to ration the food and water appropriately, and everyone agreed—even Lucy. I just couldn't bring myself to call her "Lucille". Lucy would be her nickname now.

So we had food and supplies, hopefully enough to last until pickup. Waste disposal was a little trickier, but I worked it out. You don't want to know the details. Trust me.

Boredom, however, was another matter.

The view of Earth, massive at first then shrinking into the distance, kept us occupied at first. We slept, we napped. That held our attention for a while. After everything we'd been through, I could have slept for ten days at least.

Or at least two days or so. By then, I was tired of sleeping, if you'll excuse the phrase. So we started talking to pass the time.

There was the grief to get through first. It's not like we knew any of those people very well; we had only just met Ralph and Penelope. And although I didn't know Ralph, he knew me. Or knew of me, I guess. It was a slight connection, but a connection nonetheless. They weren't our friends, but still, this brush with sudden death was something new.

And Robert. I realized I hated Robert, and it was an uncomfortable feeling. Hate was something we'd always been taught by our parents to avoid. It was as close to a guiding philosophy on Conglommora as anything else. Forgive, move on. Don't hate. It's not sustainable.

But I hated him, but there was nothing I could do about it. No closure, no confrontation, nothing. He was gone. An unfinished sentence, dangling there in the dark. It would never be finished.

Eddie. I'd known Eddie, made fun of Eddie, for a long time. Years. I didn't mean it. Didn't mean to be mean to him. What had his life been like, holding on to that incredible secret that no one would believe? No wonder he was a little crazy. Could I have helped him? Could I have gotten here years ago, long before Robert showed up, if I had just bothered to listen to Eddie, to get to know him, to talk to him?

Guilt. Another unaccustomed feeling, at least at this magnitude. Guilt at ignoring Eddie, at taunting him instead of helping him.

What *else* had I ignored?

My son? Were there things we should have talked about but never had the time? Well, we had plenty of time now. Maybe all the time we'd ever have. So we talked.

Alain and I had some fine heart-to-heart moments, veering into overt sentimentality, when Ronny started making gagging motions and begged us to stop.

It was pretty black outside now. Not as black as the void out by Conglommora—you could see nearby stars, the rest of the galaxy, the waning light from Earth's sun. But it was still dark, despite these highlights.

Ronny was getting morose. "What if Arty doesn't scan us and doesn't know to generate the big wave to pick us up?" He scratched at one of his many bites again.

A silent pause.

I countered, "And what if Arty is all set, the systems are all aligned, and it's just waiting for us to be in position?"

Ronny tried to think of a comeback, if for no other reason then to kill another minute or two. No luck. Another scratch. Another silent pause.

"And what if it doesn't?" he muttered, effectively stopping the conversation dead.

So the silent pauses grew and morphed into each other like water droplets, forming at last one long stream of foreboding quietude.

Okay, that makes it sound worse than it was, but basically we were stuck in a small jar in the dark, in the quiet, with nothing to do but worry that we wouldn't *ever* have anything else to do.

But the days did pass, with or without our cooperation. The screen beeped. It was Lucy.

"Looks like we're coming up on the transport site. Here's the data to begin braking, I think." Her confidence was inspiring.

We had run the calculations as well. Several times. Several dozen times. We even tried doing them all in our heads one day to kill a few hours. Those hours were better off dead.

Our numbers matched hers, of course, and Alain and I programmed the braking sequence into the craft, with Ronny looking over our shoulders and making snarky comments every now and then.

Braking was barely noticeable; it's not like there was a lot of scenery whipping past us. Both ships glided down to a dead stop; a few final puffs from the thrusters to balance everything out, and we sat perfectly still.

And waited.

In theory, Arty would mass the full power of Conglommora and initiate the quantum wave, which would suck us back home. But it had to know we were here. Or maybe it just tried every so often. Without the qradio, I just didn't know.

Ronny noted, "At least we aren't tied up this time."

There was that, at least. I made a face and a half an eye roll.

Nothing happened. We waited some more, expecting a magical rescue any minute now.

Nothing.

Minutes went by. An hour. We were afraid to talk, to say anything at all; afraid to jinx it.

"I'm sure Arty will scan the area or just fire up the wave," Ronny offered, unusually hopeful. I think he was trying to convince himself.

"Sure," I agreed, mostly for Alain's sake. But I wasn't so sure. What if there wasn't enough power in Conglommora to pull us back? What if this wasn't the right spot, and Arty needed the qradio to get a proper fix on our location? What if...

The what ifs were infinite. Our supplies were not. Another day or two maybe, then the little food we had would be gone. We were almost out of water already.

What a horrible way to die. Sitting here in a small bubble of metal and composites. No one would even know what happened to us. And maybe that was the hardest part. We all die in the end, but hoping that our lives *meant* something. That there was purpose, that we'd made a difference in the lives of others. I realized right then that I had lived almost none of these high-sounding words. What did my life matter, really? Would anyone even notice I was dead and gone? Alain at least had friends. They'd notice.

I refused to die like this. Unknown. Unfinished.

But maybe I wouldn't have a choice. More hours passed, anxiety and dread ramping up. Something should have happened by now. We needed a back up plan. But we didn't have one. There wasn't enough fuel to get back to Earth, and there were no other habitable bodies out here. Was there any way we could get a message to Arty, I wondered?

I turned to ask Ronny...

And before I knew what was happening, there was that infinite inside-out pulling, puking, horrible sensation that you knew would never end, would never stop until the end of space-time itself.

Really, words don't do it justice. Alain was heaving mightily this time, and it's not like we had a whole lot of room to avoid a detailed, first-hand experience of his difficulty.

We were back, back in Conglommora's space. We had made it. There was no way I was going to do that again. Earth was a gorgeous death trap that *sucked*.

We puffed over, using the last of our thrusters, and docked at Bil's—Arty must have helped them print up the appropriate adapters for the smaller landing crafts. The air whooshed in at us, fresh, wonderful air of Conglommora replacing the vomit-laden, body-odor encrusted, over-recycled embarrassment of air in our landing craft.

I seriously considered kissing the deck.

———————————

Home at last. Home at last after a long journey. Such a powerful idea. Someone should write a song about that some day. Or some long epic poem. I ate like a ponderous beast, I drank like I was draining a river. A real, Earth-sized river, not one of our pale imitations. When I'd finished, washed up, and changed into my familiar and comfortable clothes, Arty beeped.

"You did very well, Charlie," Arty congratulated me. "You and Alain both performed admirably, given very difficult circumstances."

"You're not kidding." I made the obvious statement, "We got lucky."

"It's unfortunate that you could not have recovered Penelope's body," Arty said, "A full analysis of the virus that killed her would be very valuable. As it is, we only have a limited idea of who might be susceptible."

"Only if other folks in Conglommora really want to go down to Earth, I suppose. I sure as hell am never going back," I asserted, taking another gulp of water. I never appreciated gulping a large container of water as much as I did now.

"Actually, there is a queue of people who do want to go," Arty confirmed. "Including some of your friends—Chalu in particular is very interested in studying the deep ocean, and even Ronny wants to take Janel 'camping.'"

I raised an eyebrow at that, surprised that Ronny would expose himself to those dangers again.

"Plus, I think it's a good idea to help keep an eye on the Earth humans."

"Oh?" I asked, "And what about the native Earthans? What will become of them?"

"That's a good question," Arty said, continuing a conversational mode. "Analysis suggests they will spread from the top of this continent where they are currently concentrated and ultimately retake the Earth on the whole. The migration has already started.

"Some larger tribes are moving already. Other, smaller groups are venturing forth in small boats across the other large ocean expanse. In their native tongue, they call it the 'peaceful' ocean. Such a description is poetic at best, and not meteorologically accurate. But at any rate, the native population is expanding, and expanding rapidly."

I frowned. "Is there any room for us? For the people who want to go live on Earth?"

Arty was not enthusiastic. "It is imperative that any visitors to Earth avoid contact with the natives. There is room, for now, for small individuals and groups. But in just a dozen generations, perhaps less, it will become harder and harder to avoid contact. There really isn't a viable chance of successful, large, long-term settlements. Not on land, at least."

"What do you mean?" I puzzled.

"Of the two largest oceans, one is considerably harder to traverse. It's colder, the seas are rougher. We could potentially establish an undersea colony there that would go undetected for quite some time. At least until their civilization reaches an industrial, technological era."

"That's great, right?" I was still a little confused. "I mean, that will take them, what, thousands of years, tens of thousands of years?"

"Yes, for them," Arty acknowledged, "but time is relative."

Argh, physics again. "What do you mean by that?" I asked it to clarify.

"I think I've discovered another possible reason for Earth's advanced age relative to our timeframe. You were right, it has to do with our gravity generators."

That got my full attention.

"There is an exceptionally dense neutron star cluster in a highly elliptical but irregular orbit that passes between us and Earth's solar system. Normally, that wouldn't be an issue, but somehow there's an interaction between the cluster and our gravitomagnetic generators throughout Conglommora. When the cluster is interposed between us and Earth, there is a gravitational distortion that warps relative space time. During the passage, time passes 100 to 1000 times more rapidly in the Earth timeframe than ours. Or ours passes more slowly. It depends on how you look at it.

"This phenomena isn't easily explained by any science we currently understand, but the math supports the hypothesis."

"In other words," I tried to comprehend, "there's a random thing that happens that makes the Earth age a few hundred to thousand years relative to us?"

"Essentially," Arty admitted. "At least, there's a correlation of the effects. I find no theory that adequately explains the interaction."

"What happens to anyone camping out on Earth while the neutron star thing passes by?" I asked with alarm.

"They would age according their local timeframe," Arty confirmed. "But please realize, it's not a sudden, unexpected affect. The transit of the neutron star cluster takes tens of years, and we have years of warning before it happens."

"Oh, okay," I said, pretending I really understood. "So it's not dangerous, really, unless you stay on Earth for many years during a transit."

"Even then," Arty explained, "It's not dangerous, it's just that everyone on Earth will age and die at a faster rate than their friends and family in Conglommora.

"It really is all relative," Arty concluded.

That was almost a joke. Who knew: Arty had a sense of humor.

"Well, as long as that's the only weird thing in the galaxy, I guess we're okay," I tried to joke back.

"It's not," came the reply. I didn't even answer, just raised my eyebrows in alarm.

"The time distortion doesn't explain observed readings on Earth completely, either."

"What do you mean?" This really wasn't working for me.

"Samples and scans of Earth from your visit indicated that at least some 100,000 years had passed since the exodus from Dead Earth. However, there are no known processes that would have reversed the effects of ecological damage in the given timeframe."

"So, what did it?" I swallowed hard, "Or *who* did it?"

"Insufficient data or processing power," was all Arty could say.

And yet despite the unanswered questions, the risks and outright dangers, some folks still wanted to experience Earth first-hand.

I was hanging out with Ronny. He had really, really wanted to setup a campsite on Earth. Hunting, fishing, the fabled outdoors life he'd read about as a kid. But with proper equipment, this time. Janel was a little curious, if not overly enthusiastic. The elements of history that so enthralled her were long dead and gone, so it was merely interesting, not compelling.

Arty sent them to a lush, uninhabited area of Earth, with sufficient supplies and gear. Transport had gotten easier, Arty designed some transport ships that were larger than our little landing craft, but weren't as large as house ships. Energy needs were better tuned—you didn't see the lights dim anymore when a ship went. Arty inoculated travelers against the viral and microbial threats we knew about so far and added to the list as needed.

So travel wasn't quite commonplace yet, but perhaps getting there.

"I'm telling you Charlie, it would have been great," Ronny told me. We were sitting in his living room, tweaking a new recipe of fresh-brewed algae. His arm was still encased in a clear tube; it hadn't finished regrowing yet.

"We had energy tools so we could cut trees and make a shelter, water purifier, emergency rations—even insect repellent this time." He shuddered at the memory.

"It would have been perfect," he sighed.

"But then there was the thing about the arm." I tipped my glass toward his all-too-obvious injury.

"Yeah, that. Still itches something fierce," he complained, and made a futile effort to scratch at the tubing, which had no effect at all on the flesh within.

"So, a bear, you say?" I needled him.

He nodded a chagrined nod, and Janel came through, on her way out to meet some friends.

"I don't know if it was a bear, a lion, a mastodon, or a giant carnivorous unicorn!" she exclaimed. "But there ain't no way in hell we're ever going back there again."

She didn't actually slam the hatch closed, but if she could have...

"It was a bear, I think," Ronny said, taking a sip. "At least, that's what it looked like according to Arty. If I hadn't had that stunner on me, I'd have lost a lot more than an arm." He set the drink down and looked grave.

"It's ironic, isn't it?" he asked, in a somber tone.

"How so?" I took a long draft of the brew.

"That our home, Earth, is actually an incredibly dangerous, alien planet now. After all these years, it's not really our home anymore, is it?"

I sat back and let the silence wash over the room.

"No," I agreed. "Not anymore."

Twenty-Six

THE FACT that Earth was so different wasn't a downside to everyone. Chalu was really looking forward to it.

Chalu and I had become good friends. I hadn't been back up to Sea yet, but we messaged and spoke over the streams at length about matters of philosophy, life, space, time, and such. He and one of the masters, Hoahoeh, as well as a few other hardy hands were headed down to Earth to study the ocean and perhaps even establish a more permanent colony there. He promised to stop by on his way out.

And sure enough, here was Chalu at my door of the *Neylan*, en route to the landing craft docked over at Bil's. He was dressed in regular coveralls this time, not the bare seafaring look that I'd seen on him and all his people.

"Good to see you." I beamed, with genuine delight and waved Chalu in. I introduced him to Alain, who was on his way to visit some friends, and we sat and talked a bit before his departure. I poured some of the Blue Wine that I'd learned how to trade for.

Chalu spoke of the sea on Earth and what they hoped to learn and study while there. It was a very ambitious project.

"But how did you convince Arty to let you conduct such a large study, and how did you possibly get it to agree to you establishing a colony? Arty was pretty clear that none of us on Conglommora can have any contact with the natives. For their sake as much as ours," I finished ruefully.

Chalu pulled a long sip of the wine, with appreciation. "Ah, for that, we in Sea have an advantage over most of the People." He pointed at his gill mods. "We won't be settling a colony on land."

Of course.

He grinned, from ear to ear. Or maybe gill to gill?

"We're going to build an observation station under the sea, in the middle of the second largest ocean. The natives will literally never know we are there, will never see us, will never run into us by chance.

"If all goes well, we'll expand this initial platform into a larger research community," he continued, "so that anyone who wants can come and study a real planet-sized aquatic ecosystem." Chalu, who beamed optimism and cheer on an average day, could hardly contain himself. "Can you imagine what we might find down there?" he asked.

Well, he wasn't exactly asking me. He answered his own question before I could even set my glass down.

"From the microscopic to maybe some of the largest creatures on Earth." Chalu positively blazed with the intensity of a small sun. "All could be waiting for us. Are you sure you won't come?"

I finally managed to set my glass down and answer, "No, thanks so much. But I don't have the gill mods or anything…"

"Oh, we'll have a pressurized atmosphere inside the station, of course," Chalu said. "And we'll have force fields to counteract the pressure at extreme depth, eventually. But at first we won't be so deep that we'll need that."

I jumped back in, "Even so, I feel I was pretty lucky to have survived my first visit to Earth. Granted, we were not nearly as well prepared as you'll be, and you'll be safe from the natives." I paused at the memory.

"But I've had my fill of that particular brand of adventure, I think."

"Suit yourself," Chalu replied. "But it will be *fantastic*," he proclaimed as he finished off the glass.

I'd settle for watching a stream of it, frankly.

Arty told me that Chalu and his group were the only ones headed to Earth to establish a long-term colony. But quite a few folks wanted to visit.

Ronny wasn't the only one who had dreams of "roughing it" on Earth. And as it turned out, trips to Earth were becoming a sort of small tourist trade, instead of any large-scale colonization effort. Many people were curious and wanted to try and rough it like Ronny–despite the warnings. Only a select few decided to try and live there—in isolated environs, away from the native population. Eventually, most died from various viruses or toxins, or were killed by predators, terrified Earthans, or their own naiveté.

Arty was right, and the general consensus seemed to be that Earth was a challenging place to visit. The ecosystem wasn't quite the same as it used it to be, and frankly, it just wasn't welcoming. We could mine Raw Organic from Earth, but it wasn't really worth the bother of extracting, purifying, and transporting. Too many variables in the natural world. Chalu's undersea research might improve that, given time. Maybe. And, of course, the natives aren't friendly. Why should they be?

I certainly felt that the Earth was theirs, now. It belonged to the Earthans. Not to us. Not any more. We had our chance, we left, and we had our own destiny out in the void.

Not everyone felt that way, though. There were a few who wanted to colonize full-scale, integrate with the native population despite Arty's warnings. Arty pointed out that wasn't fair to the natives, and since you needed Arty to fire up the resonance wave, for the most part these groups gave up on the idea.

Lucy, however, was not so easily discouraged.

I figured Lucy was headed back to Earth eventually. Maybe soon, maybe after a while, but definitely going at some point. She had deflected any lingering animosity over the Old Path incident by blaming that solely on

Robert: it was Robert's idea, Robert's explosives, and now of course, Robert was dead. Folks bought that story, for the most part. Case closed.

With that spotlight off of her, she'd surely try to get back to Earth somehow.

I headed over to the former Old Path section to look for her, and on a hunch, to Ashby's house in particular.

House Reardon wasn't too far from the main corridor over, and as the hatch opened, I found myself standing in his living area with Lucy, who was talking to Arty.

"I think that the hidden translator module will really help, especially with the subvocalization feature. Then we can actually help them without scaring them."

Lucy was making her case to Arty, trying to get the translation module built. Arty will generally refuse to design something that would be clearly dangerous, but this was somewhat of a gray area.

Arty asked, "How many of the people will you take on this mission to begin helping and training the natives?"

"No more than four at first," Lucy said, nodding to acknowledge my entrance. "We would start small, help them with better agricultural practices, sanitation, social issues, nothing too far from their current activity."

That seemed to satisfy whatever Arty was looking for. "Very well. The long-term survivability and welfare of the native humans on Earth is your top priority. But you must promise again, as all visitors to Earth have promised, not to reveal the existence of Conglommora or nature of yourselves."

"Yes, of course," Lucy readily agreed, "It is my mission to help them flourish and prosper, not scare them out of their wits. Remember, I've basically been trained for this style of mission my entire life—several lifetimes, in fact. You have no one in all of Conglommora who's better trained and prepared for this."

Really? I'd sure be willing to start looking.

But Arty was buying into this whole plan, as near as I could tell. And that surprised me. Arty agreed to let Lucy have direct contact. I suppose it made sense in the grand scheme of things. Protecting humans—all humans, even our cave-dwelling Earthan cousins—has always been Arty's programming. I could see sending in advisors, teachers to help the fledgling people re-take the planet. But why trust Lucy to the task?

"Ah, Arty," I interrupted, "nothing personal against Lucy here, but it was *her* and Bob who tried to blow up and take over part of Conglommora! Now you're okaying her return to Earth to take over the natives? What am I missing?" My voice rose dangerously high in pitch again. Old habits.

Lucy calmly replied, "Unfortunately, that whole incident was Robert's doing. And he wasn't himself; his bizarre behavior was a result of a fault in the memory programming, which was being corrected after repairs to the *Uten*. Another couple of weeks and he would have been perfectly fine."

"You could have tried to stop him," I countered, none too gently.

"Perhaps." Lucy took on a slightly wistful look. "But I wasn't quite myself at that point, either. I was more Ann. You didn't ever know Ann, but she was shy, quiet. Avoided conflict. Knew nothing save for the ship she was born on; the ship she died on, and her brother, Robert."

An awkward pause.

"And Grace?" I had to ask. Grimaced, more likely.

A wide smile now. "Grace has an amazing strength of will, of character. Truly a wonderful person. I... I can see the attraction. She is one of a kind."

I gulped, audibly, and damned if my tear ducts didn't decide this was a fine time to fully irrigate my eyeballs.

"But she would have wanted this," Lucy continued, looking off into the wall. "Grace's life up to now was all about nurturing life. The beasts of the field that she tended; the flowers, the crops. All about life. Nurturing it, guiding it in the right way, the intended way."

She took a step closer, still talking. I struggled to keep the tears from streaming down my face in a rivulet of loss.

"Alistaire's missions were always more politically-focused, more about working with—or around—the power structures in play. *My* mission has always been to train, to educate, to help better mankind. To bring light into the darkness. I have done this, I have trained for this, I have *experience* doing this for generations."

So that was her play: blame it on Robert. All the bad stuff, the thirst for power, for domination, blame it all on him. She was just the altruistic school teacher. Not her fault.

Yeah, right.

I didn't trust her. Not for a moment.

"Arty," I addressed the AI again, coldly and pointedly, "have you done a full risk analysis on the danger of a former Death Cult faction introduced to the humanoids on Earth?"

"Yes," came its reply. "It is reasonable to attribute Robert's violent and antisocial behavior to the malfunctions in his memory uploads because of problems on board the *Uten's* nanophotonic computer core. The neuroscans I have taken of Lucille show no such violent tendencies, but do show a marked aptitude for persuasion and instruction. Given the long history of Lucille's experience in these matters, I conclude she is well equipped for this mission and poses minimal risk."

Arty certainly has more faith in humanity than I. An aptitude for persuasion? Apparently so. There was nothing more I could do.

Lucy closed the stream and faced me now, "Why are you here? Can I help you?" she said coolly.

"I, uh," I was surprisingly tongue-tied again, "I… I came here to say goodbye to Grace."

She nodded and warmed maybe a half-a-degree. No more. "I understand. And for what it's worth, I am sorry."

She turned obliquely. "You are welcome to join us, on Earth, if you like," she offered. "Perhaps then you'll understand I only wish to help. I don't intend any harm to our cousins on Earth."

Before I even came over, and against all reason, I had thought about asking her if I could go along. Maybe *she* had the memory device, maybe I could find it, learn how to use it, figure out how to get Grace back, shove Lucy and Ann to the darkest recesses of a long-forgotten nightmare, all while surviving on Earth and then returning safely. And after a few days of wrestling with these ideas, and having them kick my ass, I came to the hard but eventual truth that it was just a fantasy. There was just no way. I didn't even know for sure that the machine even existed anymore, it was almost certainly destroyed on the *Uten*. I wasn't going to get Grace back.

There was also no way in hell I was going back to Earth again.

"Thanks, but no, Earth isn't for me. I just wanted to wish you luck, and to say goodbye."

Lucy nodded slowly, and said simply, "Goodbye, then."

She turned and walked out of the living area into the rest of the *Reardon*. My heart dropped to the floor and lay there; a pathetic throbbing bit of pain.

Ashby had wandered in for this last bit and watched her go, "Lucy is an... interesting person. Amazing accomplishments. Amazing aspirations."

The tone of his voice exposed a lot more than the words did. My heart then rolled over and died a few more times.

He had a thing for Lucy.

And Lucy either had a thing for him, too, or was just using him. Either way. Even more dead.

I wished Ashby good luck with as much politeness as I could manage, which wasn't much. A wan smile, limp handshake, and I was back in the corridor again, the *Reardon's* hatch closed behind me.

And that was that. I headed back to the *Neylan*.

Alain was eating dinner. He waved hello while reading a screen.

I got some dinner from the galley and joined him.

Epilogue

My name is Lucille Brandeis, the tall woman said. *You may name me Lucy.* She was dressed in luxurious furs, freshly skinned from several difficult kills. Ashby Reardon was proud of taking down the beasts. He was less proud of vomiting from the stench when skinning and gutting them, unused to the smell as he was. He supposed he would get used to it, as he would get used to much on the Earth of now.

She was a stranger, not one of the people of this tribe. She had been brought before the fathers of fathers: the several elders of the tribe, who stood silent and still, each with a spear in hand and a stone knife at their side.

They were different than her; her forehead, her eyes… she was beautiful, in a way their own women were not. The color of gold.

One of the fathers spoke, "I am Johg," he said with a deep, raspy voice. "Your words—you speak strangely, your words and your mouth speak different from each other, Lucy of Fur."

You see the truth, said Lucille, *I come from far away, and my words come slowly after me, as if from afar.*

Johg nodded, pretending to understand. He asked, "Why are you here? Where have you come from?"

Lucille's voice said with certainty, *I am here to bring you the light, the light of the heavens themselves. I come from there.* She pointed to the sky.

There was a gasp, not just from the fathers, but from the rest of the curious tribe gathered around.

"You come from the lights in the night sky?" Johg asked, incredulously. The father next to him jumped in, "You cannot! You cannot live on a speck of light!"

You speak wisely, and you are right. I do not live on the light itself. The light you see is as the fire's light seen through the hole in the tent. I live in the tent, in the sky.

"Hah hah har!" roared the second father, a man name Kaarg. "They do not mend their tents very well in the sky, do they!" and a round of laughter—nervous laughter—rolled through the tribesmen.

"You fell from a tent in the sky?" Johg asked, ignoring the trailing rumble of laughter and trying hard to understand.

I came as I meant to, Lucy said. *When you fall to the ground, tripped by a root or a stone, you do not mean to arrive at the ground so. But when you walk, walk to the river, walk to the hunting grounds, you do so with purpose. You may walk, you may climb the hills, you may swim the swift river, but you do so because you mean to arrive there.*

And so I meant to arrive here. By walking, by climbing down, by swimming… that does not matter. I am here, and I am here to help you.

"You fell from the sky," said Kaarg, unimpressed.

As you wish. But I fell, on purpose, to be with you here, to help you, replied Lucy.

Johg was cautious. "Help us how? My sons and their sons and their women and their children have what they need to eat, we have shelter in our tents and here in the caves when the rains come, the beasts flee before us, and our neighbors live beyond the mountain there in peace with us and others. What could you do to help us, Lucy of Furs?"

Lucy took a step closer. *Oh, I can teach you so many things, Johg of the Valley. I can show you how to find the beasts hidden in the grasses during the hunt, the fish in the fast streams. I can show you how to eat from all that you plant, even when rains leave you and do not come.*

Johg was listening now.

I can show you how to travel beyond the valley, through the wide rivers and the angry sea, to the very ends of the Earth itself; to the points of light in the sky. I can show you how to rule over all of it. To rule over your neighbors beyond the mountain, to rule over the beasts, the sea, and the air, and the sky. You, Johg, and your children, and your children's children.

I am the bringer of light.

Kaarg grew angry. "Those beyond the mountain will not wish to be ruled by us. They will fight. Lucy-fur does not bring light; she brings death!"

He stepped forward, closer to this stranger. "We do not need you. I say we feed you to the beasts of the plains, now, before your poison spreads like the snake you are!"

You cannot. Try, and I shall strike you down, as fire from the sky, Lucy replied in a remote, icy voice.

"Liar!" Kaarg roared and charged her, bringing his stone knife up to attack.

Lucy fired the modified stunner, hidden in her hand, and a crack like lightning itself shot out. Kaarg dropped. The odor of burnt flesh and hide rose with a thin tendril of smoke, like a fire snuffed out quickly and before its time.

There was silence on the plain. Death was no stranger here, but had never leapt from hand without stone or wood to carry it.

Kaarg's burnt-out husk was all that remained of him; blackened and hollow, ribs and skull smoking slightly as if freshly pulled from the very bottom of a cooking fire.

Johg spoke first, "Lucy-fur. You will show us these things, you will teach us this magic?"

Yes.

"And I and my children will rule over this land, over the beasts, over the others?"

Yes.

"And what price do you ask in trade from us for this power?" the wise father asked.

A place at your side. A voice to lead your children and your children's children.

Johg stepped forward, stepped away from the remaining fathers, and took her hand.

"For my tribe, for my family, for my children and their children, I stand with Lucyfur."

Thank You, and the Next Book

Thank you for reading *Conglommora*, I hope you enjoyed it. Please help others find this book:

1. Lend a copy to a friend
2. Write a review on Amazon, Goodreads, blogs
3. Sign up for the new releases/goodies e-mail at conglommora.com

Next Book: *Conglommora Found*

Charlie Neylan and his son Alain thought their adventures were over, as they settled into the shape of their new lives on Conglommora. But things get complicated as Alain risks his life to find answers to the secrets of Conglommora. The new undersea base, Denisova, expanded their world. So much new to study, so much to see—but safely, hidden from their descendants. The good People of Conglommora couldn't reveal themselves without jeopardizing their future. They had to remain isolated, alone. All that was left of humanity was utterly alone.

Until it wasn't.

About the Author

Andy Hunt is an author, publisher, consultant and programmer. He has authored award-winning and best-selling books, including the seminal classic *The Pragmatic Programmer*, *Learn to Program with Minecraft Plugins* for the kids, the perennially popular *Pragmatic Thinking and Learning: Refactor Your Wetware*, the Jolt-award winning *Practices of An Agile Developer*, and more. When not writing, Andy is an active musician and woodworker. Visit Andy's home page at www.toolshed.com to see what he's up to now.

Explore the ongoing mysteries at conglommora.com

Sneak Preview: Conglommora Found

Here are the first few chapters from the sequel to *Conglommora, Conglommora Found.*

Enjoy!

Andy

Conglommora Found:
Chapter One

I was back at my home, the *Neylan*, briefly, just to get a few things I wanted to have with me in Skyville. The screen in the wall lit up in the darkness and chimed at me, I made an answering gesture.

"Charlie! How are you doing, buddy?" Chalu's warm manner shone right through the screen. Even though he was down on Earth, untold light years from here, you probably could have seen him beaming with the naked eye. Chalu always seemed to glow with an unquenchable joy. The hair helped. Chalu sported multicolored strands of long hair, sometimes down to his waist, braided in parts, and always in a *wide* mix of colors.

"Hey Chalu. I'm well, just on my way back to Skyville for a while. You seem pretty excited for a guy who spends all his time underwater."

There was a pause. Communications over qradio had improved a lot, but still wasn't quite realtime. The image froze and jittered a bit. It took a little patience still, but you could pretend to have a conversation. Sort of. A dozen seconds, maybe more slipped by.

"I *am* excited. Denisova has grown so quickly, we've added so much to the station. It's more like a small city now. And we've really improved the whole docking/surface vessel thing. You really should come visit us. Bring Alain! Ahdom's been asking after him."

Ahdom was Chalu's son. Looked just like him, for the most part, with very similar features and the same burnished brown skin, although Ahdom kept his hair jet black instead of color full. He and Alain had grown to be friends over the last few years.

Chalu really wanted to get us to visit Denisova. That's what they called the new underwater base on Earth, located in the middle of one of their very large oceans.

It had started as a small research station, built just after our very first visit. But within a few years it was clear that this was an excellent way to visit Earth and avoid any interaction with the natives, our descendants. Arty, our collective AI, approved and considered it perfectly safe for us to visit Denisova.

But the Earth natives—and the Earth itself—were now over 100,000 years ahead of when we'd left, which had only been a couple of generations for us. Strange place, this universe of ours. Everything of our civilization on Earth was gone; most of it we'd scavenged in our hasty flight from the planet, the rest eroded into dust from time and nature. It wasn't our planet any more.

A lot of folks seemed to think it was nice to visit, though. There were minimum physical requirements, of course, so not *everyone* was automatically allowed to go. Arty had to approve.

For me, the thought of going back to Earth, and then staying *underwater*, was truly claustrophobic. I barely survived that first historic trip. Chalu was a good friend, and we stayed in touch even through his lengthy sojourns to Denisova, but I felt that was his adventure, not mine. Speaking of adventures...

"You still there?" Chalu asked.

"Oh, sorry. Mind wandered a bit. Yeah I haven't see Alain in a good long while now. He's still out on his Walk."

"Still?" Chalu's brow furrowed, his head tilted forward, and a few of the multicolored strands of long hair hung into his face. "I thought he was done with all that by now."

"Nope," I said with some resignation. "He's still out there. Still looking. How's your family?"

"Doing well. Sundara is almost old enough to join us, she and my wife are planning on coming down full time next season."

"And Ahdom?"

"My son takes after his father too much, I think." Chalu laughed lightly. "He wants to explore the whole of the planet, pole to pole and everything in between."

"Hah, he's welcome to it."

Chalu nodded to someone off-screen. "Be right there. Hey, I've got to run. But really, I think you and your lady friend should come on down and visit. It's safe, we've had no problems here. Nothing like your first visit to Earth!"

"There's still the joy of being sucked through the resonance wave," I commented dryly.

Chalu winced, slightly. "Yes, well, there is still that. But such a small price to pay," his eternal joy bubbled back up quickly, an irrepressible fountain. "Okay, we'll see you soon one way or another."

The screen went dark, matching the rest of the light ing on the *Neylan*. Had I always kept it so dark here, in the home I grew up? Skyville seemed so much brighter, so much more open. Granted it was a big dome instead of a just this small little ship house. But still.

I got up, ambled through the darkened passageway and into the living area. Waved my hand along the wall, a chairform popped out and I slumped into it.

So much had changed.

Maybe it was brighter in the house when Alain still lived here. Ah, probably not. He seemed to always have his head stuck in a game or vr of some sort. Well not anymore, I guess. Now he's out and about, who knows where. He pings me every once and a while, lets me know where he is and what he's up to. But not often enough, not for me. And here I am, sitting alone in the dark. Waiting for the ghosts of my past, my wife, my life...

I got up in one quick move, quick enough to leave my glum thoughts behind. Enough of this. I had plans to have dinner with my good friends Ronny and Janel, spend the night here, then set off for Skyville again in the morning. Better to be with Ronny than mope around in this empty shell of a former life. I palmed open the hatch and was back into the corridors.

Another one of those endless, mostly featureless corridors of the sort that connected all of the original ships together into the Conglommora. Ships, our houses. Ronny and Janel's place wasn't far.

I caught myself going around a junction as the gravity field shifted slightly. Midway up a narrow corridor before it met with a broad, circular tube—this was one of the spots where Eddie used to hang out. Crazy, I always thought he was just plain crazy. Ranting, incoherent. But not wrong as it turned out. Eddie had discovered the first readings of a recovered Earth. The Earth that killed him and the others on that first landing.

Guess I hadn't completely left my gloomy thoughts behind at the *Neylan*. The narrow, skinny corridor joined up with a larger, circular tube at the junction, lit in the familiar muted colors of amber and blue from the service lighting. I walked on to the last narrow corridor at the next junction, and had arrived. I took a deep breath, determined to leave my shadows behind.

The hatch slide open and Janel Q'tel swept me into their house grandly, "Welcome Charlie! Oh man we haven't seen you in... well I don't know how long. Too long, for sure. Come on in." That last bit was redundant, as she had maneuvered me halfway into their front room and sealed the hatch by now.

"Hey Charlie!" Ronny Sullivan called out from the back, "be right with you. You all sit and make yourselves some drinks."

We did, and I once again had opportunity to ask Janel what she was up to. Usually Janel's research and passion was focused on Dead Earth. Or rather, what led up to it. Geopolitics, psychology, history, anthropology, that sort of thing. It was good someone around here knew our history so well, I suppose.

Glad it didn't have to be me

Janel and Ronny seemed like complete opposites in every respect, starting with their exteriors. Janel was tall and lanky, bother her skin and hair were jet black, just like the void itself. Ronny was short, stout, with pearly luminescent white skin. But they were nearly just as opposite on the inside as well; Ronny frank and even abrasive, Janel well-studied and thoughtful.

"So what's new in the annals of Dead Earth?" I asked, after clinking our glasses of sweet-brewed algae in welcoming celebration.

"Dead Earth?" Janel looked askance. "Not so dead as we thought, apparently. I've been looking into that more and more lately, and it just doesn't make any sense." She fanned her hands out in a gesture of frustration. "Green and fertile again, no sign of pollution, radiation… no sign of *us*. No sign of our civilization at all. Nothing Arty can detect. There's no *way* Earth could have recovered so completely, not even in 100,000 years." She leaned back in her chairform. "But here we are."

"Huh." I responded with my usual eloquence. "Well, maybe it was actually longer than that. Maybe things decay faster than we think. Maybe a meteor *did* hit the planet and wiped everything clean!" I grinned. Janel punched my arm and rolled her eyes at the same time, preparing for a retort.

Ronny came in just then, bearing a mouth-watering tray of appetizers of all kinds. Bright primary colors, geometric shapes, it smelled wonderful even if I had literally no idea what it was. I asked as much.

"It's called *plenare*," Ronny said. "The folks in the outer arc are most fond of it."

I tried a bite, it had a wonderful texture—crispy and salty on the outside, light and creamy in the middle, with a tang I couldn't quite identify.

"What's it made..." I started, but Ronny waved his hands and grabbed a couple more for his plate.

"Shhhh. Don't ask. Nothing harmful."

I had my doubts, but it was really good. I took another one of the bright, electric blue ones and let it evaporate in my mouth before continuing the conversation.

"Any plans to go down to Earth? Check it out again? Visit Denisova? Chalu keeps after me to come visit," I said.

Janel shot Ronny a look. Their first camping trip to Earth back in the day ended badly, and Ronny had to regrow his arm when they got back. Still a sore point, so I try to bring it up every so often. Just for fun.

Ronny took a swig of the algae ferment. "No, no plans. I think I've had my fill. Janel talks about it sometimes. Try and get more data on Earth's recovery, find out the real story. But nothing serious."

Janel was put out. "How do you know I'm not serious?" she asked.

Ronny looked sideways at her. "Because as I remember it, you said you'd kill me with your bare hands if I ever made you go to Earth again."

"Doesn't count if it's my idea," Janel proclaimed and popped some more *plenare* in her mouth.

"Ah," Ronny acknowledged with a smirk, wisely not continuing the conversation.

Janel brought out the main courses later, and we chatted and ate through the night, like old friends who hadn't seen each other in a while. Which happened to be exactly the case. The hour grew late.

"What's wrong with recolonizing Earth?" Ronny was asking. "Get rid of the damn bears and lions, poisonous snakes and deadly viruses. We could do it, at least for a region at a time. Remake the world to suit us."

"Terraforming isn't that easy," Janel countered. "It's been tried. Remember your grandfather's story about the near-belt asteroid colonies?"

"Well that was just plain damn stupid," Ronny retorted. "They didn't have nearly enough natural resources, no Arty to keep the minerals and nutrients in balance... nothing. I could have told them they were all going to die." He drained his glass, got up for yet another.

"Ok," Janel played along. "Suppose we get all the tech right, manage to figure out to re-engineer an entire, planet-sized biosphere with all its quirks and subtle nuances. Suppose we get all that perfectly right, and remake the planet in our own image. What about the humans who already live there? What about the animals in the food chain who depend on the 'pests' you want to eliminate? What happens to all of that?" Janel asked, with more than a hint of agitation and accusation on her breath. And a fair bit of fermented algae too.

Ronny sighed. They'd had this conversation before, of course, and despite his hopes, it always ended up the same way. Our large-scale presence wouldn't be fair the humans on Earth now. Our children. Perhaps cousins, some said. Either way, the Earthans were our kin. And considering how few of us there are in the whole of the cosmos, "don't screw up the humans" was a compelling argument all by itself.

"Besides," Janel drained her glass as well. "Arty wouldn't let you, even if you wanted to."

Ronny pursed his lips, and added quietly "But Arty let Lucille go down and teach those poor natives God knows what."

The room shrunk a little. Maybe a chill came over us. Over me, certainly. I tried not to dwell on those events, on how I lost Grace, the only love of my life after my wife died, on how Grace somehow became Lucille.

Janel shook here head. "Yes, it did allow that. Arty still thinks it's a reasonable idea to have small teams go down and help the Earthans along. And who knows, maybe it's right. I don't trust Lucille, I know *you* don't trust Lucille," she said, flailing an arm at me. "But Arty runs on quantum logic, not stupid human fears."

Ronny harrumphed. "True enough, I suppose. But fear is a good thing. Keeps us safe. Arty doesn't know fear from waking up in the morning. Not in its programming. It doesn't *know* to be afraid of Lucille."

In the ensuing silence, he got up, swhooshed open a panel in the wall, and retrieved an ornate, decorative bottle, covered in delicate filigree of silver and shiny gems. The good stuff. He poured a round for us.

"It's not worried about Lucille," he continued. "I'm just saying maybe it should be."

I did not disagree.

Conglommora Found:
Chapter Two

So. Many. People. The hatch closed behind him, and he scanned as much as he could, as quickly as he could, as far as his eyes could see.

Edge to edge, he couldn't even see the floor of the dome, and really not even the walls. Just a sea of people, a giant ocean with waves of humanity of all different colors, heights, and speeds. Clothing of dark red, fluorescent green, watery blue. Skin of shining silver, gold, pink, brown, alabaster white and iridescent black. And that was just the batch immediately in front of him, elbow to elbow with almost no space in between at all.

Maybe this was a mistake, the young man thought._There's no way I can even get through here._ He struggled against the crowd, but only made it a short way inside the dome before the tide pushed him back toward the hatch he'd entered from. He tried again in a slightly different direction, but wasn't making much headway.

"Welcome to the Hive! What's your name?" shouted the girl with silver skin and matching hair.

"Alain," said the young man. He tried for as much volume as he could without actually screaming.

"What?" the girl was trying to make conversation, but it was so loud in the dome. Filled with loud, happy people, going about their daily lives. Trading, cooking, eating, telling stories, all trying to be heard over each other. Hard to hear anything other than a dull, continuous, crowd roar.

And the smells! There was a whole section of what looked like food shacks, or carts, or both, cooking a vast, mind-numbing variety of offerings. Mostly magnetic cooking, but it smelled like there were some real open fires as well.

She tried again. "What's your name?" she tried to belt out while still smiling.

"Alain Neylan," he repeated, as she turned her ear closer to his head.

She noticed the piece attached to his right ear. "You an imager?"

"Yes, that's right." Alain smiled. "I've been all over Conglommora taking images and talking to folks. So much to see." He drew a long breath and looked up at the silver dome—same color as the girl—and back down at the immense sea of people ahead of him.

"But I've never seen a crowd like this," he admitted. "I was hoping to find a place to stay tonight, but I'm not sure I can even get through this crowd."

"Oh this?" she said dismissively. "This is nothing. You should see it really packed on the local holidays. I'm Essi," she grinned, wider now. "I've got room. My place is just over there." She gestured vaguely toward the middle of the dome.

"There's a trick to navigating crowds like this. It's just a like a river back on Green Earth. Here, follow me." And with that she darted further into the crowd. Alain was startled, but dove in after her.

Sure enough, there was a flow of people within the thick of the crowd. Several flows, in fact, rushing and conjoining, losing and gaining members. Essi had a knack for finding the rivers, the eddies, backwashes; the current and flow of the crowd. Alain had a time keeping up, bumping into quite a few people with less grace than he had hoped. They didn't seem to mind, or even notice.

Finally they were swept out of the main crush and up against the hatch of a modest house. Essi palmed the wall and they entered. The sudden seal of the hatch behind them felt like earplugs; the sudden quiet was like a silver blanket, warm, enveloping, comforting.

"Wow," Alain waited a moment before breaking the stillness, "You weren't kidding. River of people, all right."

Essi motioned for a chairform, and Alain did as well, sitting next to her.

"That's really a great metaphor," Alain continued, then paused a space. "I… I don't usually tell people this, but I've seen a real river, once, back on Earth. Teeming with life, just like the river of people here in Hive."

"You've been?" Essi startled with wide eyes. "I haven't met anyone who's been down yet."

"I was lucky… I guess," Alain smiled. "I was on the very first ship down with my Dad, Charlie Neylan."

"Neylan. Alain Neylan," she echoed, then chuckled. "Well I've got a genuine celebrity here for the night! And here I thought you were just another handsome wanderer."

Alain may have blushed, may have simply stood up too quick as he started to pace.

"Oh I don't know about that whole *celebrity* business, but thanks for the lodging. I was hoping to stay at Hive for a couple of days, is that okay?" he continued pacing a little in the small room.

Essi got up from her chair as well. "Sure… plenty of room here. You can stay as long as you like," she smiled warmly.

"I don't really have any Raw to trade or anything," Alain admitted. "Well, I mean, I did, but then there was that incident back at the Chance Dome and…"

"Not a problem at all," Essi said, undimmed. "You will be *required* to tell me that story, however. And all the others. Tell me about Earth! Your trip there and back, tell me what you've seen of Conglommora, tell me…" she paused for breath, having suddenly run out. "Tell me all of it."

"All?" Alain raised an eyebrow. "Okay, I suppose. Seems a fair trade. But that's a lot of work on an empty stomach. Perhaps we should cook up some dinner first?" He nodded hopefully back toward the galley.

Now it was Essi's turn to look surprised. "What, cook ourselves? Huh. I suppose some folks do that. Not here, though. Come on," she grabbed his arm, "I'll show you how to get a proper dinner here in Hive."

She propelled him out the hatch and into the river of humanity once again, tacking against the current of bodies toward a row of free-standing cooking carts. The most incredible smells wafted past them, richer now and more focused.

Alain thought he might learn to like Hive after all.

They stood together past the third cart, nibbling on some sort of very spicy food on a stick, cooked over a real open fire with its own oxygen feed. Alain had no idea what it was, but ate gratefully.

"This is fantastic, what is it?" Alain mumbled between mouthfuls.

Essi shrugged. "Food."

He swallowed. "Could you be a *little* more specific?" Alain chided her.

"Oh I don't know what they call it. I think these folks make up new names every day anyway. That old lady over there…" She pointed, "I swear I've never gotten the same thing twice from her. And this guy," she gestured at the most recent stall featuring a very large gentleman with an equally large and bushy mustache, "I get these same things here almost every day, and he still won't tell me what they are. The names don't matter. You learn to get what you like from who you like. And where to get surprises if you want that, too!"

Alain captured a bunch of images of the stalls, of the unending crowd, of Essi.

"I don't think I've ever tasted these particular spices before," he said as they headed for a row of dessert offerings.

"As I hear it, the recipes are all closely-guarded family secrets. Most using descendants of original spice plants rescued from Dead Earth itself. But that's just talk— you've actually *been*" Essi exclaimed. "Come on, let's grab something cold and sweet and head back to my place, you can tell me all about it."

"Wow. Just wow," Essi was sitting in her living area, leaning forward, her head in her hands, her legs at an awkward, outward angle, completely enthralled at Alain's tale. They were each sipping a sweet, glowing blue concoction. "What were you thinking when the ship exploded and you were stranded? I would have pissed myself, I think. At least."

"Hah, I'm not sure I didn't." Alain sat back in his chairform, looking rueful. "That was pretty damn terrifying. Stuck in that little lander craft, the ship we came in blown to bits." He shook his head. "But you know, once we landed back on Earth and started gathering supplies, I felt better about the whole thing. I mean, it was a huge, devastating shock at first, of course. All of it.

Those first couple of folks on our crew who died on our first landing, that crazy guy Robert blowing up in the ship, and there we were, all alone, in orbit, no food, no water... nothing. But once we started *doing* something, I felt better. I thought we might really make it after all. My Dad was great through the whole thing, too, don't get me wrong. I don't think any of us would have made it back without him."

Essi finished off her dessert drink, leaned back in her chairform. "Incredible. A real, genuine adventure. Arty showed me the summary points back when all that happened, but I really had no idea what you'd been through. And here you are now, wandering all of Conglommora? I would have thought that was enough adventure to last a lifetime!" She laughed.

"Maybe it should have been," Alain pursed his lips, rolled his hands around his drink. "But I've had some pretty wild times in the darker corners out here, too. Nothing quite as dramatic," he added hastily add her worried look. "But I've been threatened, been in trouble, nearly got killed a couple of times—mostly accidents."

"Then why do you keep doing it?"

"Hmm." A short puff of a smile, and Alain looked down at his now-empty dessert cup, wistfully. "Why, indeed. A couple of reasons, I guess. I'm looking for something, I'll know it when I find it. And I'm looking for someone. A girl."

"Well, maybe you've found someone," Essi said, leaning in closer and tilting her head to one side, eyes bright and hair flowing.

"Oh!" Alain exclaimed, a little slow on the uptake. "I mean, I'm sort of looking for someone for my father."

Essi raised an eyebrow and moved back, "That's a little weird, don't you think?"

"No, no, not like that," Alain laughed gently. "It's... complicated. Family matters, I guess you could say. Here, here's a picture. Have you seen her?" He held up his shiny and made a few motions until the image came up. Essi peered over at it.

"Ah. No, can't say I've ever seen her. But I don't wander too far from The Hive, so that's not saying much. But, maybe I'm someone you're looking for, too?" Essi said hopefully.

"Just might be." Alain moved closer to her, leaned in and kissed her gently.

Essi awoke the next morning, same as any other day. But not exactly the same. She smiled, eyes still closed, vividly remembering Alain the night before. She rolled over to wake him, but he wasn't there. Must be up already.

She slid out of the bedform, still naked, and groggily wandered into the galley. It was dark. No Alain here. Now she was more wide awake, and darted to the front of her house. Nothing. His pack was gone.

He was gone.

Damn. She slumped a little in the hatchway. He had seemed so nice. But those wandering types, they do like to wonder. Well there goes plans for today, she thought.

Essi meandered back to the bedroom and pulled on a simple coverall. On a whim, she asked aloud, "Arty, where is Alain?"

Arty's voice came from the nearest speaker, "Alain Neylan is no longer in The Hive."

At least he's making good time, she thought. One other thing to do before she forgot. Essi pulled the shiny out of her pocket, stiffened it, and searched through the contacts. There was no name on this entry, just a stylized icon of a heart. She pinged the contact. A woman with dark golden hair and uncommonly deep, dark green eyes answered.

"Faith?" Essi asked.

A slight eye roll. "I've asked you not to call me that. Or call me, for that matter. What's up?"

"Some guy was through here yesterday, asking about you. Looking for you."

Faith frowned slightly. "What guy? What was his name?"

"Alain Neylan. He and his Dad were on that first mission to Earth…"

"Yeah, I got that," Faith interrupted. "What did you tell him?"

"Nothing," Essi answered. "There is nothing to tell."

"Thanks for letting me know." Faith terminated the connection and Essi's screen went dark.

She stuffed the shiny into a pocket on her coveralls and strode purposefully back to the front of her house, palmed open the hatch, and silently rejoined the massed throng of humanity in the great expanse of The Hive.

Conglommora Found:
Chapter Three

AFTER I LEFT RONNY AND JANEL'S, I headed back to Skyville. Where Ronny's place was more or less in my old neighborhood, near the *Neylan*, Skyville was a considerable distance.

On my first few trips, I walked and contorted myself through the several day's worth of corridors, connectors, and hatches. I figured a gravsled would have been more trouble than it was worth, having to stop and constantly recalibrate it every time the gravity field shifted—which was often. But the constant long walks were a little more than I could take, so I started using the gravsled anyway. I got better at the whole quick-recalibrate thing, and it wasn't so bad once you got the knack of it.

I was on approach up the last, long, lonely corridor to Skyville, gliding pretty damn fast up the straightaway. Not as fast as a hyperloop car, but maybe a little faster than I should have. I backed off as I approached the hatch, entered, and headed for the house.

The gravsled ramped its field down, gently settling onto the lush green lawn in the middle of the massive Skyville dome. I took my packages off, and the sled slid up and nestled into the niche right next to the hatch. I went inside.

The house was dark at the moment. But not dark like the *Neylan* had been. That was a dark of energies spent, of a light lost to the past. This was warmer, more comforting. A temporary dark of resting, only. Light was on the way—she'd be back shortly.

I leaned into the hatchway, looked out at the broad expanse of the Skyville dome, with its azure blue ceiling. Kind of like the sky on Earth. Close enough for everyone here, I guess. I was one of the few who'd actually *seen* the color of the sky on Earth. Not just the color, but the breadth, the depth, the richness of it all. The sky here was none of that, but it was still very pleasant.

As far as I'd seen, Skyville was pretty unique in Conglommora. Sure, there were plenty of other large domes, dedicated to different aspects of life as our grandparents and great-grandparents found it back on Green Earth. And other biospheres had large animals, too. But Skyville was a little different, because the people lived and worked right alongside the beasts. All together, sharing an endless grassy field under an Earth-like, bright blue sky.

To me, that pretty much summed up Skyville. Kind of like Earth. But not as deadly. Large, peaceful animals going about their business. Folks doing the same. Peace, quiet—but not isolated and lonely. I enjoyed what I thought was the peace and quiet living on the *Neylan*, but in hindsight, I was just disconnected. I withdrew from what friends I had after my wife Haily died, and hadn't noticed how cut off I'd become. It wasn't until Arty asked me to spy, and my son Alain and I had that whole adventure through the resonance wave back to Earth, that I really began to appreciate life again. Had to see the dark to appreciate the light, I guess. Like one of those poems I never appreciated as a youth. Some of those you just have to get older to finally understand. You have to live the light, live the dark to appreciate the subtle nuances of real life. And the light on Earth was so much more dazzling than this pale simulacrum. *That* was real light.

So, at some point I realized that the dark and quiet of the *Neylan*, which I had cherished for so long, wasn't healthy. Especially after Alain had left.

But here in Skyville, walking and working side by side with good friends under a bright blue sky, I found peace and quiet, done properly. This was where I belonged now.

Alain asked me to go with him a few times, but wandering all of Conglommora on a Walk was a young man's game. Or at least, someone else's game. Not mine. I'd had my share of adventure. Alain was welcome to dig for whatever excitement he could find out here. I did worry about him, though. He'd gotten in a couple tight spots and scrapes already, especially when he first set out. Nothing too bad—Arty is always there to protect against any serious problem, if it can. But still. A parent's worry never ends.

I hadn't heard from him for a while now. What wonders was he exploring today? The joy of surreal fabrication in the mech section, wonders of the deep in Sea? Outside of Skyville, those were my favorites. Probably not his. He was probably off with some bunch of other wild young people doing who knows what. I guess I'd hear from him in due course. I always did.

Ah, she was on her way back now. Good timing Picking her way through the fields of large animals and their droppings. Golden hair flowing behind her, golden skin. Just gold all over. I straightened up.

"Charlie! Right on time. I missed you!" We hugged, kissed deeply. I hadn't been gone *that* long, but our relationship was still in the early years. The hatch slid open and we went inside.

Some folks talk about love at first sight, and I think that was definitely the case when I first met Grace. A strange, rare, electrifying experience. Which made losing Grace—her mind, at least—very hard to take. Maybe you only get one "love at first sight" moment in your life. When Haily and I met and married, it was a slower process. Both Haily and I had a firm goal at the time to find a mate, so it was all very conscious and deliberate, but hardly instantaneous.

And now, with the latest love of my life, the process was different yet again. This one had taken some time. In

fact, I didn't even like her when we first met. I thought
we were far too different, nothing in common. I didn't
find it easy to talk to her at all. Maybe I felt out of my
league—she remains incredibly beautiful. One of the
most beautiful people I've ever seen in real life (vr models
don't count). And I'm not, frankly. So no, we didn't hit
it off on our first meeting.

Or our second.

No connection on our third, fourth, and on.

But I was spending more and more time in Skyville.
I got to know some of Grace's friends, where she worked
and hung out. She didn't have any family left. Well, there
was a sister, Faith, but she'd been on a extended Walk for
many, many years now. No one knew where she was, or
really remembered what she looked look—apparently
she was very shy if you had an imager pointed at her.
Didn't like pictures of herself. By now, she was close to
passing into myth, or legend even.

I thought getting closer to Grace's world would help
me feel closer to Grace, to the Grace I knew, but it didn't.
It *did* make me appreciate Skyville more and more, however. And as I spent more of my time there, I of course
kept running into Käthe. Which wasn't fate, or destiny,
or even unusual. Käthe was the coordinator for Skyville,
which is as close to a leader as anyone has, so of course
we had dealings with each other frequently. I still found
her hard to talk to, hard to get to know.

Until one night.

There had been an issue with contamination in the
dairy process. After milk is extracted from the cows, it's

lightly processed to remove any harmful bacteria or other contaminants. Well something had gone wrong and a few children got sick as a result. Nothing dangerous, but that sort of thing wasn't supposed to happen—and hadn't happened in many years.

With some extra hand scanners and Arty's help, we were checking all aspects of the dairy. Käthe and I happened to end up in the same place, the back of a storage area of one of the barns, filled with pipes, nanophotonic circuits, and mechanical devices.

"Anything yet?" I asked, somewhat redundantly but trying to make conversation.

Käthe put down her scanner and looked right at me. "No. Absolutely nothing. But I will keep on trying."

She was still looking at me, not the scanner. Something in the dim of my brain clicked, and I realized that maybe she wasn't talking about the dairy issue. The rest of my brain, especially the talking part, seemed to go offline and shutdown. I sputtered a little to get it going again, voicing a few nonsense syllables like a useless, damaged life form. A complete do-over. I managed to get a reasonable sentence going, something along the lines of, "you're not talking about the scanner, are you?"

"No, Charlie, I'm not." Käthe took my hand. "Charlie, you're an amazing person. Do you know how many folks I know who've led a mission to Earth? One. Who've survived exploding ships and treacherous natives? One. Who's kind, and funny, witty and fun to be around? One."

My brain exploded at the sudden notion that Käthe *wasn't* out of my league, after all. I leaned in, and kissed her passionately.

Let's just say it's a good thing we had the barn to ourselves that evening.

Even then, it took a while for Käthe and I to get comfortable with each other. She loved Skyville so much, she was really dedicated to sharing the beauty of the animals and nature with everyone. She always felt that the nature of Skyville could heal anyone, of anything. Especially me. I think in the beginning she took me on as a project in healing. If she could help me, surely she could help anyone.

And maybe she was right. I was healed. It had taken a while, and she probably was done even yet. That night had been a long time ago, and here I was still "moving in."

It may have taken a while, but I felt happy again, and perfectly safe—not like on Earth. Yes, I mused as Käthe was dealing with some late-breaking business on her screen, this was the place for me. I'll live out my years here, no more ridiculous spy missions or planetary expeditions.

I'm sure Earth was getting along fine without me.